RANCHO CUC
PUBLIC LIB

D0200121

A Touch of *Betrayal*

HEART
QUEST.

Praise for Catherine Palmer's Books

"Each of the Treasures of the Heart books is a delightful read. The energy, adventure, and romance kept me intrigued to the end. I will definitely recommend this series to my friends."
— Francine Rivers, best-selling author

A Kiss of Adventure

"This entertaining book is hard to put down."
— *CBA Marketplace*

"Elements of *The African Queen* and *Romancing the Stone* blend in this action-filled romance. Light, romantic fun."
— *Library Journal*

"I had trouble putting it down! I look forward to reading your next book."
— Jo Anne Cottone; Raleigh, North Carolina

"Your characters catch my interest from the beginning, and the background material is wonderful, but to have all of that with a Christian message is more than I usually hope for."
— Virginia Carney; Newport, Arkansas

"Your characters are so honest in their feelings toward God. I also like the fact that your books tackle tough issues, which helps me in my own walk with God."
— Sandra Grahl; Bear Lake, Michigan

"Touched me with the miracle of how God works. I needed to hear the words you wrote."
— Bridget S. Langdale; Houston, Texas

"Excellent! Filled with adventure, romance, danger, and God."
— Heather Vickers; Fremont, California

A Whisper of Danger
"At last, a Christian romance with real emotions. The only negative side to your books is that I can't get enough of them!"
— Liz Hunt; Glasgow, Scotland

"It is sometimes hard to find books that are both spiritually uplifting and entertaining. Your books are both!"
— Angela Martin; Fredricktown, Missouri

"Full of suspense and action. I had a hard time putting it down."
— Cherie Wallace; Sellersville, Pennsylvania

"A delightful romance! I was especially touched by your insights into God's will."
— Patty Goodman; Minneapolis, Minnesota

Prairie Rose
"In Rosie, Palmer has created an entertaining and humorous character. Highly recommended."
— *Library Journal*

"Begins with a bang and doesn't let up till the end. The author expertly presents the tragedy and triumph of the human experience."
— *A Closer Look*

Prairie Storm
"A fine addition to the entertaining series."
— *Library Journal*

"[This] bittersweet romance takes on themes of forgiveness and reconciliation with spiritual tenacity."
— *Romantic Times*

Finders Keepers
"A romance that tackles deeper issues."
— *Library Journal*

A Victorian Christmas Cottage
"[An] engaging seasonal collection of novellas. Entertaining."
— *Library Journal*

romance the way it's meant to be

HeartQuest brings you romantic fiction
with a foundation of biblical truth.
Adventure, mystery, intrigue, and suspense
mingle in these heartwarming stories of
men and women of faith striving to build
a love that will last a lifetime.

May HeartQuest books sweep you
into the arms of God, who longs for you
and pursues you always.

A Touch of Betrayal

CATHERINE PALMER

RANCHO CUCAMONGA
PUBLIC LIBRARY

Romance fiction from
Tyndale House Publishers, Inc.
WHEATON, ILLINOIS
www.heartquest.com

Visit Tyndale's exciting Web site at www.tyndale.com

Check out the latest about HeartQuest Books at www.heartquest.com

Copyright © 2000 by Catherine Palmer. All rights reserved.

Cover photo copyright © 2000 by Paul and Linda Marie Ambrose/FPG. All rights reserved.

Author's photo copyright © 1998 by Bill Bilsley. All rights reserved.

HeartQuest is a registered trademark of Tyndale House Publishers, Inc.

Designed by Melinda Schumacher

Scripture quotations are taken from the *Holy Bible,* New Living Translation, copyright © 1996. Used by permission of Tyndale House Publishers, Inc., Wheaton, Illinois 60189. All rights reserved.

This novel is a work of fiction. Names, characters, places, and incidents are either the product of the author's imagination or are used fictitiously. Any resemblance to actual events, locales, organizations, or persons living or dead is entirely coincidental and beyond the intent of either the author or publisher.

Library of Congress Cataloging-in-Publication Data

Palmer, Catherine, date
  A touch of betrayal / Catherine Palmer.
    p. cm. — (HeartQuest) (Treasures of the heart ; 3)
    ISBN 0-8423-5777-7
    1. Women textile designers—Fiction. 2. Anthropologists—Fiction. 3. Americans—Africa—Fiction. 4. Africa—Fiction. I. Title. II. Series.

PS3566.A495 T6 2000
813′.54—dc21
                                                        00-030244

Printed in the United States of America

06 05 04 03 02
10 9 8 7 6

Don't store up treasures here on earth,

where they can be eaten by moths and get rusty,

and where thieves break in and steal.

Store your treasures in heaven. . . .

Wherever your treasure is,

there your heart and thoughts will also be.

—JESUS CHRIST (MATTHEW 6:19–21)

Prologue

She stepped past the immigration desk at Nairobi International Airport, slipped her passport and visa into her purse, and looked for the smiling man who would be holding a placard that read her name: Alexandra Prescott. He wasn't there. She searched the line of cars waiting outside. No limousine. She studied the row of booths proclaiming hotel names: Hilton, Intercontinental, New Stanley, Norfolk. Abandoned.

Despite the late hour, the main terminal—a concrete-walled building with a cement floor—swarmed with activity. African businessmen in tailored suits greeted associates warmly. Indian women swathed in bright silk saris tended scampering children while their husbands summoned baggage handlers to begin loading mountains of suitcases. A janitor strolled across the floor pushing a long-handled broom. A shopkeeper washed the windows of his kiosk.

Alexandra fought the flutter of panic in her stomach. At nearly six feet tall, blonde, blue-eyed, and dressed in black New York City chic, she knew she stood out like a bare lightbulb. The only other Caucasian in the terminal looked like he'd gone AWOL from a halfway house. A real derelict. The man's scruffy whiskers and shaggy brown hair perfectly echoed the fashion statement he made in his dusty khaki trousers, faded shirt, battered suede boots, and baggy jacket covered with bulging pockets. Appalling.

Alexandra clutched her purse under her arm and breathed a fervent prayer. The scent of something raw and unrefined filled the air in the terminal—a mixture of spices, strong coffee, and tropical flowers. She swallowed hard. *Dear Lord, please help me.* This was not what she had expected. She was supposed to be met by a limo driver, taken to the Hilton Hotel, and greeted with a cup of papaya punch. That's what the brochure had said. Papaya punch.

She flicked open the clasp on her purse and pulled out the itinerary. There it was. Papaya punch at the Hilton. Dinner at eight. A six o'clock departure for the game park the following morning. Everything was organized. Efficient. No surprises.

Alexandra crumpled the brochure in her fist and studied the rapidly dispersing crowd. Did anyone in the place even speak English? Doubtful. She walked over to a luggage handler.

"Excuse me, sir." She held out the wrinkled brochure and pointed to the itinerary. "I expected to be met here by a representative from the Hilton Hotel. Do you know where that gentleman could be?"

The African shook his head. "Madam, you will have to talk on the telephone." He pointed to a row of pay phones on a far wall.

"I don't have my hotel's number. And I don't have any coins. I haven't exchanged my money yet."

"Madam, I cannot exchange money for you," the man said gravely. "The black market is against the law in Kenya. I will lose my position."

"No, no, I'm not asking you to—" But he was hurrying off with a suspicious last glance in her direction. Alexandra let out a breath. "Great. Just wonderful."

"Got a problem?"

It was the derelict. She could tell by the man's accent that he was American—and he was clearly the best example of the depths to which an expatriate could sink. Probably into drugs or gun smuggling. Alexandra squared her shoulders inside her silk-lined jacket as if she could somehow improve the image of her country by outshining this vagabond.

"Yes, I have a problem," she said. "My expectations have not been met."

A grin turned up the left corner of the man's mouth. "Expectations?"

"I was given this in New York." She held out the brochure. "The travel agency planned everything. And they've failed."

"Failed?"

"Is that all you can do? Repeat everything I say?" She tapped the toe of her leather pump. "Look, I'm here on business. I have a room at the Hilton, and if I can get there, everything will be all right. So if you'd just show me where to find the hotel limousines . . ."

"Let's see." He pushed back the frayed cuff of one sleeve and studied the watch on his wrist. "It's 9:00 P.M.—"

"Nine!" Alexandra slid her jacket sleeve up her arm and stared at her Rolex. "I knew the plane was late, but I thought . . . is Kenya eight hours later than New York or nine?"

"Depends on the time of year. Daylight saving time throws everything off. We don't play around with the time in Kenya, you know. Sun comes up at six. Sets at six. Equator runs right through the country." He smiled, as if this knowledge might somehow reassure her. "The exchange bank is closed, so you're out of luck there. Hotel booths are shut down. Looks like you'll have to hitch a ride with somebody."

"You mean—hitchhike?"

He laughed. "Relax, I'll take you into the city. The plane I'm meeting is due from Tanzania in a couple of minutes. If you want to visit the ladies' room, it's right around the corner there. I'll watch your bags."

Sure you will. Alexandra crossed her arms. She wasn't stupid. Let these suitcases out of her sight for a moment and the derelict would snatch them and run. She hadn't lived in New York City for six years without learning a thing or two. And as for riding with him . . .

"So, you're in Kenya on business," he said, shoving his hands into his pockets. "Let me guess. You live in New York, but you're originally from . . . Texas."

"How did you—?"

"The accent. You're a Rice graduate?"

"Baylor."

"Of course. Green and gold. Sic 'em Bears." He gave her that lopsided grin again. "You studied business, but you got a job in . . ." He looked her up and down. "Fashion merchandising."

"Wrong."

"Design."

Who *was* this man? "Fabric design," she said. "Look, I'm exhausted. Could we drop the inquisition?"

"Inquisition? I simply analyzed you, proposed a theory,

and was proven correct." He turned toward the security gates, where a line of arriving passengers was assembling. "This must be her flight."

Alexandra used the moment to study the man beside her. Despite his shabby appearance, the derelict was downright pompous. *I'll take you into the city. . . . I'll watch your bags. . . . Sic 'em Bears. . . .* As if a man like him had ever seen the inside of a university classroom. His hair had probably been trimmed with a hunting knife. And those whiskers. At least three days of dark growth shadowed a jaw that might actually look firm if he bothered to shave.

The fellow had straight teeth and bright gray blue eyes, but the getup he wore! On a fashion runway it might be called nouveau Indiana Jones . . . grungy chic. On this guy, it looked like nothing better than bottom-of-the-barrel thrift shop. Who on earth could he be meeting? A wife? A girlfriend? Hard to imagine.

"Good thing Hannah's plane was late, too," he said. "Otherwise, you'd be stuck without me."

"Too bad." She searched the crowd for the man's likely match. If the woman looked even halfway respectable, Alexandra might accept a ride with the two of them. "So, who's Hannah?"

A slow smile crept across his lips. "Hannah . . . she's my mom."

"Your mother? You're waiting for your mother?"

"Sort of." He lifted a thumb. "There she is! Hey, Hannah."

Expecting to see an elderly version of the derelict, Alexandra scanned the passengers flooding through the gates. A tiny, dark-skinned wren of a woman picked her way through the crowd and held out her arms. The man covered the space between them in two strides, picked up the old lady, and planted a big kiss on her chocolate brown cheek. An African? The man's mother was an African?

Alexandra reached for her carry-on bag. This was too weird. She had to find another way out of her predicament.

"Mama Hannah," the man said, setting the little woman in Alexandra's path, "you look great. The same as ever. How's Jessica? Did she and Rick really get back together? And what's this about Tillie? She's pregnant?"

"Grant." The old woman cupped the man's stubbly cheeks in her two hands. "So handsome. My *toto* . . . all grown up. You don't look very sick. Not as I feared."

"Just a touch of the old bug. A little fever, that's all. You didn't need to come all this way."

"I wanted to see you. And Jessica and Rick should have time together . . . time alone." Bright brown eyes turned on Alexandra. "Who is this? Grant, you did not tell me you had found a woman. She is such a beautiful girl."

"Her?" He glanced at Alexandra as if seeing her for the first time.

"He's been *analyzing* me," she explained to Hannah as the two women shook hands. "But I don't think he's actually looked at me. My name is Alexandra Prescott. I've just arrived from New York, and my limousine failed to pick me up."

"Are you afraid?" Hannah asked, searching her face.

"No. I'm just . . . just a little irked. I'm tired."

"I also am tired. Come along, Grant," Hannah said. "Pick up the bags. Take us to your car."

Alexandra tried to hide her smirk as Mr. Pompous

meekly gathered up two of her wheeled bags and the old woman's small suitcase. She felt sure Hannah wouldn't allow any nonsense. Whoever this Grant was, it appeared he could be trusted to take Alexandra as far as the Hilton Hotel.

As they began walking toward the wide exits, she let out a deep breath. This was not so bad. She had expected an adventure in Africa, inspiration for the line of exotic fabrics she was designing. She had looked forward to a change from the routine of city life, and she eagerly anticipated a break from the onslaught of another New York winter. The travel agency had let her down, but she had learned to be flexible.

And she sensed that God was with her. He had provided the derelict and his African mother—a pair of odd angels, to be sure. All the same, Alexandra was going to be all right.

ONE

As Alexandra stepped out into the African night, a sense of the mystery of the great continent prickled up her spine. No, there weren't any cannibals jumping around a fire or leopards creeping through the jungle or sahibs riding by on elephants. In fact, compact European cars cruised paved streets that led to a distant skyline of glittering lights. It might have been New York—except for the palm trees rustling in the warm breeze, the fragrance of tropical blossoms, the Swahili cries of vendors hawking newspapers and roasted corn on the cob. And overhead . . .

Alexandra stared up in wonder at the multitude of stars, billions of twinkling crystals. Constellations she had never seen before lay across the velvet expanse like expensive, Tiffany-designed brooches and necklaces. The Milky Way carved a creamy path through the midst of the heavens. And all of it hung so close, just over the tips of the palm fronds.

"Better close your mouth or you'll start catching flies." Grant took Alexandra's attaché case out of her hand before she could reply. He slung it into the back of a rusty Land Rover and slammed the door. "In Africa, those could be tsetse flies. First thing you know, you'll fall into a deep sleep—and it'll take more than the kiss of a handsome prince to wake you up."

"Grant!" Hannah touched Alexandra's hand. "He has always been a naughty boy, that one. I promise you will not find tsetse flies in Nairobi. They live in the bush country."

"That's a relief." Of course, she would be heading out on a safari into the bush country in a matter of days. She was scheduled to tour game parks, visit the coast, and even climb Mount Kilimanjaro. But tsetse flies certainly hadn't been in the brochure.

"Hop in the back, Miss Prescott," Grant said, tilting the front seat forward. "Just push some of that stuff out of the way."

Alexandra set one foot into the Land Rover and stared in disgust at the heaps and piles on the backseat—tattered books, reams of dog-eared papers, blackened banana peels, stray socks, tape recorders, and enough empty candy-bar wrappers to fill two trash cans. The smell made her gasp. Who was this guy? Some kind of international, roving garbage collector?

She cleared a space between a box of cassette tapes and a wadded-up coat. Then she sat down carefully, her knees tucked together and her toes aligned. She wouldn't be the least surprised if something came crawling out to sit on her lap.

"Oh, Grant, my *toto*," Hannah said as she climbed into the front seat. "You are worse than ever with your things. And what have you been eating? Kit Kat bars? Will you survive on those? No wonder the malaria attacked you so easily. You must become strong. Don't you know that your body is the temple of the Lord?"

The man beside her leaned over and planted another kiss on the old woman's leathery cheek. "I'm a bachelor, Mama

Hannah. I like it that way. Eat what I want, when I want. Sleep when I'm tired. Mind my own business. You know what I mean?"

As he started the Land Rover, the African woman shook her head. "I never mind only my own business."

"I've noticed that."

"Jesus Christ gave you and your three sisters into my hands long ago. How can I stand back and watch you live in this way?"

"Mama Hannah, I'm thirty-three years old."

"By now you should have a wife. Children." She looked over the back of her seat and studied Alexandra. "What do you think about this, Miss Prescott? Should this boy not find a good woman to marry?"

Alexandra cleared her throat. "Well, I—"

"Mama Hannah," Grant cut in, "you've been hanging around with my moon-eyed sisters too long. I'm happy for Tillie and Jess. I really am. But I don't want you doing any matchmaking for me, OK? I have a lot more important things to focus on. Did I tell you about the group of Ilmolelian clan members I've been talking with over near Mount Kilimanjaro? Ilkisongo area. Intriguing bunch. You'll be fascinated."

"He changes the subject," the old woman said to Alexandra. "Do you see how he does that? This boy is very smart. I cannot understand why a woman would not want to marry him."

Alexandra mustered a smile. *She* could understand perfectly. What woman in her right mind would hook up with this derelict? Sure, he had an obvious tenderness for the African woman. You could even say the man had a nice pair of eyes and a disarming grin. But his clothes . . . and this car! She had heard enough sermons to know it was wrong to judge a person by outward appearance. But she had dated enough men to trust her intuition just a little. If this Grant fellow didn't care about his health and his appearance—what would he care about?

"Miss Prescott, you have come a long way from New York to Kenya," Hannah said. "I wonder what you will do here."

"Business," Grant answered in Alexandra's place. "She's a fabric designer. Getting ideas from the wilds of Africa."

"I am certain you will make beautiful designs," Hannah said.

"I suggest you study the animals closely while you're here," Grant continued. "Scrutinize the fauna. Really look. The lines of a zebra's hide. Fascinating. The babies are brown and white, you know. Please don't give them black stripes. African elephants have big ears, huge tattered appendages. Don't draw in the tiny little flappers that Asian elephants have. In fact, you ought to visit my sister Fiona. She lives with the elephants over in the Serengeti. She could show you a thing or two."

"Your sister lives with elephants?" Alexandra asked. She was beginning to assemble a very odd portrait of this family. A derelict brother. A crackpot sister. And a mother—the sanest of the lot—who couldn't possibly be their mother.

Grant glanced back over his shoulder as he drove. "Elephants," he repeated. "Of course, Fiona wouldn't let you near her campsite. Hates people as much as I like them. She's sort of the eccentric type."

"Unlike you," Alexandra said under her breath. Aloud she added, "What exactly do you do, Mr. . . . ?"

"Thornton. Grant Thornton." He gave her that lopsided grin. "I wander around mostly. Talk to people."

"Grant, tell her what you *really* do," Hannah ordered. "We are here in the city now, and your guest must think very badly of you."

"Yep, Nairobi. City of eternal springtime." Ignoring the old woman, he steered the Land Rover around a large traffic circle. "Ten carjackings a day. That's the downside of Nairobi, Miss Prescott. That and a few random murders, the occasional student riot, and a crumbling city infrastructure. Potholes in the roads, unreliable water and electrical systems, a political structure in the throes of government reorganization. That sort of thing."

"Sounds like New York."

"The urban jungle."

"So what's the upside?"

"Flowers—bougainvillea, frangipani, hibiscus. Food—African, Indian, Chinese, Italian. Weather—no sleet, hail, snow, tornadoes, or hurricanes. Even the earthquakes keep it down to the occasional tremor or two. Best of all, I guess, would be the people. Asians, Arabs, and Europeans are interesting. But it's the Africans who turn my wheels. In one country you have four different ethnic units, more than forty indigenous groups, and just as many languages, customs, beliefs, and rituals. The place is a candy store for a guy like me. A real candy store."

In spite of the odor of overripe bananas and the sticky substance on the soles of both of her shoes, Alexandra was curious. "So, what do you really do here?" she repeated. "I mean . . . to earn a living."

"I just told you." He pulled the Land Rover to a stop in front of a round tower that rose into the night sky. "Hilton International. Swimming pool. Shopping arcade. Communications center. Western civilization. Hang on, I'll get your bags."

Before Alexandra could climb over a pair of hiking boots and out the door, the African woman reached around and touched her arm. "May God bless you," she said softly.

"May he bless you, too. Hannah, you mentioned Christ earlier. Are you a Christian?"

The brown eyes softened. "I am. And you?"

"Yes, I am." Alexandra impulsively slipped her arms around the old woman's neck. "I feel better knowing there's someone in this country who shares my faith."

"There are many believers in Kenya. But it is not we who must give you courage and strength. It is our Lord himself."

Warmth flooding her heart, Alexandra looked into the woman's dark eyes. "Pray for me," she whispered.

"Hey, are you two going to gab all night?" Grant poked his head through the open door. "Come on, Miss Prescott. I've got things to do."

"Wander around and talk to people?" Alexandra stepped out onto the sidewalk. "Thank you, Mr. Thornton. I'd offer to pay you, but—"

"But you haven't exchanged your money yet. That's OK. You've been an interesting specimen."

"Specimen?" she repeated, bristling.

He laughed. "OK, I'll stop analyzing you for a minute.

I'll look you up and down, man to woman. Yep, you're a beautiful blonde with legs that ought to be banned. If I weren't already committed, I'd ask you out to lunch."

"You said you were a bachelor."

"I'm not married—but I'm not available. My work, you know. Keeps me busy, challenges me. I'm happy. What else does a man need?"

"Let me think now. Why *do* people get together? Could it be . . . love?"

He let out a low whistle. "Don't try to trip me up, Miss Prescott. I'm a sucker for a clever woman."

"Flatter me all you want, Mr. Thornton. You'll be disappointed. I'm only in Kenya a couple of weeks. Besides, I prefer a man who woos me with flowers—not one who sticks me to the floor of his car with spilled Coke."

He was chuckling as she picked up her attaché case. A bellhop had already begun loading her bags onto a large, brass-trimmed cart. From the open glass door of the lobby she could smell the familiar scent of luxury hotel—clean floors, leather chairs, air-conditioning.

"Thanks for the ride," Alexandra said, extending her hand.

Grant took it and gave a firm squeeze. "My pleasure. Oh, and if you need another ride or anything, you can look me up in the town of Oloitokitok. It's near the Amboseli Game Park. The folks there will give you directions to my camp. It's the Maasai Oral Mythology Project. Ask for *Bwana* Hadithi, the story man."

As he spoke, he walked toward the Land Rover, his hair backlit to a burnished gold by a streetlamp. Alexandra lifted a hand. Her derelict angel. Odd how very strong and solid he looked just at this moment.

"The story man?"

"That's me," he called as he ducked into the Land Rover. "Grant Thornton."

Before Alexandra could react, the vehicle had sped away, straddling a pothole in the street and then vanishing around a corner. She stood staring at the place it had been, wondering what sort of dream she'd been tossed into.

"Grant Thornton," she repeated numbly.

"You are a friend of the Thornton family, madam?" the bellhop asked. He was a towering African with a smile that exuded courtesy. "They are well loved in Kenya."

"I don't know them. I just sort of ran into Mr. Thornton at the airport."

"Oh yes, a fine family. They have lived in Kenya many years. The father is a professor at the university. The children are scientists, I believe. One studies elephants. She is helping to stop poachers. Another works to grow crops for dry lands. The other I do not know well. Dr. Thornton— the man who brought you here—he is a good person. The books he writes are in the city library. You can read them."

"*Dr.* Thornton? He's a scientist?"

"He listens to the stories of the tribes of Kenya. He writes them down so they will not fade from memory as people move into the city and the old ways begin to vanish."

"He doesn't seem very . . . organized. I mean his car. His clothes."

The bellhop grinned. "It is not the look of Dr. Thornton that matters to the people of Kenya—his white skin or his old coat. It is his heart that we love."

Alexandra clutched her case as the man wheeled his cart toward the hotel lobby. All her education, wealth, and busi-

ness acumen couldn't outweigh the sudden sense of loneliness that swept over her. She could claim fame as a
designer. She could claim associates in the highest echelon
of New York society. But she couldn't claim that anyone
. . . even a single soul . . . loved her heart.

"Miss Prescott is a beautiful woman," Mama Hannah said as
she sat with Grant on the guest-house balcony that evening.
"We should stay in Nairobi for a few more days. You could
eat dinner with her tomorrow."

Grant took a sip of tea and hooked his heels over the
balcony railing. "Too much work to do back at my camp,
Mama Hannah. There's a big Maasai initiation ceremony
coming up. Lots of storytelling."

"You do not think she is pretty?"

He shrugged. "She's tall."

"Is that all you saw in her? She looks like you, Grant."

"Like me? No way." Crossing his legs at the ankle, he
focused on the dark wedge of city skyline between his safari
boots. Pale electric lights glimmered—nothing like the
billions of bright stars that canopied his tent. He couldn't
wait to get back to the bush.

"Alexandra Prescott is New York City from her head to
her toes," he said. "Did you see those crazy shoes she was
wearing? One misstep and she'll snap an ankle. How can
you say she's anything like me?"

"Both are tall. Blue eyes."

"Mine are gray."

"Yellow hair."

"Mine's brown." He gave her his best scowl. "A couple of years go by, and you forget what I look like."

"Your hair is golden from the sun, Grant Thornton, and you cannot deny it. You are my *toto,* and I will never forget one thing about you. I know you are smart. You are handsome. You are kind. And you are lonely."

As usual, Mama Hannah stated her opinions bluntly. Grant liked that. As a child, he'd always been able to count on her to tell him the truth. His mother's untimely death and his father's indifference toward him could have sent him into a nosedive. But Mama Hannah had always been there—the rudder in the storms that had beset the four Thornton children.

"You're right," he admitted finally. "Sometimes I get a little lonely out there in the boonies. That's one reason I'm glad you've come."

The old woman lifted her teacup to her lips. She shut her eyes for a moment as she drank. Then she smiled at Grant. "I will make tea for you, *toto.* I will see that your clothes are washed. Maybe I will even make a cake for you."

"Can you fix a pot of that stew I always liked? The stuff with the beans and cauliflower?"

"Ehh. I will fill your stomach. But I will not be able to fill the lonely place inside your heart, Grant."

"Uh-oh, I can feel a Sunday school lesson coming on."

"What do you think I will say? You are grown now. You tell me the lesson."

He leaned his head back and mentally sorted through the lists of Bible stories he had learned at Hannah's knee. He had loved the tales—loved them so much he had made his life's work collecting the mythological stories of African peoples. Even as an adult, he could hardly get through a day without two or three of Mama Hannah's little biblical parables or Scripture verses drifting at him out of nowhere. Now that she was back in his life, he knew the lessons would resume—stories about a God so real to this woman that she couldn't exist without him . . . a God so impossible that Grant could never accept him.

"The lesson for the day," he said. He closed his eyes, imagining he was seated among a circle of Maasai tribespeople, their dark skin glowing in the light from the fire that crackled in their midst. The voice of the storyteller would emerge from the vacuum of night.

"Once, there was a good man named Daniel," Grant said, keeping his words low and hypnotic. "Daniel was a chief elder in the clan of the Medes, of which Darius was the powerful *laibon*. Some of the other elders were jealous of Daniel and his influence with Darius, so they plotted against him. They went to Darius and asked him to order everyone to pray only to the *laibon,* instead of to God, *Engai.* Later, these wicked elders went and found Daniel praying to *Engai* as he always did. So the *laibon* ordered Daniel taken to the foot of Mount Kilimanjaro and sealed into a cave where there lived a pride of hungry lions. Early the next morning, the *laibon* went to the cave and called to Daniel. Daniel answered that *Engai* had shut the lions' mouths, and therefore he was innocent of any wrongs. The *laibon* took Daniel out of the cave and threw Daniel's accusers among the lions, who tore them apart."

"You tell the story well," Hannah said softly. "Although I am sure Daniel's den of lions was not at the foot of Mount

Kilimanjaro, and King Darius was not a Maasai witch doctor."

"Does it really matter, Mama Hannah? It's a story. Fiction. The tale was handed down from generation to generation in order to illustrate a point to the Jewish people. If I alter the details a little, maybe the Maasai can learn something from it."

The old woman sat in silence for a long time, and Grant knew he had offended her. To Mama Hannah, the Bible was not a collection of folktales. For her, it was truth—even the parables held such power they could change the lives of those who heard them.

It had always intrigued Grant that this African woman—thoroughly steeped in her own tribal culture as a child and young adult—had completely embraced the theology of a foreign race. What was it about Christianity that had won her over? Why did his words of callous indifference make her bristle? No, it wasn't anger he saw in her brown eyes. . . . It was sorrow.

"I apologize, Mama Hannah," he said. "I know the story of Daniel in the lions' den is important to you."

"You called it a lesson," she responded. "You said it has a point. What shall we learn from this Scripture about Daniel?"

"The moral of the story relates to your statement about my empty heart: Man needs God."

"Ehh."

"Especially if he wants to avoid being ripped apart by a pride of hungry lions."

"Now you make a joke. When you come too close to the truth, Grant, you run. Even with Miss Prescott, you cannot permit yourself to look for the good in her."

"What is it with you and that woman?" he said, unhooking his feet from the balcony rail. "It's so obvious we're worlds apart in every way. She's a New York fabric designer. I'm an anthropologist living with the Maasai. She fills her days with cappuccino and power lunches and cellular phones. I sit on the ground outside a dung-plastered hut, swapping stories with a man who has three wives and wears empty film canisters in the holes of his earlobes. Alexandra Prescott and I have nothing in common. Nothing."

"Nothing in common . . . perhaps each of you has something the other lacks."

"Except that I have everything I need." Grant stood and started toward the door.

"I see you are preparing to run again. This tells me I have come close to the truth about you."

Grant let out a hot breath and leaned against the aluminum door frame. "Look, Mama Hannah, I don't mean to be disrespectful, but I have no time to discuss things that aren't important. My work is time-consuming, and I've got to focus. Admitting a woman into my life—any woman, but especially one like Miss Prescott—would be a mistake."

"You know her, *toto?*"

"I know the type. I dated plenty in college and grad school. And I found out I don't relate to American women very well. Maybe it's because I grew up in Kenya. Alexandra Prescott and I might as well be from different planets."

"Ehh," she said, "I understand."

Grant stepped through the sliding glass door and walked across the room toward the shower as he mentally continued the argument. Foreign thoughts, ideologies, and customs just weren't compatible. You couldn't mix cultures and end up with anything but a mess.

But as he set foot on the cool tile floor, it occurred to him that Mama Hannah was an African woman with four white children and a Christian God. Grant himself was the product of an American-British marriage—a white man who lived happily among the Maasai. And Miss Alexandra Prescott was a suave New Yorker who somehow had endeared herself to the woman he loved most in all the world.

Two

Alexandra dipped her toes into the warm water and leaned back against a thick cushion at the edge of the deserted swimming pool. Sketch pad abandoned at her side, she lifted her focus to the snowcapped mountain peak hovering in the cloudless evening sky. *Kilimanjaro.* Shades of gray and teal at its wide volcanic base blended in with the unending expanse of the heavens. Never had she seen anything so magnificent.

"Practically smack-dab on the equator," a man said, sitting down near her at the poolside. "Hard to believe, isn't it?"

Alexandra glanced at him, a little irked that he had interrupted her solitude. After a trip through the Nairobi Game Park and three days of city bustle spent visiting shops and purchasing local handicrafts, she had eagerly anticipated the time she would spend here at Amboseli. The lodge, an expensive luxury resort, had few guests and not a single child among them. The surrounding game park, perched near the foot of Mount Kilimanjaro, was a reputed haven for wildlife—from lions and zebras to birds of every hue. With ten days of her tour remaining, Alexandra could hardly wait to get out into the bush country and begin sketching.

"You speak English?" Another man appeared beside her.

"I'm from New York," she said.

He smiled and nodded. "Likewise. Small world, huh?"

She gave him a cursory glance. Large shouldered and brawny, he had coal black hair and a gold stud earring in one ear. He rubbed his pencil-thin mustache with the side of a finger. Her immediate reaction was disgust.

But then she remembered Grant Thornton. *Dr.* Grant Thornton, the beloved anthropologist who was preserving the tales of the African people for posterity. She had dismissed him as a derelict. And the tiny dark-skinned woman—Mama Hannah—had turned out to be a committed Christian.

How wrong it was to judge people by their appearance. She should have learned that lesson long ago, yet she failed again and again. She knew why trusting people was so hard for her. Years ago her father's misplaced confidence in an associate had nearly cost him his company, and the lesson had not been lost on his daughter. "They're all after your money," he had told her. And he had been right. Rather than wonder whether people liked her for herself or her wealth, Alexandra had simply avoided getting close.

"Are you an artist?" the man asked.

Alexandra stirred the water with her toe. *Lord, help me start to trust. Teach me to care about others.*

"I mean, I noticed your notebook and all," he went on. "I'm kind of an artist myself. A poet, really."

"You're a writer?" she asked, deliberately turning toward him. She should at least give the man a chance. "Have you been published?"

He snickered. "Naw, I just do it for myself, you know. But you come out here to a place like this and first thing you know, the muse strikes. In fact, I wrote a little verse this morning on the way down here to the lodge. I guess you didn't notice me on the plane, but I sat behind you." He fished in the front pocket of his polyester shirt. "Would you like to hear it?"

Alexandra swallowed. No, she didn't want to listen to some stranger's poetry. In preparation for dinner, all the other guests had abandoned the pool, and she relished the silence. She wanted to drink in the evening, gaze at the mountain, and translate her emotions onto the page of her sketch pad.

"Sure," she said, forcing a smile. "Read away."

He unwadded a cocktail napkin and cleared his throat.

> "I fly up in the sky so blue;
> The mountain is below me, too.
> The green grass grows upon the hill.
> The river flows. It don't stand still.
> I think about the one I love . . ."

He stopped and glanced at her.

"Go on," she said.

"I can't ever think of words to rhyme with *love*. Wouldn't you know it? The best word in a poem and nothing to rhyme with it but *of, dove,* or *above.*"

"You're in an airplane in the poem. Maybe you could write something like . . . I think about the one I love . . . and God—"

"No, wait! I got it. I think about the one I love and all the rainbows up above."

"Nice." She picked up her tote bag, stood, and stepped

into her shoes. *Nice—if you're in the second grade. No, Lord, don't let me be so judgmental!*

"Thanks," he said, scribbling the new words onto the napkin. "I'm glad you like it. I've got a whole lot more back in my room."

"Oops, looks like the mosquitoes are coming out." She gestured to her bare arms. "I understand you can get malaria in Kenya. I guess I'll go on inside and get ready for dinner. See you later."

"How about a drink afterward?" He stood, a good two inches shorter than she was but twice as wide through the shoulders. He stuck out a beefy hand. "I'm Nicholas Jones. My friends call me Nick."

"Nick." She shook his hand. "Alexandra Prescott."

"Prescott? Like with Prescott Company? The wire hangers?"

Alexandra stiffened. Her parents had been well known in Dallas high society. But few spoke of the source of their money—plastic-coated wire hangers, wire shelving systems, wire utility baskets.

From humble roots, Alex Prescott had built his company into a multimillion-dollar enterprise. At his death, he had left his only child a dazzling fortune. She was always the center of attention. The heiress, Alexandra, and where she would go to college, whom she would date, what she would be wearing at the charity ball tended to obscure the source—wire hangers.

"My dad worked in the garment district," Nick said proudly. "Seventh Avenue. We always knew about the Prescott Company."

"Are you in clothing?" She couldn't imagine what this man was doing on a luxury safari in Africa. "Design?"

He laughed. "I'm in security."

"A policeman?"

"Bodyguard." He stuck out his chin. "I protect the personal interests of my clients."

"Ahh. So, you're here with one of your clients."

"Naw. Just came on a vacation by myself. I wanted to get away, you know. Do some thinking."

"Write poetry?"

"Yeah." He chuckled. "You know something? I like you, Alexandra Prescott. You're a good-looking woman. Smart, too. I can tell. What about that drink after dinner? Out here by the pool."

"I don't drink." She slung her tote over her shoulder. "Besides, I want to turn in early. I'm going out at dawn to study the wildlife."

She started toward the main building of the luxury lodge, but he came after her. When he grabbed her wrist in a bone-crunching grip, she came to a stop and winced in pain.

"Oh, sorry." He let go of her hand and fingered the thick gold chain around his throat. "I guess I don't know my own strength. You OK?"

She rubbed her wrist. "I'm fine. Look, let's be up-front about things. I came here to get away. I don't want any involvements."

"Who said anything about involvements? I'm not looking for a long-term deal. Not at all. I just asked you for a drink, OK? You're out here by yourself. Me, too. We're both artists."

"How do you know I'm an artist?"

"Well . . . your notebook."

"I'm a commercial designer. Fabrics. I'm in Kenya on business. I have just a few days to come up with an entire line that will be carried by Bloomingdale's, Macy's, Neiman Marcus, everybody. My time is booked solid. I'm trying to be polite here, but please—leave me alone."

"Whoa. You don't strike me as nice as I thought at first." He looked down at his feet. "I was just trying to be friendly. That's all. Just one decent human being to another."

Guilt ate into Alexandra's resolve. "I'm sorry, Nick. Really, I just—"

"Prescott! Prescott!" An African waiter carrying a small chalkboard hung with bells walked down from the lodge. "Is Prescott by the pool, please?"

"I'm Alexandra Prescott," she said. "What is it?"

"A cablegram." He handed her a small white envelope. "You will find a telephone at the front desk, madam, should you have an emergency."

Emergency! Had someone she loved died? She couldn't think of anyone she had allowed close enough to fit that category. Her mouth suddenly dry, Alexandra tore open the cablegram. It was from the brokerage firm that handled her investments. She had given her itinerary to the secretary, so the cablegram itself was not a surprise. The message inside was:

DUE TO STOCK-MARKET FLUCTUATIONS, YOUR ACCOUNT SHOWS A DEFICIT BALANCE OF -$203,127.36. TO AVOID PENALTIES AND FEES YOU MUST IMMEDIATELY DEPOSIT . . .

Two hundred thousand dollars! Alexandra stared unsee-
ing at the mountain in the distance. How could her account
be short? James Cooper, her broker, was a gifted money
manager. He had always invested capably on her behalf.
This had to be a mistake. She read the rest of the message—
a composite of dire warnings and veiled threats. In sum, it
sounded as though she was on the brink of losing everything.

"Something wrong?" Nick asked.

"I need to make a call." She looked down at her watch.
Was it eight hours earlier in New York or only seven?
Grant Thornton's face flashed before her eyes. What had he
told her? *We don't mess around with the time in Africa. Sun rises
at six. Sets at six.* A pale orange glow lit the snows of
Kilimanjaro. Six in the evening in Kenya . . . that would
make it ten in the morning in New York. Thank heaven.
She would call James Cooper.

"Excuse me," she said to the burly bodyguard. "I have to
go."

Before he could reply, Alexandra hurried up from the
pool and into the lodge, where she began trying to place a
long-distance call to the United States. Easier said than done
in the Third World. She spent an hour talking to operators,
listening to the beep of phone lines, and enduring the
repeated mechanical comment that "all international circuits
are busy at this time."

Finally her call to the brokerage firm went through.
"James Cooper, please," she said. "This is Alexandra
Prescott. I'm calling from Africa."

"Africa!" The secretary seemed stunned. "I'm sorry, Miss

Prescott, but Mr. Cooper is on vacation this week. Would you like to leave a message on his voice mail?"

It was the best she could do. Alexandra listened to the reassuring tones of the man who had been her family's financial advisor and the trustee of her own accounts since her father's death. At that time, she had been little more than a teenager, and James Cooper was the only man she had allowed herself to trust with the true status of the vast Prescott portfolio. Aware that her focus of interest lay in design rather than in finance, he had assured her that he would take care of everything, and his monthly statements to her had always confirmed his skills in money management.

"James," she said when the tape of his voice had finished playing, "this is Alexandra. As you know, I'm in Kenya. I just got a cable that says my account is short. I don't understand what's going on, James, but I want you to take care of this. Leave a message with your secretary. I'll check back in tomorrow." She paused and took a deep breath. "James, I'm counting on you."

After hanging up, she stood in silence, pondering the ramifications of the situation. Two hundred thousand dollars in deficit. How could that be? James had always been a prudent investor. Where could the money have gone? She envisioned her father's face—the strain of years of shrewd deals and risky business decisions etched in the lines across his forehead. Though they were worlds apart in personality, she had loved him deeply. She had always felt a responsibility to safeguard and increase the legacy he had left.

Very little of the Prescott Company money went into her pocket. She took pride in supporting herself financially. Her education and talent had brought her a respectable income of her own. But in the back of her mind she had plans for her father's money. Once she had garnered industry respect and a sizable clientele, she would establish her own New York design firm. Already, she was considered a major talent in the field, and if she launched out now, she could probably make her mark. But a few more years working for others would ensure success. Then she could hire skilled artists, develop her own signature lines, and build a name that would bring honor to her father's heritage.

But she could never do it without his money.

A knot was forming at the top of her stomach as she turned away from the lobby desk and studied the lodge dining room. Guests were setting wadded cloth napkins on the tables and rising to leave. She had missed the dinner hour. Great.

"Got a problem?"

Grant? Her heart contracted as she swung around. In the anthropologist's place stood the Polyester Poet. "Oh, Nick. It's you."

"Just thought I'd check on you. You've been on the phone a long time."

"I was calling the States. It's hard to get through." Why had the thought of Grant Thornton come so quickly to mind? Alexandra conjured the image of the derelict. At this moment the sight of a sensible, intelligent human being would be a blessing. She looked at Nick Jones, and her heart sank.

"Everything OK?" he asked, digging between his two front teeth with a wooden toothpick. "I don't mean to pry or nothing, but you look kind of worried."

"Just business. Some sort of mix-up with my brokerage account."

He shook his head. "And you're all the way out here in Africa. Did you get ahold of anybody who can help?"

"My broker's on vacation." She considered for a moment. "You know, I think I'll phone a guy I know in Dallas. He's an old friend of my family. Maybe he can give me some advice."

She turned back to the phone, but Nick inserted himself between her and the lobby desk. "Not so fast there. You better take care of *you* first. It's still morning in New York, and you got plenty of time to make your calls. But you haven't had a bite to eat, have you? I didn't think so. How about I put in an order with the hotel kitchen, and then we'll take a walk by the pool while they fix it? I don't mean to intrude on your private business, you understand. But you and me . . . we're the only two Americans in the place. I reckon we ought to stick together, huh? What do you say?"

The last thing Alexandra wanted to do was go for a walk with Nick Jones. "It took me nearly an hour to get through to New York—"

"Yeah, and if you start trying to call again, you're gonna fade away from hunger. Am I right? OK, so put this in my hands, babe. I'll take care of you. Not horning in or nothing. Just seeing to the welfare of my fellow American. Now sit down over there on that chair. I'll get you a sandwich. How about it? Ham and cheese?"

"Fine. OK." Alexandra rolled her eyes as he walked toward the kitchen. Just what she needed. A hero wanna-be. Rescue the damsel in distress. Only she'd never been the wilting-violet sort. She hadn't inherited her father's interest in mechanics and high finance, but she certainly had his backbone. She would get to the bottom of this mess. And she didn't need Nick Jones's help to do it.

The thought of valuable stocks being sold off in order to bolster an account deficit she hadn't even known was there sent another knot into her empty stomach. She would have no choice but to leave the lodge in the morning. The hotel personnel could help her find a travel agency and book a flight out of Nairobi. By the following day she'd be back in New York—back in charge.

Staring out into the black African night, she tried to form a prayer. God had given her this life, these responsibilities. She needed his advice. *Father, you're the only one I can trust. Please, Lord, show me what to do about my dad's money. Don't let them sell off the stocks.*

It seemed a little shallow to pray about money. All the same, she couldn't make her dreams come true without it. *Her* dreams . . .

"Two ham and cheese sandwiches coming up. Fifteen minutes max," Nick Jones said. He sauntered toward her, a slight smirk on his thin upper lip. "Come on, Alexandra. Let's get you out into the moonlight. A walk will do you good. Clear your head."

Alexandra considered protesting again. If he got ideas that this gallantry act of his appealed to her . . . still, she would be grateful for the sandwich. The other guests had apparently retired to their rooms or the hotel's bar, and the place was deserted. A walk around the pool actually would give her time to think—assuming Nick didn't start reciting iambic tetrameter again.

"Cooler than you'd think," he said, slipping his arm around her waist. "Dumb, I guess, but I figured it'd be hot as blazes at the equator."

"Maybe it's the altitude." She attempted to politely shrug him away.

His hand settled on her hip, holding her firmly in place at his side. "Snow at the equator. Kind of brings on the muse, doesn't it?"

"I'm really not in the mood for poetry."

"Me either." He rubbed his free hand down her bare arm. "You got goosebumps, pretty lady. I bet you won't have those when you get to the beach."

Alexandra stiffened. How did he know she was going to the coast? She hadn't told him her itinerary. "Nick, listen—"

"Hey, let's walk over to the edge of the patio. Did you get a look at the water hole down below there this afternoon? I counted fifteen deer."

"Antelope." He was leading her determinedly toward the shadowed stone wall that rimmed the lodge enclosure just beyond the swimming pool. For some reason, the pressure of his hand on her waist sent a curl of panic through Alexandra. She didn't like people coming so close. Especially someone she hardly knew. Again, she tried to push away. "Listen, Nick—"

His hand clamped over her mouth, cutting off her words. "We're outta here, baby," he said. Half lifting her from her feet, he exited the pool area through an iron gate and started down the steep slope toward the water hole. Obviously a path used only by hotel staff, it was narrow and unlit. Terror poured through Alexandra. She stumbled over an exposed root as she tried vainly to push away from him.

He left the trail and began dragging her through the tall grass away from the lodge, away from safety and reason and all that was civilized.

Horror mingling with determination to escape, Alexandra bit down hard on the man's finger. He didn't flinch. What could she do to stop him?

As he continued on, moving her farther and farther from the remnant of artificial light, she shuddered, nauseous. This couldn't be happening. She had to get away. Had to fight. *God, give me strength!* She kicked his shin and rammed her elbow into his stomach.

He marched doggedly onward, his fingers and thumb crushing into her cheeks. "You don't want to fight me, OK?"

Dragging her now, he moved toward a faintly moonlit outcrop of rock she had not noticed during the day. "You fight me . . . it's only gonna hurt worse," he continued. "I can make this nice and quick. Or not. It's kind of up to you."

Oh, God! The prayer was wrenched from Alexandra's heart. *God, help me! Help me!*

"See, the thing is, you made a mistake." He lugged her around the rock. "You trusted somebody you shouldn't ought to have trusted. Never trust nobody, baby. That's the rule I live by."

Alexandra swallowed and tried to force herself upright. If she could somehow trip him. Or distract him. Or outsmart him. *Oh, Lord, he's so much stronger than I am! You've got to save me!*

Nick Jones continued to haul her out onto the open plain

beyond the rock. By now, they were well away from the hotel. No one would hear her screams.

"This looks like a good spot," he said.

Struggling to breathe, focus, concentrate, Alexandra searched her surroundings. A huge tree overhead. A strange pointed mound of dirt nearby. Grass. Lots of moonlit grass. A weapon? Anything?

Dear God! Give me something to fight him with!

"I never killed anybody in Africa before," Nick said. "I did a guy in Mexico one time."

Alexandra moaned as he threw her to the ground beside the tree. He stood over her, one leg on either side, pinning her in place.

"Nick!" Her mouth finally free, she sucked in a breath. Reason with him. Logic. "Nick, think about this. People saw us together. We're the only Americans."

"Don't try to talk me out of this. I done it a hundred times." He flexed his arms and began stretching his fingers. "Truth is, I like what I do. It moves me—kind of like an inspiration, you know? You ought to read the poems I got about it. This one is gonna be real different. Out here, see, the animals will finish off what's left. That way I don't get the blame. No fingerprints, no nothing."

Oh, God, he's going to kill me! Kill me!

He set his hands on his hips and looked down at her. "You wanna choose? A gun's best, but I ain't had time to acquire one. I got a little knife that's quick across the throat. I got some wire. That way you black out before you go. Or I can just snap your neck. Kinda like a chicken. It's fast."

"Nick . . . Nick . . . please . . ."

"I'd pick the knife if I was you."

"Please!" *Give me time, Lord God, give me time. Help me!*

"Just don't fight me. I hate that. Wears me out, and then I got to walk all the way back to the hotel." He reached into his pocket and pulled out a length of curled electrical wire. Looming over her, he tested it, snapping it taut twice and then winding one end around the meat of his hand.

"OK, baby. Just relax." He squatted over her and slipped his hand behind her head. "Pretty hair. Good thing it's short. Now, I'm going to wrap this wire around your neck—"

"In the tree!" she shrieked, pointing up into the branches, where a dark spotted shape crouched. "It—it's . . . it's a l–l–leopard!"

"Huh?" He straightened quickly, looking up into the tree.

"Move!" She threw her body sideways, fearing the lurking creature as much as the man.

Knocked off balance, Nick grabbed at her. "You little—!"

"It's going to pounce!" She wrenched herself out from under him and scrambled on her knees around the tree trunk. As she rose and started through the tall grass, she suddenly knew she could never outrun the man, never hide from the leopard. She ducked her head down and sank to all fours again. *Dear God, dear God.* Sliding, staying low, she crawled toward the pointed mound. *Hide me, Lord! Hide me in the darkness!*

"Where'd you go, you crazy chick?" he roared. "I told you not to try nothing, didn't I?"

She slipped behind the hillock and clung to it for a moment, breathing hard, arms stretched wide, fingers digging into the soil. The warmth from the dirt soaked into her skin. Why hadn't the leopard followed? What should she do?

Go, Alexandra. Go again. Run.

Moonbeams silvered the long grasses. A soft breeze barely ruffled their tips, like waves on a sheltered lake. If she kept low . . . stayed down . . . maybe she could crawl away from the human monster, crawl to . . . to what? At the lodge, Nick would find her again. She couldn't go there, and this place was a leopard's territory. Where to hide?

She started off again, sliding along on her belly like a snake, hardly rustling the grass. Where could she go? So many animals lived out here. Leopards. Lions. Cheetahs.

In the midst of her panic, the face of the wise old Mama Hannah suddenly shone like a beacon before her. As Alexandra crawled through the brush, she could hear Nick Jones nearby, calling her name, cursing her, swearing he'd find her and kill her. Sometimes he moved closer, and she stopped. She curled into a ball, hiding herself in the darkness like a hunted animal.

When his voice sounded from farther away, she crept on. Thorns pricked her palms; sharp grass scraped her bare arms; stones cut into her knees. *Father God, help me. Help me get away. Keep me safe. Show me where to go.*

The answer floated always just ahead of her. Mama Hannah. Somehow, she must find Mama Hannah.

THREE

When the lights of the luxury lodge were no more than pinpricks in the distance, and when she could no longer hear the voice of the demon who wanted to kill her, Alexandra stood and began to run.

As she ran, a thousand questions tumbled through her mind. *Why me? Why now?* Had Nick Jones focused on her, planned his attack, stalked her to the lodge? All the way to Africa? Or was it just a terrible coincidence that had put her in the path of a psychopathic murderer? Should she return to the safety of the lodge? Could anyone there protect her from him? What if she stayed in the wilderness? Would that leopard attack her?

Mama Hannah. Maybe Alexandra was delirious in her fixation on an old woman she barely knew. But Mama Hannah—the embodiment of kindness, security, faith—seemed the only answer to her questions. So she simply ran on in the direction of Mount Kilimanjaro. The great mountain loomed over her, its snowy peak bathed in moonlight. Dr. Thornton had said his camp lay near the foothills. But how could she find a single tent in the midst of this wilderness? Were there roads out here? People? This was nothing like New York, of course. Even Texas, with its wide-open spaces, couldn't compare with the vast emptiness surrounding her.

Lungs bursting, she finally slowed to a trot. Reality sank in. She had survived. God had brought her through! It suddenly hit her that he had heard her prayer for help, and that maybe—just maybe—it was her heavenly Father who had provided the mysterious leopard. Relief sent tears streaming down her cheeks. She continued walking, crying, praying, through the darkness. The moon rose high overhead, silver and bright like a new coin. The image brought her previous concerns to mind—an account deficit, an absentee stockbroker, the threat of losing everything. How paltry her worries seemed now. It hardly mattered if she lost her money. She had almost lost her life.

As her pace slowed, fear again crept over her. She spotted a moonlit tree in the distance. Climbing into its branches would not offer much protection in a country known for its big cats. She had half convinced herself that God had sent the leopard when she thought she heard a sound behind her. Her spine prickled as she swung around and searched the darkness. Was that a rustle in the grass? The leopard? A lion? Or Nick Jones?

She began to run toward the tree. She reached it, scanned the upper limbs, and then grabbed the first branch. Thorns tore into her palms. Gasping in pain, she huddled at the base of the trunk. A dead branch covered with thorns lay nearby. She gingerly picked it up and propped it beside her. *Her weapon.*

Determined to fight fatigue, she leaned against the tree and stared into the darkness. What was out there? What lay ahead of her? Whom could she trust?

Before dawn Alexandra was up again, jogging through the grass in her flimsy slip-on shoes. She carried her thorny branch, swinging it around her now and then to ward off some imaginary enemy. As light gilded the land, the animals came to life. Herds of brown-skinned gazelles mingled with zebras. Strange cowlike beasts with humped backs and long gray beards eyed her beneath their curved horns. Antelope in coats of burnished copper lifted their heads to regard her. She didn't know the names of any of them, and the memory of Dr. Thornton's admonitions ate at her.

"I'm supposed to design fabrics, and I don't even know what I'm looking at," she muttered as she trotted along. "I don't know where I am. I don't know where I'm going."

Worry gnawed at her insides. What if Nick Jones rented a Land Rover? What if he was coming after her even now? She was clearly visible in the open grassland. The perfect victim. But did he really want *her*—or just easy prey?

Shuddering, she moved ever forward, running when she could, walking when her blistered feet protested too much. The sun rose, burning down on her fair skin. Flies danced around her eyes. Thirst dried her mouth and parched her throat. Hunger clawed at her stomach. She saw no vehicles, no houses, no people. Nothing but endless grass dotted with wildlife—zebras, gazelles, giraffes. It was hopeless. As she moved ever toward the mountain, Alexandra gradually realized the monster probably would get his wish after all. She would die.

The sun slipped toward the west. Three vultures began circling overhead. Their shadows made dizzying patterns on the grass, and she blinked to clear her vision. Her feet ached. The thorn branch dangled in her hand. Her steps dragged. *Stop and rest? Try to find water? Keep moving?* She couldn't think clearly.

She passed a herd of elephants. Huge gray creatures lifted their trunks to sniff the air. Her scent would intrigue them. Intrigue the others, too . . . those with claws and fangs. She tried to swallow, but her tongue stuck to the roof of her mouth.

I'm going to die, Lord. It won't matter about designing for Bloomingdale's and Macy's. It won't matter about the account deficit. Nothing will matter. The animals understand I'll get too weak, and I'll lie down . . . and then they'll come.

She wiped a tear off her cheek and licked the salty moisture from the back of her hand. Kilimanjaro loomed in the distance, still so far away. No matter how many steps she took, it never got closer. Like an apparition . . . a hope . . . a promise . . . it hovered just out of reach. Too far to save her.

I look up to the mountains—does my help come from there? My help comes from the Lord, who made the heavens and the earth!

Alexandra closed her eyes and stumbled on. No help from the mountain. No help from Mama Hannah. No help from anyone. Only God.

"Lord, Lord." Her mouth formed the words again and again. She sensed the wild animals watching. Waiting. The thorn branch would do no good. "Lord, Lord, Lord. Lord, save me. Save me."

A sudden chill of fear forced her eyes open. She stopped. Just ahead of her a dog crouched low. Round-eared, black-faced, it bared a set of shiny white teeth. Long mottled hair in shades of tan and black covered the beast. And then she saw another behind it. Exactly the same colors, muzzle, teeth. And another. Three stood just to her left. Two to her right. She turned. Four dogs crouched behind her.

Dear God, it's a pack. They're wild. They'll tear me apart! Please help me. She stiffened, gripping her stick with both hands.

"Nice dog," she said in a low voice.

The animal's neck ruff lifted. Its lips curled back in a snarl. It gave a loud growl and rushed her. She screamed.

Something flew through the air, piercing the dog's flesh. The canine yelped and fell. The other dogs lunged at her, barking wildly. Alexandra lashed out with her thorn branch, shrieking, shouting. Again an object zipped through the air, and another dog dropped bleeding at her feet. At that, the pack fled, their mottled coats vanishing in the grass.

Unable to stop screaming, she sank to her knees, wracked with nausea and sobs. The two dead dogs lay prone, their bright blood staining the yellow grass. And then a pair of small brown feet appeared between them.

"Epuonu mbaa too muroishi," said a husky little voice.

Alexandra lifted her head. A boy, no older than eight or ten, stared down at her, his brown eyes bright with curiosity. He wore a length of red fabric tied toga-style over one shoulder and a choker of red and black beads.

She brushed a hand over her eyes. "I thought . . . thought I was dead," she choked out. "You . . . you ran them off. Killed them. Who are you?"

"Isuyian," the boy said and pointed at the two dead dogs. *"Owuaru."*

"I don't understand . . . but thank you—for what you did. The dogs. You saved my life."

"Isuyian." He squatted near one of the dogs and pulled his short spear from the animal's side. Then he walked over to the other dog and jerked out a sharpened stick. With a smile that revealed a pair of missing lower incisors, the victorious hunter regarded Alexandra with a shy gaze.

She struggled to her feet. "Do you know a man by the name of Grant Thornton? Dr. Grant Thornton?"

The boy stepped toward her and bent his head. *"Na kitok,"* he said.

Alexandra stared down in bewilderment at the youngster. "Uh . . . *na kitok.*"

He giggled. *"Aa. Na kitok,"* he repeated. Then he took her hand and gently placed it on his head. *"Iko."*

"Iko," Alexandra said.

The boy lifted his head and beckoned her with a long, skinny arm. *"Ilotu!"*

As she followed him through the grass, she realized he had been guarding a small flock of goats when the wild dogs surrounded her. Now he began to drive his flock with a thin stick. Relieved to be in the company of a human carrying a spear—small though the boy was—she walked beside him.

It was impossible to communicate. "Do you have any water?" she asked. He smiled. "Do you have food?" she asked. He smiled. "Where are we going?" she asked. He smiled.

At one point, he stopped and lifted the dry gourd that hung by a leather strap from his shoulder. He pulled off the leather lid and took a long drink. At the sound of liquid gurgling down his throat, Alexandra nearly wilted.

"May I please have a drink?" she asked, pointing at the gourd. "I'm thirsty."

The boy offered the container. When she caught a whiff of its contents, she nearly collapsed again. Sour milk mixed with something else. Something with a really nasty odor. She shut her eyes and took a swig.

Gag! What was the stuff? The boy chuckled at the face she was making and took his gourd away. Alexandra clasped her hands. "I'm sorry," she said. "I'm not used to it."

"Yooz-toot."

"Used to it."

The boy shook his head and laughed as though this was the funniest thing he had heard in quite some time. "Yooz-toot," he said over and over. Then his face sobered, and he bent over and gently touched her skinned knee with a fingertip.

"*Osarge,*" he said. His brow furrowed. "*Aainyo?*"

"A bad man chased me."

The boy shook his head in obvious pity. He regarded her for a moment, then patted his chest. "Mayani," he said and pointed at her. "*Eira ng'ai?*"

"Alexandra."

"A-link-anda," he repeated slowly. Then he beckoned again. "*Ilotu.*"

She'd hardly had time to absorb the exchange before he was off again, driving his little flock ahead of him. So, his name was Mayani, she thought as she hobbled along in her useless shoes. Her rescuer.

Why had God sent a child? Why had she been given

someone who couldn't even speak to her? She had no idea where he was taking her—though she felt sure it couldn't be to Dr. Thornton's camp. That request had passed right over Mayani's head. If he was taking her to his village . . . to a group of Africans . . . people just like the boy . . . with horrible things to drink . . . and nobody who could speak English . . .

"Alinkanda!" he called just ahead of her. *"Ilotu!"*

As the boy ran excitedly on, Alexandra moved more slowly. In the distance she now could see a circle of flat-topped igloos made of mud. None of them was taller than four feet, and none possessed a window. Around the arched doorways played naked children tended by bald-headed women. Like some otherworld assemblage of plaid Scottish tartans, Indian paisleys, and Italian checkered tablecloths, the people's togas displayed an amazing variety of patterns—all in red hues.

A few elderly men loitered in a circle playing some sort of game with stones. Mayani approached them head down. One of the men rose and laid his hand on the boy's head. They spoke for a moment, then the man lifted his focus to Alexandra.

"Alinkanda!" Mayani called.

She hesitated. Were there cannibals in Africa? If she went into this village, would she be jumping from the frying pan into the fire? *Dear God, what should I do? You've brought me this far—alive. Shall I trust them?*

Her earthly father's voice echoed in her head. *Don't trust anyone, Alexandra.* And her mother's voice: *They're nasty people. Nasty.*

The last time she had made an attempt to trust someone,

she had ended up in Nick Jones's clutches. She swallowed and looked for an escape. No choice but the wilderness presented itself. She squared her shoulders. *OK, Lord, I'm going to trust you in this. Guard me!*

The African man walked toward her, Mayani following respectfully. He was an old man, his head bald as a coffee bean and his eyes framed in a pair of thick, round, silver-rimmed spectacles. In the tops of his ears, he wore mismatched beaded loops. His earlobes, stretched to form huge holes, displayed a second pair of ornaments. One was a set of double iron bells. The other was a small round plastic bottle with a red lid. As he approached, she realized that the printing on the bottle read Tylenol.

"*Yieyio,*" the man said.

Alexandra bent her head as she'd seen the little boy do and repeated the word he'd taught her. "*Iko.*"

He did not put his hand on her head, but he began to ask her questions. She shook her head. "I don't know what you're saying. I am American."

"*Amedika?*"

"Yes. I speak English. I am looking for Dr. Grant Thornton. Dr. Thornton. The storyteller." She searched her brain. What was the name of the town he had mentioned? "Walkie-talkie?" she said.

"*Totona penyo!*" The old man motioned her to wait. He walked to the nearby compound of huts and spoke at length with the other men. Finally, they all rose and solemnly approached her. Clad in red plaid wool blankets despite the heat, they made an intimidating group. Still, Alexandra decided to hold her ground.

"*Iko,*" she said as they approached. This struck two of the dignified elders as so hilarious that they dissolved into giggles. The others managed to restrain themselves.

One man stepped forward. "Alinkanda?"

"That's my name. Alexandra Prescott. I don't speak your language."

"On the contrary, you speak it quite well," the man said in a clipped British accent. "We simply find it a bit humorous that you have stated a portion of our traditional greeting in the wrong order."

Alexandra stared at the man. "You speak English?"

"I should hope so, my dear. I hold a doctorate in political science from Oxford University. Sambeke Ole Kereya, at your service. Dr. Kereya, if you like, although I won't insist on it. You may call me Sambeke." He smiled, revealing his set of missing lower incisors.

"I'm . . . I'm pleased to meet you, sir," Alexandra managed.

"I realize it must come as a bit of a shock to hear me speaking. You see, at age twenty-three I was sent off to England. It was 1968, and an official in the Kenyan government thought it would be a jolly idea to bring a dose of civilization to the Maasai. That's the name of our tribe. After studying Western civilization for eight years, I decided we were much closer to the ideal out here on the plains. And so here I am. Now, may I inquire as to your presence in these parts?"

"I'm . . . I'm looking for someone. A Dr. Thornton."

"*Bwana* Hadithi! The storyteller. Of course." He regarded her solemnly. "But it would not be like Dr. Thornton to lose one of his students in the bush. Are you certain he is aware of your presence?"

"I'm not a student. I met him at the airport. He's . . . he's the only person I know out here . . . and . . . and . . ." The memories of Nick Jones's attack flooded in, and Alexandra struggled to focus. "I need to . . . need to get help."

"You've been injured. Mayani tells us wild dogs attacked you."

"Yes."

"But I think . . ." He studied her. "I think the wild dogs did not chase you into the bush."

"No. There's a . . . a problem. . . ." She swallowed. "Sir, may I come into your village? I'd like to sit down. I'm very . . . very thirsty."

Sambeke turned and began to speak to the women who had gathered shyly behind their men. They hurried forward and led Alexandra toward the huts. Her request might have been a mistake, she realized right away. Every inch of bare ground inside the village was covered with a thick layer of dried cow dung. Some not so dry. The odor nearly knocked her flat, and the flies . . .

"Kule naailang'a?" a pretty young woman asked, presenting a gourd to Alexandra.

"Uh . . . is this the same drink Mayani has?"

"Kule naailang'a is boiled milk," Sambeke said, "mixed with cow's blood. I think it will not be to your liking— though I must tell you that it is the foundation of our diet. In fact, *kule naailang'a* provides all essential amino acids required for human growth and development. We Maasai have almost no incidence of malnutrition, heart disease, or digestive disorders."

He gave her another gap-toothed smile, and then he imparted further instructions to the women. They regarded Alexandra in astonishment for a moment—probably having just learned that she didn't like *kule naailang'a*—and then went off to fetch her something else. Alexandra studied the surreal scene for a moment. She had been attacked by a mad poet, had walked for almost twenty-four hours through the wilderness, and now was standing in a village where the people lived on cow's-blood milk shakes. One of her hosts carried a Tylenol bottle in his earlobe. And another held a doctorate from Oxford. Could she be dreaming all this?

"Now, my dear Miss Prescott," Sambeke said. "Whilst the women are fetching fresh milk, may I inquire as to your business in our country?"

"I'm a fabric designer." She glanced at the assortment of red printed fabrics and realized her own ideas hadn't come close to reflecting the true adornment of Africa's people. "Anyway, I was touring. I was staying at the lodge in Amboseli."

"A popular place."

"Yes, but I was . . . I was abducted."

"Drugged? Robbed?"

"No. The man wanted to kill me."

Sambeke's dark brow creased. "This is not at all typical of the rare but unfortunate attacks on tourists in our country. Robbery is the usual motive."

"The man is not an African. He is American."

"You don't say? In our culture, one would rarely see such barbarity against a helpless woman. And all crimes are punished with sufficient severity to be an effective deter-rent." He turned and related the news to his fellow elders, who shook their heads and clucked in disbelief.

"So, Miss Prescott, you wish to find your friend Dr. Thornton?"

"He's not really a friend. I just thought . . . thought maybe he could help. I need to get back to the States."

"But of course. Do you have any idea where Dr. Thornton is making camp these days? We have not seen him in our *kraal* for some time."

"He's near a town. Something like . . . walkie-talkie?"

"Oloitokitok!" He laughed. "Ah, it is not far! Perhaps two days walking."

"Two days?" Alexandra looked down at her expensive designer shoes—flat heeled with a taupe linen fabric covering the vamp. Grass, burrs, dust, and dung coated them. Inside, her toes were blistered and her heels rubbed raw. Then she studied the shoes of her host—a pair of soles cut from rubber tires, thin straps made of inner tube. They looked infinitely more comfortable than hers.

"We will set off tomorrow morning. In the meantime, I should be delighted to welcome you to stay the night in the home of my wife. Miss Alexandra Prescott, please meet Loiyan."

"*Na kitok,* Alinkanda," the woman said, stepping forward.

"*Iko.*" Alexandra gave a little bow because it seemed appropriate. "It's nice to meet you, Loiyan."

Her head shaved, her ears loaded with earrings, and her neck stacked with beaded collars, the woman held out a dried gourd filled with frothy white milk. "*Kule nairowua,*" she said softly.

"Warm milk," Sambeke announced proudly. "Fresh from the goat."

Alexandra took the gourd and lifted up yet another prayer for divine help. Then she bent to take a sip.

"Delicious!" Grant Thornton announced from the low-slung canvas chair beside the fire. He dipped his spoon into the bowl and took another bite of stew. As he ate, he proudly surveyed his two tents, the blazing campfire, his Land Rover, and the spreading acacia trees that sheltered his domain. "This is great. You keep up this fine cooking, Mama Hannah, and I'm going to need a new belt."

"You do not wear a belt," the old woman said. "And you are too thin. Have you been drinking that terrible drink of the Maasai?"

"*Kule naailang'a?*"

"The soured milk and blood."

"I'll have you know, a well-respected Maasai gentleman once told me that *kule naailang'a* provides all the essential amino acids—"

"Do not talk to me of acids, Grant. You need vegetables. Potatoes and beans and cauliflower."

"But not those green ones! Please don't make me eat those nasty green ones!"

Hannah chuckled. "You believe I mother you too much."

"Nah," he said. "Well, maybe a little. I mean, I've had to shave every day since you've been here."

"The better to see your handsome face."

"And then there's the matter of laundry."

"I do not think you had washed those socks for three months."

"You may have a point there. On the other hand, I've been living in Maasailand. To get laundry water, I have to dig a hole in a dry riverbed. I prefer to use that precious commodity for making a cup of coffee or giving myself the occasional shampoo."

Mama Hannah leaned back in her canvas chair and studied the man across from her. "Why, Grant?" she asked softly. "Why do you choose to live in this way?"

"It's my job."

"It is more than that."

"OK, I really like the people. The Maasai are incredible. Strong, powerful, self-sufficient. I admire them."

"You wish to be self-sufficient. You wish to need only yourself. But the Maasai live in a clan. Others just like themselves live all around to give help, comfort . . . and love. You have no one."

"I don't need anyone."

"The Maasai depend upon each other. And they depend on their faith in God, the one they call *Engai*. But you?"

Grant set down his spoon and let out a sigh. Not this again. "Mama Hannah, if I ever need a god, maybe I'll invent one to call on. But things are fine. I can take care of myself."

"Ehh," she said—that enigmatic response that drove all the Thornton children nuts.

Grant picked up his spoon again and began to eat. "So, you want me to tell you a story? I just heard a new one about two brothers who quarreled. The Maasai saying goes: *Etaarate ilmoruak are alasharra nejoki obo olikae, olpurkel osidai, nejoki olikae, osupuko.* To settle their argument—"

"I will tell *you* a story about two brothers," Hannah cut in. "One brother asked to be given his inheritance even before his father's death. The loving father gave the young man half of his wealth. But the boy went into the city and spent it foolishly on sinful living."

"This is the story of the Prodigal Son, Mama Hannah," Grant said. "It's Judeo-Christian, OK? That means it originated in the Middle East, and it has an entirely separate contextual portfolio from my African studies. It's a good story, a valid story, but I've already heard it. If you want to tell me a Kikuyu legend—something from your own tribe—I'll listen."

The old woman looked down at her lap. Guilt crept over Grant's heart. If Mama Hannah loved the Bible stories so much, he ought to let her tell them.

"I'm sorry," he said. "The Maasai say that we begin by being foolish, and we become wise through experience. You're a lot wiser than I am, Mama Hannah. If you want to tell me the story of the Prodigal Son, I'll listen."

"The young man who ran away found it better to live with a father who might despise him than with pigs," she said gently. "People need each other. It is God's plan."

"And I have you."

"Grant, my *toto,* you will not have me forever. I have not seen your sister Fiona in many years, and Tillie will have her baby soon. One day, I will go away from this place."

"I'll miss you. But truly, Mama Hannah, I don't need—"

"*Bwana* Hadithi! *Bwana* Hadithi!" One of the young boys from the nearby *kraal* came running toward the camp. He babbled in such rapid Maasai that Grant could hardly make sense of his words. When he finally did, the message was all but unbelievable.

"The Maasai at a *kraal* west of us found a white woman

46

two days ago," Grant translated for Mama Hannah. "She was walking around alone in the bush country."

"We should go to her!"

"They're bringing her here." Grant stood and tucked in his shirt. This was just wonderful—some wacky tourist had gotten separated from her group. Now he'd have to spend countless hours taking her to find help. "They're about half a mile away, and she's not doing well. She's apparently deteriorated a lot during their journey. They're terrified she's going to die on them. I'm going to have to go out there. You'd better stay here."

"I will prepare the cot."

"*My* cot, no doubt."

"Would you put the poor woman on the floor?"

"No, no, of course not." He probably would have, but Mama Hannah would be horrified. "I won't take the Land Rover. There's no road that direction, and the riverbed is in the way. This might take an hour or so."

"You must carry a lantern."

"Just hand me the flashlight."

"But, Grant—the animals. This is their time for feeding."

"It was my time for feeding, too." He looked down at his bowl of half-eaten stew. "Keep that hot for me, would you?"

Four

The sun was almost gone when Grant spotted the band of Maasai warriors in the distance. They moved much more slowly than was usual for a people accustomed to traveling by foot. He could see that they were carrying something. A cowhide suspended among them held a still, almost lifeless figure.

"*Lo murran!*" Grant called in greeting.

"*Ipa!*" came the traditional response.

One in their midst jogged toward him, and he recognized the man as his close friend Kakombe.

"My brother, we have brought her of the English," Kakombe said in the Maasai tongue. "At first she walked, but then she grew weaker. Now we fear she is ill. If she dies, we do not know what to do. The government will not permit us to put the body of one of the English into the grass for the hyenas to take away—as we do the bodies of our own people. This is a great trouble. You must help us."

Grant watched the other warriors approach with their burden. "What illness do you see in her of the English?"

"Her skin has been attacked by *Engai Na-nyokie,* the red god of anger. She wears his marks. We believe he wishes to possess her. He will take her to death."

Grant frowned. He knew that while some Maasai had

become Christians, most worshiped their traditional deity. They believed *Engai Na-nyokie* was the avenging aspect of his character, while *Engai Narok,* the black god, was the benevolent protector. The red god expressed himself in violent lightning and in famine. The black god revealed his nature in rain and in times of bounty. Why would these warriors believe the red god had attacked the person they carried?

Grant stepped toward the cowhide litter and understood at once. The woman's face, unprotected from the equatorial sun, had been scorched and blistered. Her eyes had swollen shut, and her cheeks were flaming. Grant's first guess diagnosed it as a serious case of heatstroke.

Worse, the woman obviously had endured some kind of physical trauma. A scratch on one arm was caked with dried blood on which flies clustered like a string of black beads. Round purple contusions marked her flesh. Grant lifted the blanket in which the men had wrapped her and flicked on his flashlight. The woman's sunburned arms led to torn palms and tattered fingernails. Her bruised legs looked like a pair of knobby canes, and the soles of her bare feet were raw.

"Do you know the woman's name?" he asked, kneeling beside the litter and taking her wrist to check for a pulse.

"Sambeke Ole Kereya talked to her in the tongue of the English. She is called by the name of Alinkanda."

"Alinkanda?" Grant stroked his thumb over the woman's battered fingers. "Ma'am," he said softly in English. "Can you hear me? My name is Grant Thornton."

Her puffed eyelids opened slightly. Two feverish blue eyes focused on him. "Grant," she mumbled.

"Good, you're conscious. Listen—we're going to take you to my camp. We'll get some liquids into you, cool you off, see what we can do about those feet. You're going to be all right. We'll take you back to your tour group—"

"No!" Her fingers gripped his hand. She struggled onto one elbow, her eyes wild. "No . . . not . . . man . . . can't . . . man . . ."

"Hold on, now. Calm down." He eased her back onto the cowhide litter. "Just relax, OK? Nobody's going to take you anywhere until you're better."

Standing, Grant faced the leader of the warriors. "What happened to her, Kakombe?" he asked in Maasai. "Did someone in your *kraal* injure this woman?"

"No, my brother!" All the men clustered forward, eager to reassure him. Their leader spoke for the group. "A pack of wild dogs tried to attack the woman, but one of our boys drove them off. A brave child. He killed two dogs. We have been most honorable in the care of her of the English."

Grant studied the woman again. He had always trusted the Maasai as truthful and fair. It wouldn't be like them to harm a defenseless woman. And they clearly knew the government would not be pleased if an American should die in their care.

"Enough talking. I delay you, you delay me; we depart without profit," Grant said, repeating a common Maasai proverb. "Let us take her of the English to my camp. Maybe she will be able to tell us what happened on her journey."

Grant took part of the cowhide near the woman's head and began to walk. He hadn't seen anyone so sick, swollen, and miserable in a long time. She needed a doctor. Probably a hospital.

Though he was sympathetic to her plight, he guessed she was probably just another tourist who had gotten into trouble through carelessness—like those who stepped out of their cars to take a closer gander at the lions, those who ignored warnings to take their malaria medicine, those who photographed the native people without offering to pay for the privilege. They treated Africa as though it should conform to them instead of the other way around.

The thought of driving this woman all the way to Nairobi in his Land Rover made Grant groan inwardly. In less than a week, the Maasai of the nearby *kraal* would be holding a major ceremony marking the confirmation of elderhood. Grant had never been invited to witness *Eunoto,* but if he could convince the elders to let him attend, he knew the experience would be invaluable. Not only would he be able to gather more stories and traditions, but he would also enjoy seeing the initiation of Kakombe and several other close friends during the ceremony.

The gas lantern hanging from Grant's tent pole shone like a guiding star in the dark night. As the group approached, Mama Hannah emerged from a second tent, her yellow cotton dress drifting below her knees in the breeze that swept down from Mount Kilimanjaro. She hurried toward the warriors.

"Grant?" she called.

"It's us, Mama Hannah. Do you have the cot ready? She's in pretty bad shape."

The warriors carried the cowhide into the lantern light and set it gently on the ground. "Oh, look at her skin!"

Mama Hannah said, kneeling and pulling back the blankets. "The sun has burned her. She is so—" Her words stopped, and she looked up at Grant. "But this is Miss Prescott!"

"Who?"

"Alexandra Prescott! This is the woman we met at the airport in Nairobi. Do you not recognize her?"

Grant scrutinized the woman. "I don't think this is Alexandra Prescott. She had that New York look. She was . . . sleek and elegant . . . and . . ." On the other hand, the hair was the same. She was the right height. If you could picture the face and the eyes in a different light, you might actually be close to the image of the woman whose memory had played through his brain in flickers of shadow and light.

"Miss Prescott?" he asked. "Is that you?"

Her puffed lids opened again, and she mumbled something.

"It is she. Carry her into the tent, Grant," Hannah ordered. "Take that blanket away before she smothers. Bring me some water. Do you have clean water? I don't want anything dug out of a riverbed."

Still bewildered that he hadn't recognized her—while Mama Hannah had known right away—Grant slipped his arms beneath Alexandra. Her body was so feverish that he could feel the heat through her clothing. He tucked her against his chest and stood.

"Relax now," he said. "I'm taking you into the tent."

"Don't . . . the man!"

"What man?" He started walking with her, but she began to writhe.

"Man . . . here . . . he's—"

"Nobody's here but the warriors and us." He drew her

closer. "We're going to take care of you, Miss Prescott. I promise we won't let anybody hurt you."

"Dogs!"

"No, there aren't any wild dogs around. You're safe. Mama Hannah's going to wash you up in a minute, and . . . and . . . hey there, don't cry."

"Mama Hannah?"

"I am with you," the old woman murmured as Grant laid Alexandra on the narrow aluminum-framed cot. She pushed back the injured woman's hair and placed a dark hand on the feverish forehead. "'Have compassion on me, Lord, for I am weak,'" she recited softly. "'Heal me, Lord, for my body is in agony. I am sick at heart. How long, O Lord, until you restore me?'"

Grant walked outside toward his precious container of clean water. He could hear Hannah's soothing voice coming from the tent. It reminded him of the crooning of Maasai women as they sang their prayer songs:

> *Naomoni aaayai*
> The one who is prayed for and I also pray.
> *Nairkurukur nesha,*
> God of the thunder and the rain,
> *Iye oshi ak-aaomon.*
> Thee I always pray.

Mama Hannah wouldn't like it if she knew he compared her devotion to Jehovah to the Maasai's veneration of *Engai*. But to Grant, it was all so much mumbo jumbo. Alexandra Prescott would get better if she rested, drank a lot of water, and took a round of antibiotics.

Infectious germs could be seen through a microscope. So could the medicines that would attack and destroy them. But God . . . *Engai* . . . was ephemeral. The Indescribable Color, the Maasai called their unseen deity. Christians called him the Holy Spirit. Either way, scientific evidence was definitely lacking.

Grant filled a bowl from the twenty-gallon plastic tank of city water he had hauled from Nairobi on his last visit. Then he went over to his own tent and dug around in his first-aid kit. By this time the visiting Maasai warriors had wandered to the nearby *kraal* to seek shelter for the night with others who were preparing for the initiation ceremony.

"'He lets me rest in green meadows.'" Hannah's voice sounded through the canvas tent wall as Grant approached. "'He leads me beside peaceful streams. He renews my strength.'"

"But can he do anything about a bad sunburn?" Grant asked, pushing back the flap that was intended to keep mosquitoes outside. "How's the patient?"

"Calm." Hannah touched Grant's arm. "This is more than a sickness of the body. Something terrible has happened to our friend."

Friend? We don't even know this woman, Grant thought. He knelt beside the cot and slipped his hand behind her neck. "Time for a drink of fresh water, Miss Prescott."

She moaned and placed her swollen lips on the rim of the cup he had poured. As she gulped the cool water, Grant pondered what on earth could have happened to the sophisticated lady he had met in Nairobi. An unexpected stab of fear ran through him. What if she was sicker than he thought? What if she took a turn for the worse? She was acting a little shell-shocked, and the burn was pretty serious—not to mention the scratch on her arm and those flies. . . . He should take her to Nairobi as soon as possible. Better yet, he could drive her to the lodge at Amboseli Game Park. Small planes regularly flew in and out of there. She could be in a Nairobi hospital by tomorrow night.

"Miss Prescott," Grant said. "Can you hear me? Can you understand what I'm saying?"

She nodded.

"You've been badly sunburned. I suspect you may have heatstroke. You may need professional medical attention. I'd like to drive you over to the lodge at Amboseli and put you on a plane—"

"No!" Her eyes flew open, and she gripped his arm. "Not there! The man . . ."

"You are upsetting her again," Mama Hannah said. "Come, Miss Prescott. Take some more water. Grant, you wash her face while I go to the other tent and prepare some broth from the stew."

"I'll do the broth," he said quickly.

"You bathe her."

When Mama Hannah spoke in that tone, Grant knew there was to be no argument. He set the bowl on his lap and dipped a rag into the water. Brushing back strands of the woman's blonde hair, he stroked the wet cloth over her forehead. She moaned slightly.

"Miss Prescott . . . Alexandra," he said in a low voice. "Can you tell me why you left your tour? Has someone tried to hurt you?"

"Man," she muttered.

"Which man? Was it one of the Maasai? The African warriors?"

She shook her head. Her eyes opened. "Jones."

"A white man?"

"The lodge."

"Someone attacked you at the lodge? One of the guests?"

"Jones. Nick Jones." She reached up and laid her hand over his. "Please . . . Grant. Don't take me there."

He studied the dark bruises on her skin. "Look, I'm going to drive over to Oloitokitok tomorrow morning. With a white woman disappearing from a lodge and her tour, this is going to be all over the news. The police are searching for you already, I'm sure. I'll tell them what's happened, and they can haul the guy into custody."

"No—"

"Yes, Alexandra. If some maniac is out there attacking women, the authorities need to know about it."

"Please, Grant." She swallowed hard. "Can't talk. More water."

He helped her take another sip. "You'd better rest. Mama Hannah will be in with the broth in a minute."

"The man," she said, catching his sleeve before he could move away. Her voice was deep and hoarse as she spoke. "If you tell anyone, it'll get into the newspapers. Then he'll know I'm still alive. Where I am. He'll come after me. He wants to kill me."

"Kill you? Why would anyone want to do that?"

"I don't know."

"That settles it. Whether you approve or not, I'm going to the authorities with this."

"Please don't." Her face tensed with emotion. "He swore he'd find me. He has a wire. A knife."

"This is unbelievable. You're a couple of tourists, right? So what's the guy's problem? He chases women all the way to Africa to kill them? I don't get it."

Grant continued bathing her swollen skin in silence. The whole thing made no sense—unless Alexandra had been involved in some kind of relationship with the jerk. A love affair gone wrong. Maybe this Nick Jones had gotten too serious too fast. Or maybe he had wanted more than she was prepared to give.

But to threaten to kill her? Leave her out in the wilderness to die? That went beyond anything Grant could fathom.

"How long have you known this Jones fellow?" he asked.

"That evening. Sitting by the pool. Bad poetry." She squeezed her eyes shut. Her words were barely audible. "A cablegram came. I had to make a call. A deficit. He ordered me a sandwich. And I told him I didn't want to . . . to go . . . and he grabbed me . . . the tree . . . under the tree . . . the leopard." Her eyes opened. "I saw a leopard."

Grant scowled. What on earth was she babbling about?

"It's the strange part," she said. "A leopard in the tree."

"In the game park? I don't think so. Leopards prefer dense bush like the forests on Mount Kilimanjaro. I doubt you'd ever see a leopard in Amboseli."

"Yes," she insisted as a tear squeezed out of the corner of her eye and began to slide down her cheek. "Yes, I'm sure."

"Do you make her cry now, Grant?" Mama Hannah asked when she walked into the tent. "A woman so ill, and you cause her to weep?"

"I was just asking her a few questions."

"The scientist. Always the scientist." The old woman motioned Grant away from the cot and bent over Alexandra. "I bring you warm soup. This is made in the way of my tribe, the Kikuyu," she said softly. "It is not like the food of the Maasai. We are farmers, and they are owners of cattle. This soup is rich with beef and good vegetables. Potatoes, beans, cauliflower. You will try it?"

Mama Hannah cradled Alexandra's shoulders and lifted the spoon to the injured woman's lips. "It will warm your stomach," the African coaxed her. "Your body must become well first. Then your spirit will begin to heal."

Feeling left out and—if the truth be known—a little stupid, Grant hunkered down on a camp stool and studied the two women. Hannah was right, of course. He shouldn't have begun with a barrage of questions. The correct response to a woman in Alexandra Prescott's condition was tenderness. But Grant couldn't recall the last time he had needed to display a gentle side. In fact, he wasn't sure he had one.

Mama Hannah was correct in referring to him as a scientist, always a scientist. He liked to analyze things, not feel them. He preferred objects that could be measured and quantified rather than emotions that needed nurturing. He liked people as the subjects of his objective anthropological studies. But he had made it a policy never to become too involved in their lives. It was one more reason he steered clear of relationships with women. They tended to need things he didn't know how to give.

This Alexandra Prescott was a perfect example. Attractive. Talented in her field. Probably intelligent. Under certain circumstances he might consider her a candidate for lunch out or maybe even a movie. But right now she needed the kind of gentleness better suited to Mama Hannah. She needed warmth, compassion, empathy. Grant felt pretty sure he didn't have a drop of those qualities anywhere in his body.

"Better?" Mama Hannah murmured. "Is your stomach warm?"

"The soup is delicious." Alexandra was sitting up against the pillows now, her flushed face looking slightly more reminiscent of the woman Grant had met in Nairobi. "Thank you. Both of you."

"We are happy to care for you," Mama Hannah said. "Are we not, Grant?"

"Sure. But I still think she needs a doctor." From his camp stool, he examined the younger woman. "That burn is pretty bad in some places. Blisters across the nose and cheeks. And the bruising looks serious, too."

"I'll be all right," Alexandra whispered. "I have to take care of this on my own. Is there a telephone I can get to?"

"There's a little grocery store in Oloitokitok. Sometimes the phone there works. You don't want me to talk to the police. Who are you planning to call?"

"Grant, it is her business!"

"Mama Hannah, she's in my camp. It's my business, too. People are probably looking for you, Miss Prescott."

"*Alexandra*. Let them look." She crossed her arms. "I need to call the States. My broker needs to know—"

"Your broker!" Grant stood, frustration sending hot trails down his spine. "Look, I'm sorry this Jones fellow attacked you. Sorry you've been trekking around in the bush. But if your primary concern is the status of your stocks—"

"The cable I got at the lodge was—" She cut herself off, visibly tucking away her true emotions. "My broker is the only person who needs to know I'm alive. He's a family friend. He does overseas business all the time, and he'll know who to contact to quietly end any search that may be going on. He can also arrange my flight back to the States."

Yeah, and take about a month doing it, Grant thought. Some New York City stockbroker wouldn't have the first clue how to deal with the kind of mess Alexandra Prescott had gotten herself into. All kinds of government red tape would be involved. Maybe even the United States consulate. In the meantime, Grant would be stuck with her.

"You trust this broker of yours to know what to tell the Kenyan authorities?" he asked. "You trust him to help you get out of a foreign country—even though you think some killer is stalking you?"

"Trust him?" She dampened her lip. "Well . . . I have to trust someone, don't I?"

"Trust *me,* then."

"You?"

"Why not?"

"I don't know you."

"Yeah, well, take me on faith. I'm not interested in killing you. In fact, I'm very interested in getting you some help—like a doctor, the police, a trip to the airport, that sort of thing. I have a lot of work to do, Miss Prescott— Alexandra—and the truth is, you can count on me to get you up and out and moving on as quickly as I possibly can."

She glanced at Mama Hannah, and a smile hinted at the corner of her lip. "I think he wants to get rid of me."

"Ehh," the old woman said. "But he tells you to have *faith* in him. This certainly is a new subject for Dr. Grant

Thornton. Perhaps you should allow it and see what happens."

"Is he trustworthy?"

"Hey, did I suddenly leave the room?" Grant asked. "Talk to *me* if you want to hear an honest answer. Of course I'm trustworthy. Ask any Maasai in Kenya. If *Bwana* Hadithi says something, he means it."

"*Bwana* Hadithi is an anthropologist." Alexandra looked down at her bruised arms. "I need to get to safety as soon as I can."

"The Lord is your safe haven," Mama Hannah said. "He will see you through this."

"Yes, that's true," Alexandra acknowledged.

"Wait a minute now. A guy tries to kill you—and you're willing to rely on some kind of religious dogma?"

"I'm a Christian, Grant," she said. "I trust God."

"I've got news for you. God doesn't fill out government forms. He doesn't negotiate missed airline reservations. And he sure doesn't drive the only Land Rover in fifty miles."

"You're right. But he did send a leopard to save me from Nick Jones. He led me through the darkness. He rescued me from the pack of wild dogs. I'll just have to trust him to see me through this."

"Fine. Go the Jesus route. If you want to count on—"

"He brought me here to *you,*" she cut in, her voice gentle. "So maybe I *can* trust you."

Grant stared at her, suddenly feeling a little sheepish. He'd built a great trap of an argument—and stepped right into it. Now Alexandra saw him as divine provision in her time of need. God's pawn. Not only that, he'd practically forced her to accept his assistance—help he didn't really want to give.

"Thank you, Dr. Thornton," she said, suddenly looking very tired. "I appreciate what you're doing for me."

He nodded. "Sure. Anytime."

As he left the tent, he could feel the jaws of the trap closing around his heart.

FIVE

Alexandra lay on the cot and stared up at the expanse of green canvas over her head. More than a day had passed since the Maasai warriors had brought her to Grant Thornton's camp. In that time she had hardly budged, gratefully accepting Mama Hannah's tender care. Though her body still craved rest and nurture, she knew the interlude couldn't go on. It was time to reenter the land of the living.

Morning sunlight streaming through the acacia trees created a display of spiky shadows across the canvas tent. It would make a perfect pattern for sheets, upholstery, even dresses, Alexandra thought. Even though the world of fabric design and high fashion seemed light-years away, she missed her sketch pad. Gazing up, she tried to memorize the shades of green and the interplay of the long thorns.

Her concentration was jarred by the animated voices of Grant Thornton and a group of men walking into the camp clearing. She paused in her study of the tent and listened for a moment. Though she couldn't understand their words, Alexandra found herself drawn to the sound of Grant's low-pitched voice. When he used the African language, his words rolled comfortably in the same rhythmic, melodic tones she had heard among the Maasai as they carried her the long miles.

Now *that* was poetry.

The men laughed, their deep chuckles tumbling over each other. Grant said something, and they laughed again. How wonderful to speak another tongue with such ease, Alexandra thought. She had studied a little French in high school and college. But she doubted she could order a drink of water—even if she were standing in the middle of Paris.

"Ayia taa," Grant said, in what sounded like words of farewell to his friends. *"Irragie naishi o kule."*

"Toomono," came the response.

"Knock, knock. Anybody home?" Grant's head appeared between the flaps of Alexandra's tent. "Hey, you're looking better today. Mama Hannah sent me over to—"

"Ol-oibor siadi!" one of the African men called to him.

"Just a sec." Grant vanished for a moment. *"Nyoo, Kakombe?"*

"Inotie enainotie le-nkipika te minjani," the man said. At this, the other Africans burst into hearty guffaws.

Shaking his head, Grant stepped into the tent. "Ha-ha," he said. "Big joke at my expense."

"What did they say?"

"Kakombe—he's a friend of mine—he says I have what the son of Engipika got in the deserted *kraal."* Grant pitched a stack of folded clothing onto the end of the cot. "Here's a pair of my trousers and a shirt. Mama Hannah wants to wash that dress of yours."

Alexandra pushed herself up onto one elbow. "Who's the son of Engipika?"

"It's just a saying. Don't worry about it."

"I want to know what it means."

"It refers to a Maasai legend."

"Tell me the story."

He shrugged. "One day a man named Ole Engipika was eating meat when he was attacked by his enemy. He escaped with the meat, but he left his weapons behind. He ran into a deserted *kraal* to hide, but he soon discovered that he wasn't the only occupant. A lion leapt up and growled at him. Deciding he'd better leave, he turned around and saw a snake coiled around the gatepost—the only exit. Then he looked into the distance and saw his enemy coming fast."

"So what happened?"

"Nobody knows how Ole Engipika escaped. That's the point of the saying. *Inotie enainotie le-nkipika te minjani* basically means, 'Buddy, you are in a fix.'"

Alexandra looked into his eyes. "It's me, isn't it? The African men think I'm a problem for you."

"Yeah, but not in the way you probably imagine. You've got to understand that the Maasai are totally structured by clan and family. They can't figure out why I like to live alone out here. They can't believe I'm happy without a wife or two and a bunch of children. Your coming along when you did . . . well, they tend to view things from a sort of superstitious perspective."

"They think God sent me to you?"

"Very perceptive." He gave her that crooked grin. "Don't worry about it, though. You and I both know the truth. So, if you'll pull on those clothes, I'll drive you up to Oloitokitok to use the phone. Then we'll figure some way to get you back to Nairobi."

Alexandra slid her feet over the side of the cot. As her toes touched the tent floor, she winced and glanced at the flat-heeled shoes the Maasai warriors had carried all the way from their *kraal*. "I'm not sure I can get into those things. My feet are still swollen."

"Here." Grant set a pair of sandals made of rubber tire soles and inner-tube straps beside the cot. "I traded a ball-point pen for these. They're high fashion in the bush."

Alexandra stared at the shoes. "Thanks . . . I think."

"No problem. Meet me at the Land Rover in ten minutes."

He started out of the tent, but she called to him. "Grant, when the man stopped you a minute ago—what was the name he called you? It didn't sound like *Bwana* Hadithi."

He raked a hand through his mop of light brown hair. "It's just a nickname. You know . . . sort of a joke."

"Another joke? These Maasai seem to have a good sense of humor. So, what do they call you?"

"*Ol-oibor siadi*. It's a play on my name. There's a species of gazelle known as Grant's gazelle."

"*Ol-oibor siadi,*" she said. "I'll try to remember that in case I get lost again."

"I wouldn't if I were you. They'll . . . uh . . . they'll laugh."

"I don't see what's so funny about a gazelle."

A strange flush of color crept up the back of Grant's neck. "That particular gazelle has a patch of white near its tail. *Ol-oibor siadi* means 'he of the white behind.'"

"I see." It was all Alexandra could do to contain the giggle that rose up inside her.

"It's a pun," he went on, his voice assuming a scholarly tone. "The Maasai enjoy riddles and wordplay. In fact, that subject actually comprises one of the chapters of the book I'm writing. The Kikuyu were the first to call me *Bwana*

Hadithi—a straightforward description of my role as a collector of stories. But the Maasai like to play with words. So the nickname they've given me fits their anthropological profile. *Ol-oibor siadi* refers to Grant's gazelle on the one hand . . ."

"And on the other?"

"The fact that I happened to be spotted swimming in the river one day—without anything on—which amused the folks around here to no end. So, that's the explanation."

"Anthropologically speaking."

"Are you laughing at me?"

"Me?"

"Because I did bring you those fine shoes. *And* I'm your entire source of hope for getting out of this mess."

"I thought *you* were in the mess," she said, slipping her feet into the sandals. "Ole Engipika in the *kraal,* remember?"

He regarded her for a moment. "The Land Rover," he said. "Ten minutes."

As Grant walked out of the tent, she sang out, "Yes, sir—he of the white behind."

"We're going up Mount Kilimanjaro?" Alexandra asked.

Grant steered the Land Rover along the narrow dirt road. "The town of Oloitokitok sits at an altitude of about five thousand feet. But you won't feel like you're on the slope of the highest mountain in Africa. It's deceptive."

"And you're sure they'll have a telephone?"

"One. If we're lucky."

He glanced over at the woman beside him. Expecting to read dismay in her blue eyes, he was bemused at the look of fascination he read there. Alexandra was leaning forward in her seat and gazing up at the imposing vista of the snow-capped dormant volcano. In the open window her blonde hair blew away from her sunburned face, revealing high cheekbones and a finely sculpted chin. Lips parted, she looked breathlessly eager—as if the journey itself excited her, and not just the prospect of using a telephone.

"Take a look at the trees," he said. "You reach a certain altitude on the mountain, and all of a sudden they start cropping up."

"What kinds are they?" she asked.

"Those with the pink flowers are called Cape Chestnuts. That's a eucalyptus. And that one—with the big, orange-red blossoms—is a Nandi Flame Tree. Like it?"

"It's beautiful."

He could almost say the same about his companion. Since he'd first met her, Alexandra Prescott seemed to have changed in a rather interesting way. It wasn't so much the sunburn—though that pale face he'd spotted at the airport could have used a little color. It wasn't even the change of clothes. He had to admit she did look pretty cute with his khaki trousers gathered up and held on by a piece of tent rope around her waist. But there was some-thing else different about Alexandra . . . something he couldn't quite put his finger on. Maybe it was just that she'd lost the big-city look. Earthiness became her.

"What are you staring at?" she asked warily.

"You."

"Why?"

"You've changed since the first time we met. Must be the shoes."

Her face sobered. "What do you mean? What are you saying?"

"Nothing." He focused on the road. "Just that I like the trousers. Especially the rope. It gives them kind of an avant-garde look, don't you think? They make a real statement." He playfully tugged on her shirtsleeve. "What would you call it in the fashion industry—that rugged outdoorsy feel?"

When he turned to give her a wink, she reached for the door handle. "Let me out," she said in a clipped voice. "Stop the car right now."

"What?" He eased up on the gas pedal. "What's wrong?"

"I'm not going." She threw open the door and stumbled out of the moving vehicle.

Grant stepped on the brake. Leaving the Land Rover idling, he jerked open his own door and jumped down. "Alexandra?"

"Stay away from me!" She was backing down the road, a stick in her outstretched hand. "I don't . . . I won't . . ."

"Hold on, Alexandra." He took a step toward her. "I didn't mean anything."

"No. Don't come near me!"

"Look, stop walking away, OK?" The panic in her eyes told him what he hadn't seen before. He had somehow terrified her.

"I was making conversation about the trousers," he said. "All I want to do is take you up to Oloitokitok to use the telephone. I'm trying to help you."

She stopped fifty feet down the road. From that distance

she looked so fragile, like a bruised flower. "You can trust me, Alexandra," he called. "I promise I won't hurt you."

All of a sudden her shoulders sagged, and she covered her face with her hands. She shook her head. "I'm sorry."

"It's OK. You've been through a lot." Grant walked slowly toward her. Her body shook slightly as she wept into her hands. He continued, "I didn't realize how my words sounded." As he finished speaking, he reached out and laid a hand on her arm.

She jerked backward with a gasp. "Don't touch me again! Don't . . . don't you . . ."

"Sorry!" He held up both hands. "I'm not touching you, see? I'm not going to hurt you."

Heart hammering, he shoved both hands into his pockets.

She was frantically brushing away the tears that spilled from her eyes. "I don't know what's wrong with me," she choked out. "I had this awful feeling you were taking me away to . . . to . . ."

"I'm not taking you away. I'm driving you up to Oloitokitok. You asked me to get you to a telephone."

"Yes, that's true." She tucked the ends of her hair behind her ears. "But the way you were talking . . . you sounded like him."

"I'm not him."

"I'm so confused. You can't possibly understand what it's like for me here. You speak the language, and you wear these clothes. The people like you. They trust you."

"I trust them. They're honorable people—most of them." He paused. "I'm an honorable man, Alexandra. I won't hurt you."

"Just don't touch me."

"I won't, OK?" He looked into her blue eyes and saw the fear begin to fade. "Do you think you can get back into the Land Rover?"

She nodded and began walking beside him. "I'm a mess. Do you think I'm nuts?"

He glanced at her and then turned quickly away. "What am I supposed to say? I'm half scared to even look at you again."

"You can look at me." She gave him an embarrassed smile. "It was sort of a flashback or something in the car. It was weird. Nick Jones . . . we met beside the swimming pool. I didn't want to leave the lodge . . . but . . . but . . ."

"You'd better not talk about it."

"I need to talk about it."

Grant stole another peek. That was exactly the kind of thing he didn't understand about women. First Alexandra couldn't even think of the attack without going off half-cocked. Just a misspoken comment from him had sent her into a tizzy. Now she *needed* to talk about it.

"At the edge of the pool," she said, "he started forcing me to walk down toward the water hole. I told him to let go of me. And then he was pushing and shoving me. I tried to scream, but he covered my mouth. I couldn't get away."

Grant stopped walking. At her words, something powerful rose up inside him. Something so overwhelming he could hear his own pulse hammering in his temples. This woman—alone, afraid—had been abducted. Terrorized. And then what? Grant wasn't sure he could hear what the man had done to her next. The force inside him demanded action. *Take her in your arms, Grant. Hold her tight. Protect her. . . . And kill that creep!*

"It was dark," she said, her head bent. "I couldn't see much. He threw me down under a tree. Then he said he was going to kill me. . . . I could choose the way I died."

"Why?" Grant demanded. "Why was he going to kill you?"

"I don't know. He said he'd done it dozens of times. There was a man in Mexico—"

"Is he a serial killer or something?"

"I don't know, Grant. I told you I had just met him. He . . . he said he had a knife and a wire. Or he could break my neck—"

"The guy's a barbarian!"

"Break my neck like a chicken's." She covered her face with her hands again. "I don't know what I did wrong! Why did he pick me? I was just sitting by the pool sketching. And . . . and I listened to him read a poem . . . but I wasn't encouraging him. I didn't like him. I don't want . . . don't want any man to . . . to . . ."

"Alexandra." Grant reached out to her. Then he stopped, squeezed his hand into a fist, and hammered it into the side of the Land Rover. "You didn't do anything wrong. The man is deranged. He probably picks his victims at random."

"In Africa? Why here? I expected snakes and lions. Dangers like that. But a serial killer from New York?" She was knuckling away tears again as fast as she could. "I should tell the police. Identify him. Protect other women. But if he finds out I'm alive . . . he said he'd come after me."

"That was just a threat."

"No!" She looked up at him, her blue eyes rimmed in red. "Grant, I really think he wanted to kill me. *Me*. He said something by the pool that haunts me now. He knew I was planning a trip to the beach."

"Almost every tour through Kenya includes a stop at the coast."

"But he said it with such confidence. Like he *knew*." She shook her head. "He knew all about my father's business, too. Not even our closest friends talked about what Daddy did."

"What did he do?"

"He made hangers."

Grant frowned. "Something wrong with making hangers?"

"Prescott Company," she said. "Did you have any idea that was hangers?"

"I've never even heard of Prescott Company, Alexandra."

"See what I mean? But Nick Jones knew! He knew everything." She shuddered. "I think he picked me out. I think he'd studied me. And I . . . I'm scared he may be looking for me right now."

Again Grant had to restrain himself to keep from touching Alexandra. She looked as though she might shatter into a thousand pieces without the most gentle handling. Something inside him urged him to give her that—to cradle her, soothe her, tuck her away from every fear and every evil. It was a new feeling, a compulsion that startled him in its intensity. For years now, Grant had looked after himself. Only himself. For the first time, he needed to touch another human being—and she had forbidden it.

"He won't find you at Oloitokitok. It's sixty miles from the main highway and the nearest town of any size. If this

Jones fellow has any idea that you're alive, and *if* he really wants to kill you, he'll assume you'd do what anybody in their right mind would do: Go back to Nairobi and get out of the country as fast as possible. He's not going to look for you in some podunk village at the foot of Mount Kilimanjaro."

"But what if he does?"

"Then he'll have to deal with me, right?" Saying it felt good. Grant had no permission to put protecting arms around Alexandra. But let that Jones creep show his face, and he'd regret it.

"Why would you do that for me?" she asked.

"Why not?" He leaned back against the Land Rover and crossed his arms over his chest. "You're a person. I'm a person. It's the right thing to do."

"But I . . . I'm not sure I can pay you for all this. My money . . . my passport . . . I left everything at the lodge in Amboseli."

Grant couldn't hide a scowl. "Do I look like the kind of man who does things for money, Alexandra?"

"Well . . ." She looked him up and down, taking in his faded khakis and denim shirt. It was the first time in years that Grant had felt the least bit uncomfortable about his appearance. "Maybe not. But I don't know of anyone who *doesn't* do things for money."

"Meet Grant Thornton," he said, "whose total worldly wealth consists of one Land Rover, two tents, five shirts, seven socks, and four pairs of trousers—one of which you're wearing." At the look of incredulity that crossed her face, he couldn't hold back a chuckle. "I'm helping you because you're in a tight spot, Alexandra."

"But—"

"I don't care if you could pay me ten thousand dollars—or ten dollars. My friend Kakombe is bringing his father over from the *kraal* to meet me this afternoon. He's a respected elder. If he gives his permission, I'll be issued a formal invitation to an *Eunoto*—an elder-initiation ceremony. To me, that opportunity is worth more than any amount of money you could offer."

"I see."

"Now if you wouldn't mind getting back into the Land Rover, I'll drive you the rest of the way to Oloitokitok so you can call this broker who's so important to you. I don't want to miss my afternoon meeting."

Without answering, she climbed in and shut the door behind her. Grant walked behind the vehicle, wondering if he had somehow put his foot in his mouth again. Probably. He'd never been known for finesse. Well, if she was mad, she'd get over it. In a day or two he'd pack her off to Nairobi, and Alexandra Prescott would never cross his mind again.

All the same, her silence made him feel increasingly uncomfortable as the Land Rover climbed the mountain. "Are you OK?" he asked finally.

"Yes," she said.

"What are you thinking about?"

"Those seven socks you own."

He glanced over to find a grin tugging at the corners of her mouth. "I think a vervet monkey stole number eight off the clothesline," he said. "That's what I get for washing them."

Her laughter filled the Land Rover with a warm, joyful sound that danced into his chest. It twined with his powerful need to protect and formed a slender vine that began to curl around the edges of his heart. And suddenly he wasn't so sure about anything.

Alexandra stood inside a cement-block office in the little town of Oloitokitok and listened to the overseas telephone operator tell her—repeatedly—that all international circuits were busy at this time. Across the room, Grant was speaking to an African man about the pipeline that carried water from the snows of Kilimanjaro down to the main highway and the town of Emali. From there, it was piped to Nairobi—melted snow that was a primary source of drinking water for an equatorial city.

The whole experience of Africa seemed unreal to Alexandra. Things had come at her so unexpectedly that she felt off balance. She was supposed to be on a planned tour. Hotels. Meals. Guides. Everything had been scheduled and organized to maximize her exposure to the Dark Continent.

Exposure to the Dark Continent? What a joke! She had gotten to know the real Africa by walking alone through the brush in the middle of the night, being attacked by wild dogs, drinking milk and blood from a dried gourd, and traveling on a cowhide stretcher carried by a band of native warriors. Oddest of all was how natural this world seemed to the American man who had become her guide and helper.

As she stood listening to the operator try to place her call, Alexandra studied Grant Thornton from a distance. He stood chatting with the official, his hands illustrating the point he made with his words. How badly she had misjudged him that evening at the airport. Grant wasn't a derelict. He fit perfectly into this life. He blended.

If she looked at him from that perspective, Alexandra realized, Grant was a very attractive man. Tall and broad shouldered, he had the build of an athlete. He was clearly accustomed to walking long distances, and he knew how to survive in the most rugged environments. He willingly ate whatever was on hand, whether it was a handful of candy bars or a hearty African stew. Comfortable with himself, he wore clothing that fit his lifestyle.

She recalled the tailored, starched, and pressed business-men she passed on the streets of New York. The choking neckties. The women with their moussed and sprayed hairdos. The tight skirts. The uncomfortable shoes. Odd that such apparel had once seemed so right, so perfect, in her mind. Now it seemed almost silly.

She glanced at the tire sandals strapped to her feet, and a bubble of giddiness rose up inside her. What on earth would her associates think if they could see Alexandra Prescott now? She wiggled her toes. No polish. She hadn't had a dusting of powder on her face for days, and her skin was still a bright pink. What must Grant think of her? She glanced at him again, and at his acknowledging tip of the head, something warm curled around the pit of her stomach. Startled at her own response, she turned away, her hand damp on the receiver.

"Hello," a voice said on the other end of the line. "James Cooper and Company. May I help you?"

The real world slammed back into place. "Yes, I need to speak with James Cooper's secretary, please," Alexandra said. "I'm calling long distance."

"I'm sorry, ma'am. Mr. Cooper's secretary is on vacation this week. May I take a message, or would you prefer to speak to Mr. Cooper's voice mail?"

"This is Alexandra Prescott. Did he leave any messages for me?"

"One moment, please." An infuriating silence passed before the receptionist returned to the phone. When she did, her voice was clearly flustered. "Uh, Miss Prescott . . . Mr. Cooper did leave you a message a few days ago. Would you like for me to read it?"

"Of course."

"It says: 'Alexandra, please don't worry about anything. I'm taking care of things on this end. Relax, and have fun.'"

"That's it? He didn't say anything about my account?"

"No, ma'am . . . but yesterday he called in and left word with us that he had heard you were missing . . . missing in Africa."

"I had a problem, and I left my hotel without telling anyone. I know the authorities must be looking for me."

"Are you all right?"

"I'm fine," Alexandra said. "Listen, tell James I want to talk to him. Tell him . . . . tell him I'll try to call him in two days. Nine o'clock in the morning New York time. I need to talk to him. This is urgent. I need money. I need airline tickets. I need him to use his contacts to call off any search for me here in Kenya. He's got to help me get out of this country. Do you understand what I'm saying?"

"Yes, ma'am. Yes, of course," she said. "I've written down everything. Where are you calling from? I mean, in case you don't call him, maybe he could call you."

"I'm in a little town in southern Kenya." Alexandra spelled the name from the sign on the store across the street. "O-l-o-i-t-o-k-i-t-o-k. But there's no way he can reach me here. I'll call him in a couple of days—either from here or Nairobi."

"Yes, Miss Prescott. Uh, ma'am . . . are you sure you're all right?"

"I'll be all right when I can get back to New York." She wound the cord around her finger, reluctant to let go of the sound of normalcy. "It's hard to get through on these international phone lines. You make sure James is waiting for my call, OK?"

"He's staying at a ranch in Arizona. I can't give you the number, but he checks in every day. I can try to patch you together."

"Tell him I need to know about my account. Specifics."

"All right, Miss Prescott. Is there anything else?"

Alexandra searched her mind. Anything else? A thousand questions raced through her thoughts. Is it snowing there? How's the food at that little bistro down the street? Are the trains running on time? What's the best play on Broadway these days? Could you send out for some Chinese?

"That's all," she said softly. And her heart whispered, *Don't forget about me.*

"I'll convey your message, Miss Prescott."

"Good-bye then." Alexandra pressed down the plunger and heard the line go dead.

"*Memsahib* Prescott?" The African official touched her on the arm.

"What?" Her heart hammering, she searched the room. "Where's Grant?"

"He has gone to the petrol station," the man told her. He gave her a friendly smile that revealed his two missing lower incisors. His shoulder-length earlobes dangled as he handed her a bottle of warm Coca-Cola. "You wish to drink, madam? Very good. Just like America!"

Six

Late that afternoon Grant sat outside his tent with five elders from the nearby *kraal*. Kakombe, who had remained at the *kraal* with his fellow warriors in preparation for the *Eunoto,* had also joined the meeting. The discussion of whether to allow Grant to attend the ceremony had gone on for hours, in traditional Maasai fashion. Each elder wanted to have his say before a consensus was reached. They had permitted Grant to sit in on the meeting. He was allowed to speak on his own behalf and explain why he wanted to go to the initiation rite and what he planned to do with the information he obtained.

Eventually, his backside numb and his legs cramped from sitting on the low wooden stool, Grant found his attention wandering toward the spreading acacia tree under which Mama Hannah and Alexandra Prescott were seated. The older woman had her little Bible in hand. She looked up from her reading, and the two women appeared to discuss something for a few minutes, nodding their heads and chuckling over some bit of humor they had shared. Then Alexandra began to sing. Soon Mama Hannah joined her. The lilting sound drifted over to the Maasai elders, who stopped their discussion to listen.

"What do they sing?" Kakombe's father, Sentero, asked Grant in the Maasai language.

Grant absorbed the song for a moment. "It's called 'Zacchaeus Was a Wee Little Man.' It's a children's song about God."

The men grunted in understanding. In the *kraals*, their women often sang about God. "But who is this Zacchaeus?" Sentero asked. "Was he an elder? Did God, the powerful knowing one, speak to him?"

"Jesus Christ spoke to him."

The men conferred for a moment. "Yes, Jesus Christ is the Son of God," Sentero announced. "Jesus Christ is the one who offered the great sacrifice. Instead of slaughtering a bullock or a goat, he permitted himself to be sacrificed for the sin of the people."

"Who told you the story of the sacrifice?" Grant asked.

"We heard the news from the great missionary Cummins," Sentero said. "He was the man who first brought the message of Jesus Christ to the Maasai of Kaputei and Ngong-Magadi."

Grant nodded. Though he'd never met Harold Cummins, he knew the fellow had been teaching and starting churches in Maasailand since the mid-1970s. The tribespeople revered the man.

"Sambeke Ole Kereya and I were among the first to step into the water for baptism," Sentero went on. "By the time Cummins left us to live the years of his elderhood in America, thirty churches were meeting under the acacia trees or in small buildings. More than one thousand Maasai came to believe the words Cummins spoke. Oh yes, we know all about the Son of God."

"And you believe this?"

"Certainly," Sentero said. "We Maasai have always

known about God, the splendor of the morning. We did not know his Son. Now many of us do."

Grant felt inwardly numb as he turned toward the women singing under the tree. These Maasai elders believed in Jesus Christ? The same Jesus Christ whom Mama Hannah worshiped? And Alexandra Prescott had obviously bought into the story, too.

"There is some confusion among us on this matter," another elder acknowledged. "We do understand about the great sacrifice. But Cummins and some of the others who believe in the Son of the Creator have told us that no man may marry more than one wife. How can this be so? A man must marry as many wives as he can afford, so that his children can care for his cattle."

"You are asking the wrong man this riddle," Sentero said. "This friend of ours does not have even *one* wife!"

The men chuckled heartily at that. Grant grinned, accustomed by now to their gentle teasing. All the same, it bothered him that Christian teachings were infiltrating the Maasai culture so swiftly. Following the trail Cummins had blazed, other missionaries had spread throughout Maasailand, and their congregations of believers were growing in size and strength. Just as rapidly as beaded leather togas had given way to red checkered ones, the old beliefs were evaporating in the heat of this faddish new religion.

"Did Cummins also tell you this Son of God became alive again after his great sacrifice?" Grant asked. "Alive— after he was dead?"

"Oh yes. A wonderful thing!"

"You believe it?"

"Do you not?" Sentero regarded Grant solemnly. "You,

85

the man of many stories, do not know which ones are the truth?"

Grant shifted uncomfortably. If he admitted he believed all mythologies were merely a means by which people explained their world, the Maasai would be offended. They would be reluctant to tell him any more of their legends—and they certainly wouldn't invite him to the upcoming ceremony.

"You must join us in the *kraal* tonight," Kakombe's father said. "Sambeke Ole Kereya will arrive with other elders from his *kraal*. They are coming to unite with us for feasting, singing, and dancing. Because he studied in England for a time, Sambeke knows much more than I do about the Son of God. He can read the Bible, and this I cannot do. You may ask Sambeke all your questions. After he tells you, then you will understand why we believe. You will know in your heart that this is true."

"And what about *Eunoto?*" Grant asked. "May I also be permitted to attend that ceremony?"

The elders looked at each other, silently seeking a consensus. Finally Sentero nodded. "Yes, you will come," he said. "And you will bring her whose hair is the color of the first milk of a cow at milking time. She of the English is the woman God has sent to become your wife. Everyone in the *kraal* will want to look at her."

"My *wife?*" Grant glanced at the woman under the tree.

"Oh yes," Sentero said. "It is clear to everyone. But now we must go."

Their meeting adjourned, the elders stood. Grant followed them toward the edge of the clearing. At least he'd been officially invited to the ceremony. Now if he could just figure out how to send *God's gift* to Nairobi so she could catch a plane back to the States . . .

"Oh, mother of Grant Thornton." Kakombe's father stopped beneath the acacia tree to give Mama Hannah the traditional Maasai greeting. "Please tell us—who is this man Zacchaeus of whom you sing?"

When Hannah and Alexandra turned to Grant for an explanation, he translated the question. "Just tell him it's a children's song, Mama Hannah," he added. "They've invited me over to the *kraal,* and I want to talk to—"

"Zacchaeus was a very small man," the old woman interrupted, looking directly at Sentero. "He was also a very bad man—a cheater and a thief. But he wanted to see the Lord Jesus Christ, who was traveling to the man's village." Stopping her narration, she spoke to Grant. "Tell this man what I have said."

Grant dutifully translated her words.

"The Son of God must have been very angry with such an evil man," Kakombe's father said. "Did Jesus Christ command Zacchaeus to pay a fine of a bullock or a young heifer? Or did he call a council of elders to discuss this matter?"

Grant translated again, aware that the communication was growing frayed. Mama Hannah attempted to ignore the elders' questions and go on with the story, but they began to discuss what the proper fine for cheating and stealing should be. They asked Mama Hannah exactly what it was that Zacchaeus had stolen, so that they could set the appropriate fine. When she tried to explain about tax collecting, the elders demanded to know where this terrible Zacchaeus was living now so that they could exact vengeance. One man began flicking his wildebeest-tail fly whisk around in the air and uttering loud, agitated grunts. Grant spoke back and forth, translating, mollifying, trying to explain—until suddenly Alexandra stood.

"Zacchaeus was a wee little man," she sang, acting out the childish gestures that went along with the song. "A wee little man was he. He climbed up in a sycamore tree, for the Lord he wanted to see."

She pointed up into a nearby tree. The elders nodded in understanding. Then Alexandra sang again, gesturing along with the words. "As the Savior came that way, he looked up in the tree. And he said, 'Zacchaeus, you come down, for I'm going to your house today.'"

The elders burst out laughing. Clustering around Alexandra, they begged her to sing the song again. Grant was ordered to translate the words. The Maasai agreed that the Son of God was a most amazing man to love as terrible a person as Zacchaeus enough to visit his *kraal*. And then, while Alexandra sang, all the elders began acting out the song themselves—portraying the little man, pretending to climb into the tree, and shaking their fingers.

"Oh, Grant Thornton," Sentero said after Alexandra had repeated the song seven more times. "We all agree that he whose robe has many folds has given you an intriguing gift. There is no day in which good is not born, and there is no day in which bad is not born."

"What do you mean by telling me this proverb?"

"We believe," the man explained, "that this woman God has sent to you is very ugly—with hair the color of new milk, with long, thin legs like the limbs of a young tree, and with skin like the snow of Kilimanjaro on which the setting sun casts its redness. We are very sorry for you about that. But this woman is a most clever singer! Her voice is like that of the laughing dove. Also, she is kind to the old woman. One day she will be strong enough to build a good house for you and bear many sons. We believe she will make a fine wife for you. Now this we command: You will bring the woman tonight to the *kraal*. In two days' time, you will bring her to the *Eunoto*. She will sing the song about the bad man who climbed the tree in order to see the Son of God. May he carry you under his wings."

So saying, Sentero turned and began his dignified stroll back to the *kraal*. The other elders moved along beside him, clearly satisfied that all was well. Grant set his hands on his hips and regarded the women.

"Well, I hope you two are happy," he said. "You just added a Judeo-Christian story to the lexicon of Maasai legends I've been trying to keep pure for years."

"Yes, I am very happy," Mama Hannah answered. "Now the old men know that God loves all people—even the bad ones."

Grant rolled his eyes. "And before I can put a stop to it, Zacchaeus will be transmuted into some high-paid government official trying to steal Maasai cattle while climbing thorn trees."

"The men seemed to like the song," Alexandra said, "but I had this feeling they were talking about me. What did they say?"

Grant pondered his answer for a moment. She gazed at him with wide blue eyes, and he felt a wave of tenderness curl inside him. For some unknown reason it mattered to this New York fashion designer what a bunch of old Maasai men thought about her.

"They said you have hair like fresh cream," Grant said. "You're as tall and willowy as a young tree, and your skin is as lovely as snow. They think you're intriguing." He met her eyes. "And so do I."

Alexandra wasn't at all sure she wanted to go to the Maasai feast with Grant Thornton. She didn't like the idea of walking around on fresh cow dung in the dark. She didn't relish the thought of what she might be offered to drink. She was still very sore and tired from her recent ordeal. And she didn't want to leave Mama Hannah alone, even though one of the young Maasai warriors had agreed reluctantly to miss the feasting and stand guard near the tents. The main reason Alexandra didn't want to go, though, was Grant himself. In the past couple of hours, the man had become downright obstinate.

"I don't see why you refuse to drive me to Nairobi tomorrow morning," she said as she followed his flashlight beam through the tall grass toward the *kraal*. Though he clearly didn't want her along, he had insisted she come because the Maasai elders had requested her presence. "The city is only a hundred and fifty miles from here, isn't it? That would take us three hours at the most. You could be back by evening."

"You flew from Nairobi to Amboseli National Park, didn't you?" he asked.

"Well, yes, but—"

"Driving it will take a good part of a day. At their best, the roads in Kenya are two-lane highways covered with potholes. At worst, they're dirt tracks. Depending on the time of year, they're nothing but mud. If I leave in the morning, I'll have no choice but to spend the night in Nairobi. The *Eunoto* ceremony lasts only four days—starting day after tomorrow. You'll just have to wait."

"But I need to get out of here. I have to arrange a ticket back to the States. I have to call my broker." She stumbled over a knot of grass roots and caught Grant's arm to keep from falling. The flashlight swung in a crazy arc. "Sorry. I tripped."

He stopped. "Look, Alexandra, I sympathize with you. This isn't what you expected when you booked your tour. But you've got to understand I have a life here. My research depends on a thorough accounting of all the Maasai ceremonies. All of them. *Eunoto* doesn't come around but every fifteen years or so. I can't miss this."

"So what am I supposed to do—sit under a tree for four days while my finances are in chaos?"

"What are you talking about?"

"Look . . . something has gone wrong. I told you I got a cable right before that . . . that man . . . attacked me. Things are a mess, and if I don't get back there to straighten them out, I could end up broke. I know that doesn't matter to you, Mr. Seven Socks, but it does to me! I have plans for that money."

He was flicking the flashlight on and off, its beam aimed at her rubber-tire sandals. "So that's what this is all about?" he asked finally. "Your money?"

"My father's money." She shoved her hands into the

pockets of her borrowed trousers. "It's like those stocks are a treasure chest. I have to protect it. It's a lot of money, Grant. My father worked very hard to earn that treasure, and I'm not about to stand by and watch it be frittered away. I've never been poor—and I never intend to be."

"Poor." He snapped off the light. "Exactly what is the meaning of that word?"

"Hey, turn the light back on."

"Look up, Alexandra." He tilted her chin with his fingertips. "You don't need a flashlight on a night like this one."

She blinked up at the awesome expanse of shimmering stars. The earth beneath her feet reeled away, miniaturized suddenly by the enormity of the great inky sky overhead. Never—even on the darkest night at the Texas ranch where she'd grown up—had Alexandra seen such majesty. The constellations stretched their arms in exhilaration. The Milky Way frothed and bubbled through the blackness. And the moon glittered in a white almost too bright to bear.

"You don't need diamonds when you've got stars," Grant said in a low voice. "You don't need silver when you have the moon."

Alexandra lowered her focus to his face. His skin was silvered by the light, his hair lifting a little in the cool breeze that swept down from the mountain. He gave her a slow smile. "Africa," he said with a shrug. "What more could anyone need?"

She took the flashlight from his hand and ran her fingers down the warmed metal. "I know you don't understand. You're happy with your tent and your seven socks. But I don't live out here, Grant. I live in Westchester County, New York. One month's payment on my condominium would keep you in groceries for a year. If I want to make my dreams come true—and I do—I need the money my father left me. I want to start my own design firm. I can't do that with the moon and the stars. I need capital."

"You *need* it?"

"Yes, I do. My parents didn't bring me up to become poor. They instilled certain ideals in me. I want the financial legacy they left me to grow. I don't want to end up like these people out here—with nothing but a strip of cloth on my back, bare feet, and a house made of cow dung."

He jerked the flashlight out of her hand and flipped on the beam. "These poor people," he said and began walking away. "An old British lady once asked me the meaning of the word *civilization*. And now you come along with your notion of poverty. So who's poor? Who's rich? Who's civilized? Who's a savage? I say I'm rich, and the Maasai are civilized. I say you're poor, and the citizens of New York City are savages. What do you make of that, Miss Prescott?"

"Well, I—"

"The world's upside down now, see? You're in Africa, the Southern Hemisphere, the Dark Continent. In Africa, darkness is light." He spread his arms to encompass the glittering heavens. "And light—" he snapped off the flashlight again—"is darkness."

"You're crazy."

"Am I?"

"Yes, you are."

"I'm *different. You're* crazy. My seven socks have driven you crazy. Africa has driven you crazy. You're the one who's crazy, Miss Prescott."

As drums and chanting filled the night air, Alexandra

stopped just outside the wall of dried thorn brush that formed a protective barrier around the Maasai *kraal*. She didn't want this twisted conversation. She didn't want this primitive bunch of Africans. She didn't want this frustrating, challenging, stubborn American who thought he knew everything. She wanted normalcy—her nice, clean condominium and her silver Volvo, her tidy bank account, her sleek office and leather portfolio, and her orderly schedule. She just wanted to go home.

Dear God, she breathed in prayer, *take me out of this place. Please help me get back where things are normal. And please, please make this infuriating man shut up!*

"Coming into the ballroom, Miss Prescott?" he said, holding out a hand. As she reluctantly took his fingers, he gave her a polite bow. "May I have the first dance?"

Alexandra walked into the *kraal* and stopped in disbelief. She had been to dances—plenty of them. She had danced at her high school prom. She had danced at her debut into Dallas society. She had danced at charity balls, wedding receptions, gallery openings, and galas. But she had never seen anything like the sight that greeted her just inside the thorn fence.

The women appeared to be wearing their brightest togas and all their beads. The men had on their loincloths. They faced each other in two long rows—men on one side and women on the other. Then they leaped high into the air to the rhythm of the song.

"It's like something out of a Tarzan movie," she said. "Half-naked natives leaping around a fire."

"They're dancing," Grant clarified. "And they're not naked."

Alexandra gawked at the incredible height the men reached, thrusting out their necks and surging their shoulders upward. "If the NBA recruiters ever got a look at these guys . . ."

Grant laughed. "Come on. It's fun."

"But my feet!" she protested as he drew her toward the crowd of dancers. "My feet are still sore, and I—"

"Leap as high as you can. They'll love it. How tall are you, anyway?"

"Five-ten," she replied, before adding the part she had always hated. "And a half."

"A Maasai dream come true." He positioned himself opposite her and began to move to the beating drums. "The taller the better. I'm six-two, and most of the Maasai men are my equal in height. Have you noticed?"

"It must be all that milk and blood they drink."

Alexandra joined the group of women who parted shyly to allow her among their ranks. As they danced, their flat, beaded collars bounced up and down to the rhythm. She listened to the song—a high-pitched, chanted phrase followed by a deep chorus of response—and tried to feel the beat. Slowly she began to attempt the bouncing and head-thrusting movements the other women demonstrated.

"What are they singing about?" she asked Grant during a pause in the song. "Sounds emotional."

"War," he said. "The government won't let the Maasai fight anymore. It's been a big problem for the warriors."

As she tried to match the women's movements, Alexandra studied the interplay of colors, the incredible swirl of pattern, and the array of fabrics, feathers, and beads. Although the scent on the people's skin was unpleasant to her at first, she found she quickly grew accustomed to it, focusing instead on the acrid smell of wood smoke from the fires and the fresh breeze drifting down from the mountain. The women beside her gingerly fingered her clothing and hair, giggling in amazement and whispering among themselves as they danced.

When Alexandra touched the toga of the woman beside her, she was greeted with a broad smile. In moments, the Maasai had unfastened one of her smaller bead collars and slipped it around the visitor's neck. Then she demonstrated how to make the collar flip up and down in time to the music.

"Did you see this?" Alexandra asked Grant, who had been leaping up and down in a sort of contest with some of the other men. "That woman over there—she gave this necklace to me."

"These are generous folks," he said. "They'll want to feed you some meat in a little while. It's been grilled over an open flame—not bad, really."

"Oh, Grant, I don't think so. I'm mostly vegetarian, and I try to avoid fats. Cholesterol, you know, is—" Alexandra glanced around her, realizing how silly her words sounded in this situation. "If you'll excuse me, I think I'm going to sit down and rest my feet."

She moved over to an empty stool beside one of the low mud dwellings. Again, she felt terribly off balance. Her thoughts reeled from deficit brokerage accounts to murderous stalkers to houses made of cow dung. Nothing was right. Nothing was in order.

Covering her eyes with both hands, she bent her head. *Dear Lord, what's happening to me? What am I supposed to do?*

*Now Grant tells me I can't leave this place for six more days. I'm
frightened of that horrible killer . . . and I'm touched by these odd
people . . . and I'm fascinated with a man who is so foreign . . . so
different. . . . Oh, Father, I need some help here. I need some
guidance. I'm feeling so—*

"Ah, good evening, Miss Prescott! And how are you this
fine night?"

She lifted her head to find Sambeke Ole Kereya standing
over her. The Oxford-educated Maasai had donned a knit
wool cap with a pompon at its point, and he was wrapped
up like a burrito in a deep red blanket. Beside him stood
little Mayani, the boy who had saved her from the wild
dogs' attack.

"Sambeke, Mayani!" she cried, starting to stand. "You've
come all this way."

The elder motioned her to remain seated while he squatted on the bare ground beside her. "Oh yes, my dear. The
ceremony of *Eunoto* is a very important event for our tribe.
Every able Maasai in the area has been traveling to this *kraal*
for many days. The warriors, you see, are to become junior
elders."

Alexandra laid her hand on Mayani's head in greeting,
and then the child knelt at her side. "Junior elders?" She
looked up at Sambeke. "I'm afraid I don't understand."

"Of course not. You have nothing with which to compare
such an event. It is a great step into a new stage of life."

Alexandra's debut flashed across her mind—a lavish party,
thousands of dollars spent, and a fancy dress that now
languished at the back of her closet. "What does it mean,
really, this *Eunoto* ceremony? Does it actually make a differ-
ence in the warriors' lives?"

Sambeke chuckled. "Until now, these men could not marry! After the ceremony, they will wed, have children, and put their spears aside in favor of the fly whisk and the walking stick."

"I see."

"Poor Dr. Thornton," the elder said, shaking his head. "We Maasai feel great sorrow for him. He is of the English, you see, and as you well know, their culture leaves much to be desired. A real pity—few ceremonies, no feasts, and so little structure upon which to base one's life. Indeed, a Maasai always knows who he is and where he belongs in the organization of the clan. But our dear friend, whom we respect greatly, has no cattle at all, and he certainly has no hope of obtaining a wife. I'm afraid that even within his own culture, the man is a hopeless case."

Alexandra tried to hide her grin as she watched the tall anthropologist listening intently to something one of the Maasai was telling him. "Why do you say Dr. Thornton is hopeless?" she asked. "Just because he has no cattle and no wife?"

"What more is there in life? Only God—and Dr. Thornton refuses to believe in the One of Many Colors. His scholarly mind and his search for fact and measurement have become a barrier to discovering what is real truth. He is a good man but a very sad case. Perhaps you can bring joy and hope into the life of our friend, Miss Prescott."

"Thanks, but I don't think I'm qualified. Besides, I'm going back to America in a few days."

"Really?" He seemed surprised. "You have seen the beauty of our life, and you would choose to leave us?"

"It's just that I have . . . my own life. I'm designing a new line of fabrics."

"Why?"

"Because it's what I do. It's my job."

"To make pictures on cloth? Oh, Miss Prescott, we elders have been discussing you all this day, and we believe that God has brought you here for a very important reason."

Alexandra was incredulous. "You've been discussing me? Why?"

"You are to do something much greater than make pictures on cloth."

"But that's what I *like* to do."

He shook his head sadly. "You do not have a husband, Miss Prescott."

"No, and I'm not interested in marriage, Sambeke."

"Why is this?"

"Men I meet seem to be after my . . . my money." Suddenly Grant's words flashed into her brain. *You don't need diamonds when you've got stars. You don't need silver when you have the moon.* "Most men, anyway. I can't trust them. If I ever did marry, I would want the man to love me for myself and not for my wealth. Can you understand that?"

"Oh yes. Yes, indeed. In Maasai culture, however, such issues are irrelevant. Marriages are made for the good of both parties. And that is why, Miss Prescott, I have come to help you." He stood solemnly. "I have been commissioned by the elders to arrange a good marriage for you."

"A marriage? To whom?"

"To Dr. Grant Thornton," he said with a smile, "of course."

SEVEN

"Marry Grant Thornton?"

Alexandra glanced up to find the man himself staring at her from across the *kraal*—a look of shock that mirrored her own written across his face. Evidently, he had just been offered a similar proposal by the elderly Maasai man who stood beside him.

"No, no, Sambeke," she said, standing quickly. "You don't understand how we do things in America."

"On the contrary, I do understand. Lest you forget, I spent many years of my life in the so-called civilization of the West. I can tell you, my dear, that we Maasai have very few instances of unhappy marriage, while you people have great numbers of divorces. Now why is that? I will tell you. First, it is because you choose mates from the heart, while we choose from the mind. Second, we provide love and support for the marriage and the children throughout the lives of our people. The threads that bind us together are many and strong. Yours are few and pitiably weak."

"I agree with what you're saying to some extent, Sambeke. But you must understand that I barely know Dr. Thornton. He and I come from two different lifestyles, and we have very little in common. I can't possibly marry him."

"Wrong! If the two of you would simply reflect on it,

you would see that you have a great deal in common. You are both good people, both strong and healthy, both very lonely. Were Dr. Thornton a Maasai, tomorrow he would be joining his friend Kakombe in the ceremony that ends warriorhood and signals the age of marriage and family. It is time for our beloved anthropologist to settle down and wed a fine woman."

"Maybe so, but I am not that woman."

"Balderdash! You are well within the years for bearing children, my dear. And you have no provider. No protector. We all saw how easily an evil man was able to abduct you and leave you to die in the wilderness. But with a good husband like Dr. Thornton, you would always be safe, cared for . . . and loved."

Alexandra rubbed her forehead. She could see Grant making his way through the dancers toward her. How embarrassing.

"Thank you, Sambeke," she said in a low voice. "I appreciate your concern for my future. Really I do."

"Then you will consider this matter. You have six days. After that time, we will perform the ceremony of marriage."

"Sambeke, you old warthog," Grant said on arriving. "What are you up to now?"

"Where is the greeting of respect that I should be accorded?" The old man gave a grunt of disapproval. *"Old warthog* is certainly not an honorable address for a Maasai elder."

"It's an appropriate address for somebody who puts his nose into other people's business. You and Sentero have cooked up quite a scheme this time, haven't you?"

"I am sure I do not know what 'scheme' you are talking

about. Now, will you listen to the wisdom of your elders, as a young man should? Or will you continue in the foolish pattern that has brought you no wealth, no security, and no future?"

Grant folded his arms over his chest and shook his head. "Wisdom is not always white headed, Sambeke."

"You address me disrespectfully, yet you throw a good Maasai proverb at me? Then I shall retort: It is unlikely that you will find a gray head who is unwise."

"You and Sentero have great wisdom," Grant said, his voice more gentle. "I have sought your counsel in many matters, my teacher."

"But this you choose to ignore?"

"May I cut in here, gentlemen?" Alexandra spoke up. She was beginning to feel like a heifer being bartered at a county fair—and not a very prized heifer at that. "I'll make my own decisions about my future, thank you. Right now, I'm tired, and we've been away from Mama Hannah for hours. I'd like to get going, please."

"Of course, my dear," Sambeke said. "In a moment." He turned back to Grant. "Now, Dr. Thornton—Sentero, the other elders, and I shall not let this matter rest until it has been resolved. You have lived near our people many years, and we consider you almost as one of our young warriors. I'm afraid that none of the elders is willing to assume the role of adoptive father for you. You are simply too unorthodox. And the young lady cannot expect to find a good Maasai father quickly either. This unfortunate fact, however, allows you to dispense with the giving of gifts and all other matters related to the marriage dowry. It leaves merely the giving of the silver chain and the performance of the ceremony. You *do* have a chain?"

"I do not have a chain, and I—"

"I might have known!" He parted his blanket and slipped a waist-length silver chain over his head. "Here you are, then. You owe me a young goat for this, my dear man. Give the chain to Miss Prescott when the two of you have worked out the details of your future union. When the *Eunoto* ceremony has ended, we shall be more than happy to perform a wedding. Good night to you both!"

"May you lie down with honey and milk," Grant said as the old man strolled away with young Mayani at his side. "Clueless," he muttered as he slipped the chain into his pocket. "Completely clueless. Sambeke lived in England for years, and he still looks at things only from the Maasai point of view. I'm sorry he cornered you, Alexandra. He's just trying to be helpful."

"I understand the elders' concern," she said. "But what I do with my future is none of their business."

"Bunch of busybodies, if you ask me." He chuckled, shaking his head. "Look at them over there discussing the two of us. I'll bet you never thought you'd wind up with a marriage proposal on this trip."

"I never thought I'd wind up with any of the things that have happened to me."

"Your basic disaster, huh?"

"More or less." She started toward the *kraal* gate with him. "So, are you still determined to stay here through the entire ceremony? The venerable elders are going to expect an answer about your future state of matrimony."

"Could be worse. I'll deal with it one way or another."

"Why *don't* you marry, Grant?" she asked as they walked toward the faint lights of the camp. "Mama Hannah seems to think it's a good idea. Surely there's some woman who wouldn't mind living out in the bush. Maybe you could find another researcher or something. Even *I* used to love camping with my father."

"Even you—the big-city lady?"

"I spent a good part of my childhood on a Texas ranch, buster. I love camping, OK? The tents, the fresh air, the sunshine. Because of my business, I work in New York. But I like being out in the wild. There's bound to be a woman somewhere who could tolerate you and your life-style enough to marry you."

He laughed. "I'm flattered. But no thanks. I'm a happy camper just as I am. What about you? You've got money, looks, education, and talent. Surely those New York junior executives are champing at the bit to slip a diamond on your finger. Besides that, Sentero assures me you're in your prime childbearing years."

"Oh, he does?" Alexandra lifted her chin and soaked in the vision of the starry night sky as they walked along side by side. "The truth is, I've always felt different from most people. I haven't ever really fit. In school, I was too rich for the regular kids, and I was too artsy for the highbrow bunch. I chose a career in design, but my coworkers are intimidated by the money thing. Everyone who isn't intimidated is trying to manipulate it away from me. I really can't trust anyone. I'm sure you wouldn't understand what that's like."

"I trust people. But I know what it's like to feel different. Try growing up as a white kid in Africa with Mama Hannah for a mother. When I got to college, I could speak five languages, and I'd been to the Nile, the Sahara, and the top of Mount Kilimanjaro. But I didn't know how to work a Coke machine."

"You're kidding!"

"Go ahead. Laugh at my pain."

"I'm not laughing."

"You're laughing." He reached over and poked her in the ribs. When she let out a giggle, he did it again. "There you go again."

"You rat!" She gave him a gentle shove, and he caught her fingers.

"Oops—I forgot. No touching." He dropped her hand. "Sorry."

"It's OK. I'm better, I guess. At least I think I am."

"You mean you semitrust me—another human being? You don't think I'm after your money?"

"You'd be smart to go after my money. If you want permanent funding for all your anthropological research projects, you ought to reconsider Sambeke's idea."

"Last I heard, your finances were in chaos. Maybe you ought to listen to Sambeke and make a play for me."

"The Man with Seven Socks."

"Don't forget I now own a valuable silver chain." He pulled it out of his pocket and dangled it in front of her. "You are getting very sleepy, Alexandra. Very sleepy. You are in a trance. When you awaken, you will have a strong affinity for blood milkshakes and canvas tents and anthropologists."

"Get that chain out of my face, Houdini. I can't see where I'm—" She stopped and peered at the campsite. One of the lanterns was swaying in a widening arc as the tent pole that held it snapped back and forth. "Look at that, Grant. What's going on?"

He swung around. "Mama Hannah," he breathed. "Someone's in her tent. Stay here!"

Grant broke into a run, the flashlight beam swinging across the grass as he dashed toward the tent. Suddenly terrified, Alexandra glanced behind her. Images of shadowy creatures reared up from the brush. Wild dogs. Wild men. She couldn't stay alone in the bush—there was no place to hide, no safety. She clenched her fists and sprinted after Grant.

"Loomali!" he was shouting to the Maasai guard. "Loomali—*kaji negol?* What's going on? Who's there?"

Alexandra saw a shadow emerge from the tent a second before it collapsed in a puff of canvas. Grant let out a bellow of rage. "Hey—who are you? What have you done to my mother? Stop!"

Dear God, is it him? Is it Nick Jones? What's happened to Mama Hannah? Her palms clammy, Alexandra threw herself down in the deep grass. *Oh, God, save us! Save us!*

She covered her head with her arms as she listened to the shouts—Grant, another man, and then another. English words mingled with Maasai. The sounds of scuffling echoed across the darkness. A heavy weight slammed into something metal. More shouts, more cries.

Alexandra squeezed her eyes shut. She had brought this. She had brought the killer to Grant's campsite. *Oh, God, what shall I do?* The *kraal!* She should run back to the *kraal* and call the warriors. How could she make them understand what was happening?

Sambeke would know.

She forced herself to her feet. But which direction was the *kraal?* She searched the darkness for familiar markers. In the campsite clearing, the men thrashed around the fallen tent. Was Mama Hannah still inside it? What if she needed help? Someone should go to her. Alexandra bit her lip. She didn't want to be anywhere near the clearing. Nick Jones would see her and attack again.

But Mama Hannah might be hurt. At the very least, she would be terrified. Alexandra swallowed at the knot of fear in her throat. *Lord, I'm so scared! Help me!*

She gritted her teeth and started toward the clearing. Grant's tent was still standing, its lantern swinging as the silhouetted men brawled around it. The other lantern lay on the ground. A patch of burning kerosene spread across the grass toward the crumpled tent.

Fire!

Where did Grant keep his water? Alexandra raced to the edge of the camp and located the heavy plastic tank. Hurling her shoulder against it, she managed to topple it to the ground. Then she rolled it toward the fire. As she neared the tent, she could see a huddled shape moving beneath the canvas.

"Grant?" Mama Hannah's voice called weakly. *"Toto?"*

Terrified to respond for fear that the attacker might hear her, Alexandra uncapped the tank and allowed the sloshing water to gurgle out onto the licking flames. Then she plunged toward the tent.

"Mama Hannah!" she whispered. "I'm coming for you!"

She found the tent opening just as a car started up at the edge of the clearing. Was Grant running away? Or was Nick escaping? Determined to help the only person she could truly trust in this wilderness, she tunneled under the folds of canvas. In the utter darkness, she bumped into the edge of an overturned cot, then crawled over it. She banged her forehead on the corner of a metal trunk.

"Ouch! Mama Hannah?"

"Alexandra, I am here!"

"I'm coming for you. Hold out your hand." She reached into the void and felt the touch of warm fingers. "Are you all right, Mama Hannah?"

"Oh, Alexandra, my *toto!*" Mama Hannah's arms slipped around the younger woman. "I have been praying for you! But now I see you are well."

"Praying for *me?* What about you?"

"God is with me," Mama Hannah whispered. "'The Lord is my light and my salvation—so why should I be afraid?' It is for you I fear, and for my Grant."

Alexandra huddled under the tent, her head on Mama Hannah's shoulder. "Nick Jones is out there," she said, listening to the frightening silence outside. "He came for me. He's going to hurt us."

"Pray, child. Pray. 'You are my God! Listen, O Lord, to my cries for mercy! O Sovereign Lord, my strong savior—'"

"Mama Hannah?" Grant's voice broke through the murmured prayer. "Where are you, Mama Hannah?"

"Here, *toto!* We are in the tent."

"Who's with you?"

"Alexandra. She is protecting me."

The tent began to lift overhead, and Alexandra struggled to push away the sagging fabric. Mama Hannah was the protector, she sensed—and not the other way around.

Alexandra had been so frightened. She was frightened even now. But the old woman's calm voice and gentle words of hope and comfort gave her strength.

"Come with me, Mama Hannah," she said, rising to a crouch. "We need to get you out of here."

"Oh, *toto,* allow me to sit until the tent has risen. The man caused me a small injury."

"What did he do? Did he hit you?" Alexandra fell to her knees again as Grant emerged through the tent opening with the flashlight. He wedged the central tent pole into the canvas peak and propped it up, then he swung the flashlight beam toward the two women.

"Mama Hannah, your head! You're bleeding." Grant sank to the ground and gathered the old woman in his arms. "I'm here now, Mama. How bad does it hurt?"

"It is nothing, *toto.* The man had a knife, and he believed his weapon would make me speak to him."

Grant stripped off his shirt and began dabbing it against Mama Hannah's temple. "He cut you to make you talk?"

"Ehh. He said he would like to slit my throat. But I asked him, 'Sir, how then will I speak to you?' I think he is not a very clever man."

"It must have been Nick Jones," Alexandra whispered, feeling faint. "Oh, Grant, she's bleeding so much!"

He pressed on the wound where the knife had sliced through skin and muscle. "The guy's a demon. He tied Loomali up and strung him from a tree by his arms and legs. Humiliating. The poor man's gone back to the *kraal* to get help."

"Grant, I'm so sorry," Alexandra said. "This is all my fault. I never should have come here."

"Forget it. The main thing now is to take care of Mama Hannah. We've got to get her to a doctor."

"Toto, the wound is not so bad."

"Alexandra, press this against her head," Grant said, ignoring Mama Hannah's protest. "I'm going to my tent for my first-aid kit."

"What about Jones?"

"He's gone. He didn't get what he came for."

Me, Alexandra thought as Grant disappeared through the tent opening. *He came for me. He tracked me out here to the middle of nowhere. He tried to force Mama Hannah to tell him where I was. And soon he's going to kill me!*

"'I am trusting you, O Lord, saying, "You are my God!"'" Mama Hannah murmured as Alexandra cradled her. Her words gradually began to stumble and slur. "'My future is in your hands. Rescue me from those . . . from those who hunt me down . . .'"

"Mama Hannah?" Alexandra said, hearing the panic in her own voice.

"I need to rest, *toto.*"

"Please try to stay awake. You've lost a lot of blood." She fought back tears. "This is terrible!"

"Do you blame yourself for the work of an evil man?"

"Shh, don't try to talk. Are you in pain?"

"Yes, very much. I think it would be good to sing." She hummed for a moment. "Let us go to heaven."

"Heaven?" The word sent a chill of terror racing through Alexandra. "Mama Hannah, please don't die!"

"Relax," Grant said calmly, coming back into the tent. "'Let us go to heaven' is an African way of introducing a song. You're not going to die on us, are you, Mama Hannah?"

"Sing to me, *toto*. Sing to your mama."

Alexandra could see Grant struggling to maintain his composure as he lifted away the bloody shirt and pressed a clean bandage to the old woman's head. "I don't know any songs," he muttered. "You're bleeding here, and I can't . . . can't . . ."

"Jesus loves me, this I know," Mama Hannah sang in a wavering voice. "Sing to me, *toto*."

"Jesus loves me, this I know," Grant sang, his voice rough-edged. "For the Bible tells me so. Little ones to him belong. They are weak . . . but . . . but . . ."

"They are weak," Alexandra finished, "but he is strong."

"Mombasa." The manager of Kilanguni Lodge eyed the injured woman lying on a pallet of blankets in the back of Grant's Land Rover. "We have a small airplane leaving our runway for the coast in fifteen minutes. The plane is only half full, and I think I can hold it for you. But you'll have to hurry."

Grant considered a moment. "I'd rather take her to Nairobi. The hospital there is bigger and better equipped."

"We won't have a plane going to Nairobi until tomorrow evening. It is your choice."

Grant shook his head. There was no choice.

Mama Hannah had faded during the overland trip from the campsite to the lodge at Tsavo West National Park. Even now, Alexandra huddled over her in the backseat, trying to keep her alert and encouraging her to take small sips of water. Every time Grant thought about the brutal beast who had attacked a helpless old woman, fury surged through his veins like wildfire.

"Hold that plane for us," he told the manager. "And radio ahead to the hospital. I want the best doctors they've got. Have them standing by."

"Yes, Dr. Thornton. Of course." He hesitated a moment. "I think it would be appropriate to bring the police into this matter. The disappearance of the tourist from Amboseli Lodge several days ago created quite a disturbance. The news of the search for her has been in all the papers. Now this attack on your camp. Such things are very bad for tourism."

"The woman who disappeared from Amboseli is sitting right there in the backseat," Grant said, cocking a thumb at Alexandra. "Look, I want you to put Miss Prescott on that plane to Nairobi tomorrow. And watch her closely. The man who wounded Hannah Wambua is the same one who attacked Miss Prescott."

"The same man? Do you have a name?"

"Nick Jones. Tourist from New York. If the police don't track down that guy, I will." Grant opened the back door. "Alexandra, there's a plane to Nairobi tomorrow evening. You can stay here at the lodge until then. You'll be safe."

"Yes, madam, I will assign a guard to you immediately," the manager said as he hurried toward his office.

Alexandra tucked a strand of hair behind her ear. "I'm not leaving," she said firmly. "I'm going with Mama Hannah, Grant."

"In ten minutes I'm putting her on a plane to Mombasa. That's three hundred miles from Nairobi. If you want out of this trouble—and out of this country—now's your chance."

She looked into his eyes. "I'm not leaving her, Grant. I can't."

"Why? Because you blame yourself for what Jones did?"

"Because I care about her."

"I care about her, too, and I'll see that she gets safely to the hospital. You get back to the States, where you belong."

"You're the one who should stay here. Attend the Maasai ceremony that's so important to you, and I'll go to the coast with Mama Hannah. I've got a forty-five-day visa. I can stay with her until you come."

Grant hesitated. He hadn't given the *Eunoto* ceremony much thought in the urgent hours of driving to the lodge. Missing the elder initiation would be a blow. It could hamper his research by years. His financial backers were expecting a report on the rite. They were also expecting regular articles and a book. Without the account of the *Eunoto,* he could lose his funding—and his job.

Torn, Grant looked down at Mama Hannah. Her head on Alexandra's lap, she was clearly struggling to contain the pain she felt. She had squeezed her eyes shut, and her rigid lips were clenched in agony. In one hand she clutched her little Bible. In the other she gripped Alexandra's fingers.

"I'm taking Mama Hannah to the hospital," Grant said.

Alexandra's blue eyes softened. "Then let's go."

The tiny plane thumped and bounced over pockets of air until Alexandra felt like she was riding a bucking bronco.

She couldn't imagine the depth of misery Mama Hannah must be feeling as she lay on a stretcher in the narrow aisle. Grant sat grim-faced, holding the old woman's hand and staring blankly at the back of the seat in front of him. Beside him, Alexandra rested her head on the tiny oval window and prayed for Mama Hannah.

What was the Scripture the old woman had quoted when the Maasai had carried Alexandra into Grant's camp? *"Have compassion on me, Lord, for I am weak. Heal me, Lord, for my body is in agony."*

As she prayed, Alexandra let her eyes wander. Thin clouds like swaths of cotton batting from a torn quilt drifted past the window. Below them, vast waves of golden grass swept in an unending sea. To the south, Mount Kilimanjaro's snowcapped peak glowed like a ruby in the sunrise as the airplane gradually left it behind. Barely visible on the ground, herds of wildlife grazed—antelope, zebras, elephants, and gazelles. It was going to be another beautiful day in Kenya.

Alexandra shut her eyes. She was so tired. The night attack had brought back memories of Nick Jones and fears for her own safety. She couldn't imagine how he had tracked her to the tiny campsite. What if he found her again? What if she had endangered Grant and Mama Hannah all over again by insisting on going with them to the coast? Alexandra had the terrible feeling that if the plane didn't stop jolting she might be ill. But she had to keep her thoughts focused—focused on Mama Hannah. *Pray, Alexandra, pray.*

"Dear Father," she murmured. "Please guard us. Please protect us."

"Huh?" Grant turned to her, bleary eyed. "What did you say?"

"I'm praying."

"You're wasting your breath. This is going to take a doctor."

Alexandra swallowed at the harshness in his voice. "You don't believe in God's power to heal?"

"I don't believe in God. Period." He scratched his unshaven chin. "How did you fall into the religion thing anyway? Parents?"

"In the beginning. But as the years went by, my faith became my own. I believe in Christ because I see the effects of his presence in my life."

"I hate to mention this, but your life includes a maniac killer."

Alexandra sobered. "Terrible things happen to people all the time, Grant. Cancer, abuse, freak accidents. God doesn't promise us a life free of problems. But I knew he was with me in the bush when Nick Jones attacked me. God led me toward Sambeke's *kraal*. He sent Mayani to protect me from the wild dogs. Even if I had died out there, God's presence would have given me strength to the end. And hope. How can you exist without hope?"

"Hope of an afterlife, you mean? Come on, Alexandra. Do you have any evidence of heaven?"

"I don't need evidence. I have faith."

"Yeah, well, I need proof. I'm a scientist, remember?"

"You needed faith to get on this airplane."

"I happen to understand aerodynamics. Besides, I don't have a lot of faith in this airplane. I'm wagering that if it hits one more bump, the whole thing's going to come apart."

Alexandra leaned back against the seat and closed her eyes. She had never been any good at explaining her faith in

Jesus to other people. Through prayer, Bible reading, the church, and the circumstances of her life, she had experienced God's powerful presence. But to make Dr. Grant Thornton understand the fullness of life in Christ? Impossible. If Mama Hannah's genuine and unpretentious faith hadn't been able to convince him, Alexandra Prescott certainly couldn't.

"Look, I didn't mean to offend you," Grant said. "I really appreciate what you did for Mama Hannah—going to her in the tent last night even though you knew Jones was after you. You even put out a fire."

Alexandra opened her eyes. "Just call me Wonder Woman."

Grant searched her face, his head resting on the seat just inches away. "So, what's going to happen to you?"

"I don't know. I'm going to hope the police catch Jones before he finds me again."

"You're going to need a lot of faith. He's pretty determined. Strong and sneaky, too."

"He's obviously no slouch at tracking, either. If I knew why he had chosen me it would help."

"Maybe he's attracted to beautiful women."

"Ha." Alexandra instinctively touched her peeling nose. She wished she could take Grant's comment as a compliment, but she knew she was a mess. "I think it's the money."

"How is killing you going to get Jones any money? If he's after money, he ought to kidnap you and demand a ransom, right?"

She shook her head. "I don't know, and I'm too tired to think it all through. I just can't believe what he did to

Mama Hannah. I have no doubt he would have killed her if we hadn't walked up when we did."

"He's got you running scared, hasn't he?"

"Scared, yes. But I'm also angry. Every time I think about him threatening her—and cutting her—I get furious."

He nodded. "If I could get my hands on that guy, I'd make sure he never hurt either of you again."

Alexandra looked into his gray blue eyes. A spark of something unexpected flickered to life inside her. "Do you mean that, Grant?"

"Of course I mean it. Mama Hannah is my mother. And you're . . . well, you're beginning to seem . . . hard to ignore."

"Such a compliment."

"OK, I'll admit it," he said. "I kind of like having you around."

Alexandra smiled, but her expression quickly turned serious. "Grant, I've always believed that the greatest love a person can have is to lay down her life for people she cares about. After what happened to Mama Hannah, I believe Nick Jones is capable of *anything*. He's not going to stop, and he's not going to care who gets in his way. I think you and I both know what I have to do."

"Tell me anyway."

"We've got to trap him," she said. "And I have to be the bait."

Eight

"Miss Prescott?"

A tall African in a gray police uniform awakened Alexandra out of a troubled sleep. She lifted her head from Grant's shoulder and tried to focus on Mombasa Hospital's waiting room and her unexpected visitor.

"Is your name Alexandra Elizabeth Prescott, madam?" the policeman asked. "Are you a citizen of the United States of America? Are you visiting Kenya on a tourist visa? And is this your passport?"

At the sight of the familiar little blue booklet, Alexandra nodded and sucked in a breath. "Where did you get my passport?"

"The manager of the Amboseli lodge sent it to us some days ago along with your other baggage. Your schedule listed Mombasa as your next stop. The manager felt that you might choose to continue your journey to the coast. We are holding your things at the main station." He tucked the passport into his pocket. "I need to speak with you now, Miss Prescott. Please follow me."

Grant slipped a protective arm around Alexandra's shoulder. *"Bwana,* we're waiting to hear the results of a surgery. Can this wait?"

"Are you Dr. Thornton?"

"That's right."

The flicker of a smile crossed the man's somber features. "I am glad to meet you." Then he sobered again. "I must speak with you also, Dr. Thornton. We received word this morning that there was an attack on your camp near Mount Kilimanjaro last night. I must ask that you and Miss Prescott accompany me to police headquarters to file a report."

"*Bwana,* I respect your request, but I can't go anywhere until I find out how the woman in that operating room is doing. *Mchomwa mwiba hawi mtembezi.*"

At this, the officer couldn't hold in his grin. "'He that has a thorn pricking him will not be a walker.' What they say about you is true, Dr. Thornton. You speak our language as one of us, and you understand our customs. Is the patient your close friend?"

"She has been a mother to me. I don't want to leave until I know her condition. Could you question us here?"

The officer studied the waiting room for a moment. "Very well. But you will be expected to stop at headquarters later today."

He pulled a chair across the bare tiled floor and took out a notebook. For some reason, Alexandra found she didn't mind in the least having Grant's arm around her. In fact, she welcomed it. His broad shoulders had come to symbolize a sort of Rock of Gibraltar to her. His voice comforted her down deep, where fear and hunger and exhaustion had formed a big knot. And when he touched her fingers, a blessed warmth flowed through her heart.

"Miss Prescott," the officer said, all business again. "Please recount for me the experience you had at the lodge in Amboseli National Park."

Alexandra took a deep breath, dreading the ordeal of dredging up the haunting memory. But she knew she had no choice. She began with the poolside encounter that led to the attack under the tree. Then she told the officer about the wild dogs, the Maasai, and her torturous journey to Grant Thornton's camp.

"Why did you not contact the authorities when you and Dr. Thornton drove up to Oloitokitok, Miss Prescott?"

"I was afraid if I told anyone that I was alive, Nick Jones would come after me again. I wanted to grow well enough to leave and get on a plane back to the United States." She thought for a moment. "But I did tell someone. I phoned my financial advisor in New York and told him to contact the Nairobi authorities and call off the search for me."

"Your disappearance is the subject of much speculation and a thorough, ongoing investigation."

"I'm very sorry, sir." Alexandra rubbed a hand over her eyes. "I *am* all right, and I didn't intend to cause trouble."

"Dr. Thornton, do you have anything to add to this woman's testimony?"

Grant's fingers tightened on Alexandra's shoulder. "Only what happened last night in my camp." He briefly related the attack on Mama Hannah and their subsequent flight to Mombasa. "We want this Nick Jones stopped. Do the police have any idea where he might be?"

The officer shook his head. "This is private information, of course. But allow me to assure you that you will be among the first to know when we apprehend this man."

"We'd like to help you capture him," Alexandra said. "Officer, Nick Jones is after *me*. Where I go, he's bound to follow. We know he was near Mount Kilimanjaro last night. He'll easily find out I flew to Mombasa, since lots of people at the lodge saw us there with Mama Hannah. Jones probably suspects the police will be looking for him at the airport, so I would think he is driving. How quickly could he get to Mombasa?"

"By this evening, madam."

Alexandra swallowed. "OK, why don't I stay someplace where he thinks he can find me alone? If he senses I'm vulnerable, he'll try again."

"I believe you should leave this matter to the police. It would not be wise to place yourself in unnecessary danger."

"You don't understand. I'm convinced Jones can track me anywhere, sir. No matter where I go, I'm in danger. I might as well do my part to help you catch him. I'll book a room at a small place somewhere on the beach. Not a fancy hotel because it would be too public. If we could find some sort of—"

"Bungalow," Grant cut in. "The Thornton family has owned a little cottage on Diani Beach for years. You can stay there."

"I will speak to my supervisor about this matter," the officer said. "It is possible he will agree to your request— with our constant protection, of course. By day, you would be followed by an armed detective. We would post a guard near your room at night. In Kenya, it is a common practice to hire a night watchman. The man would not suspect."

"I can do the usual tourist things," Alexandra continued. "But I'll make myself vulnerable. I'll lure Jones to attack me, and then you can step in and catch him."

Grant frowned. "I don't like it. This isn't some detective show on television, Alexandra. This is reality here. Jones is strong. He managed to disarm a Maasai warrior, who was carrying a spear and a fighting stick. Then he strung up Loomali from a tree limb like a piece of meat. Jones told you he worked as a bodyguard for a living, so he knows the tricks of the trade. And he was smart enough to track you to a camp on the back side of nowhere. You're risking your life playing cat and mouse with a man like that."

"The police will be near me everywhere I go," she said.

"Indeed," the officer avowed. "The man may be clever and strong, but Dr. Thornton knows our Swahili proverb: *Taritibu hushinda nguvu*. Persistence overcomes strength."

"Grant, it makes sense," Alexandra said. "Jones is going to try to get to me. I might as well set him up."

"Not without me, you won't."

"What are you saying, Grant? Stay here with Mama Hannah. She needs you."

"*You* need me, Alexandra." His gray eyes crackled. "If Jones wasn't afraid of Loomali and his spear, he won't be afraid of me. But he picked the wrong place to cross me. We'll do this thing together."

"Grant, really, I don't want you to risk—"

"Dr. Thornton?" A white-coated African doctor pushed through the double doors. Alexandra and Grant leaped to their feet. "The surgery was successful, and Ms. Wambua is in the recovery room. She received a deep laceration over the left eye extending down toward the ear. The temple muscle was partially severed, but we have stitched it. We expect full recovery. She did lose a great deal of blood, however, and she is weak. I would like to perform a transfusion."

"No way." Grant shoved his hands into his pockets.

"Not with AIDS in the blood supply. You'll have to try something else."

Alexandra took a deep breath. "Use my blood, doctor," she said softly. "I'm O positive—the universal donor. And I don't have AIDS."

Grant gaped at her.

"Come with me, please, madam," the doctor beckoned. "I will need you to sign release forms. Dr. Thornton, please wait here."

Alexandra started for the double door, but Grant caught her hand. "Wait a second," he said. "Why are you doing this?"

"Don't ask. You won't like the answer."

"Tell me."

"Jesus commands us to love each other in the same way he loves us. I'm happy to give Hannah my blood."

"Come, come, madam," the doctor called. "We must hurry."

Alexandra squeezed Grant's hand. "See you in a bit."

It took the rest of the day to get out to the Thornton bungalow. After giving blood, Alexandra was ordered to rest at the hospital for several hours. The doctor had examined her thoroughly and treated her peeling skin and blistered feet before he finally agreed to release her. The attending officer drove Alexandra and Grant to the police station after a brief stop at a local restaurant for lunch.

After recounting the details of her ordeal a second time, Alexandra had to go through her papers and every item in each of her bags to identify her possessions. That done, the police allowed her to try to call her broker in the States. She couldn't get through. By the time the police had arranged for an undercover detective and a night guard, Grant had rented a small car. He drove them to a supermarket, where they picked up a supply of groceries, and then they set out for Diani Beach.

Night fell, and Grant greeted the police guard before showing Alexandra to the room that would be hers. A large living room and dining room that opened out onto a huge verandah separated her side of the house from his. She went through her luggage again and was relieved to note that her sketches and designs were intact; evidently no one had touched a thing. She ate a snack, took a long shower, and fell into an exhausted sleep, aware only of the sound of crashing surf outside her window.

She awoke midmorning to the arrival of Mama Hannah, whom Grant had fetched from the hospital. Hearing the low tones of conversation coming from the living room, Alexandra eagerly ate a banana and got dressed.

She tucked a pair of sunglasses into her pocket and then hurried to join Grant and Mama Hannah. In the expansive, open-air room, the old woman was stretched out on a long striped sofa, her white bandage taking the place of her usual nylon scarf.

"Good morning!" Mama Hannah cried warmly, extending a hand.

Alexandra took the gnarled brown fingers and kissed them gently. "They let you go."

"God is good," Mama Hannah said. "And so are you, *toto*. How can I thank you for such a gift?"

"You don't need to thank me. I'm just grateful you're well enough to leave the hospital. How do you feel?"

"Ehh, they have given me enough medicine to make an elephant believe he could dance on the clouds at the top of Mount Kilimanjaro. I have no pain. I also cannot walk unless Grant holds me. My steps are like those of a woman who has drunk too much *pombe*."

"*Pombe?*"

"African honey beer," Grant said.

Alexandra turned to him, but the question on her tongue froze solid. Grant Thornton looked positively rakish this morning. His faded denim shirt and jeans brought out the color of his eyes. He had rolled up the shirtsleeves just far enough to reveal thick golden hair that covered his forearms. Though he had combed back his damp hair, a single curl fell onto his forehead. With his clean-shaven chin and a sparkle in his eyes, Grant would have knocked any woman flat. Alexandra was doing her best just to breathe.

"Fermented honey," he said, giving her a lopsided grin that sent a shiver down to the tips of her toes. "I doubt if Mama Hannah's ever tasted *pombe* in her life."

"I have not," the old woman said. "But I have seen men staggering down a street just as I stumbled through that hospital. Grant, I think I must sleep again now. My head swims."

Grant knelt beside the sofa and drew a lightweight blanket up to Mama Hannah's chin. "The armed guard is right outside, and I'll be here with you, too. Just rest."

"No, no. You must take Alexandra out to the beach. Show her the water and the ferry and even the old town.

Take her to see Fort Jesus. You are both too young to stay by the side of a sleepy old woman all day. Go now."

Grant lifted his focus to Alexandra. "Have you seen the beach yet?"

"No, but I'd rather stay here, if you don't mind."

"*I* mind," Mama Hannah said. "Go away, both of you, and let me sleep. I am not afraid. 'Oh, how I wish I had wings like a dove; then I would fly away and rest! I would fly far away to the quiet of the wilderness.' This was the song of David, and it is now the song of Hannah Wambua. Shoo!"

"Shoo?" Grant frowned as the woman's eyelids dropped shut. "You sure are a feisty little thing, you know that?"

"Ehh." She held up a hand, and one eye slid open. "Grant, you must protect Alexandra. She is a treasure. The man . . . he is . . . wanting to hurt her. 'In a little while, the wicked will disappear. . . . Though you look for them . . . they will be . . . gone. . . .'"

"She's asleep," Alexandra said. "Do you think she knows something about Jones that she hasn't told us? Maybe he admitted why he was after me."

"I'll talk to her about it when she wakes up," Grant said. "For some reason, she feels very protective of you. It's weird how the two of you bonded so fast."

"Not really."

"The Christian thing, right?"

"The night we met at the airport, Mama Hannah told me she was a believer. After Jones attacked me, all I could think about was finding her. She was a light in my darkness. Sort of a vision of sanity and truth and everything good."

"I know what you mean," he said. "She's been like that

to me during a lot of hard times. Let's go out to the beach for a few minutes. Give her some peace and quiet."

Alexandra nodded and accompanied him through the living room's wide opening created by folding glass doors. The policeman stood guard at the edge of the verandah. In a low voice, he assured them he would watch Mama Hannah. The undercover officer would follow them on the beach. They would know him by his green thongs.

Comforted somewhat by this knowledge, Alexandra descended the wide concrete steps to the bungalow's front yard. Beyond the verandah, tufts of hardy grass quickly surrendered to hard sand. Huge coconut palms swayed overhead, their fronds rustling in the breeze that blew in from the sea. Brown hairy coconuts lay scattered across the ground. Alexandra walked the short distance to the water's edge.

As she and Grant emerged from the palm grove, she had to stop. Overhead, the sky gleamed a rich shade of azure, curving like a giant lapis lazuli gemstone. At the horizon, the sky dipped into turquoise water dappled in shades of indigo, teal, and mauve. A long line of white waves broke against a distant reef that stretched north and south as far as the eye could see. Near the shore, crystalline water unrolled like a transparent carpet over sand as pure and white as salt.

"I've never seen anything so beautiful," Alexandra said. "And I've traveled a lot."

Grant's smile reflected pride in his homeland. "The Indian Ocean. You ought to see what's in the water. It's unbelievable down there."

She studied his face. "You love this place, don't you?"

"My family came here on holiday every August. Dad,

Mom, when she was alive—and after that Mama Hannah—three little sisters, and me." He chuckled. "What a crew."

Alexandra let out a deep breath as they walked onto the soft warm sand and began to stroll along the shore. For the first time since arriving in Kenya, she was beginning to relax. The equatorial sun warmed her skin through her gauzy blue tunic and skirt. Wind feathered her hair away from her face and neck. She regarded the man at her side. As hope and strength returned to her body, Grant Thornton began to invade her thoughts.

"Tell me about your sisters," she said. "I grew up as an only child. What was it like to have siblings?"

"With Tillie, Jessica, and Fiona around, things could get pretty crazy. Lots of laughter. Some tears. They drove me crazy most of the time, but I love my sisters." He laughed softly and shook his head. "Tillie's the youngest. She was a little scalawag with long blonde braids and skinny legs—always planting things. That's what she does now. She's an agroforester in Mali, West Africa. She's hoping her trees will hold back the Sahara and make the ground stable for crops. A while back she married some kind of renegade writer. I haven't met the guy, but I have a hard time believing any man is good enough for Tillie."

"Pretty special, is she?"

"A gem. Then there's Jessica, the artist of the family. She's a very sensitive and tenderhearted girl. She just hooked up with her husband after a ten-year separation. They've got a great kid. I don't know how it's going to work out. Rick ran off and left Jessica after they'd only been married a short time. I couldn't understand why she married him in the first place. He drank too much—always riding around on his motorcycle and shooting off his mouth. Mama Hannah says he's cleaned up his act. Found the Lord or something. I'll believe it when I see it."

"Sounds like two humdingers for brothers-in-law. What kind of a guy did your third sister pick?"

"Fiona's not married. She doesn't like people much."

"Is this the sister who lives with the elephants?"

"Yep. She's a gifted scientist. Her research has broken a lot of new ground."

"But she hates people?"

"More or less. It goes back to our childhood. She had a hard time of it. . . . I guess we all did. Anyway, she's afraid to trust anybody. Sort of like you."

Alexandra glanced at him. "I've been working on that. My most recent effort at trusting people landed me Nick Jones, remember?"

"I thought *I* was your most recent effort."

She shook her head. "OK, OK. I have to admit, I trust you."

"How much?"

"A little. How much do you want?"

"More." He stopped walking. "Alexandra, on the road to Oloitokitok you asked me not to touch you."

"That's true." She paused. The hem of her skirt fluttered against her ankles with the same breathless beat her heart suddenly began to play. "I did say that."

"But in the airplane you held my hand," he said, slipping his fingers through hers. "So that must be OK."

"I guess that's OK." His hand was warm and firm, reassuring in its strength. "I don't mind."

"And you didn't mind at the hospital yesterday when I

put my arm around your shoulders." Still holding her fingers, he slid his free hand behind her back, turning her into his embrace. "Kind of like this."

"No, I didn't mind." She could hardly breathe. He stood barely two inches away, and the fresh scent of his clean hair and skin drifted around her. *Did* she mind? Did she want this? Could she allow him to get this close?

"And I've been wondering a lot," he murmured near her ear, "whether you would be too troubled by . . ." His lips brushed against her temple. "By the touch of my mouth . . ." It grazed across her cheek. "On your skin . . . like this . . ."

He bent and pressed his lips to hers in a gentle kiss, over in a breath and as tempting as sweet honey. Alexandra hung suspended against him for a moment, looking up into his denim blue eyes and trying her best to draw air into her lungs. His mouth wore the hint of a smile as he awaited her response.

"Like that," he said in a low voice. "Which is what I've been wanting to do for a long time now."

"You have?"

"Yeah." And he did it again, only this time longer.

Alexandra floated in the sensation, something brand-new and so unexpected she felt dizzy. Kisses had never felt the way they did with Grant Thornton. Instead of binding, his arm around her was an emblem of security. Rather than demanding, the brush of his mouth on hers was a gift. Though he held her tight, so tight, he didn't possess her. Instead . . . somehow . . . he set her free.

"Yes," she whispered.

"Yes, that troubles you?"

"Yes, I trust you. And yes, it troubles me, too."

He searched her eyes. "I won't hurt you, Alexandra."

"Not on purpose."

"Not ever."

"I suspect you will. These things never work out well for me."

She stepped out of his arms and began walking again. How could she explain to a man whose real estate consisted of two tents what it felt like to be respected and desired only for your bank balance? Grant couldn't understand such a thing, and Alexandra knew he would never treat her that way. Yet any feelings between them were an unnecessary complication. They lived in separate worlds, had opposing belief systems, and would never see each other again after she flew back to New York.

"You're analyzing this thing. I can almost hear your brain clicking," Grant said, matching her stride. "That's my job, you know. I'm the scientist."

"So analyze."

"Gladly." He held up a hand and began to tick off his fingers. "A, beautiful woman—that's you—finds herself in the company of B, dashing stranger—that's me, of course. The two ingredients are mixed. They form a slightly unstable, highly volatile combination. And then—"

"Boom! Big explosion. That's how my science experiments usually ended."

"Then you didn't mix your ingredients carefully. Things like this require gentle handling."

"So what's C?" Alexandra asked. "What's the result of your experiment with A and B?"

"Undetermined," he said. "More kissing required."

Alexandra giggled as Grant swung her into his arms again

and demonstrated. This time, she welcomed him, sliding her hands up his back and allowing herself to savor the moment. Crazy, yes. Doomed, no doubt. But it felt wonderful—deliriously wonderful—to drink in this man. His strength warmed her. His intelligence intrigued her. His wit delighted her. And his mouth . . . oh, his mouth . . .

"You've been fooling me about this loner business," she said against his cheek. "You must have been practicing this."

"You're the first woman I've kissed in six years."

"Something pretty bad must have happened six years ago."

"Nothing happened. Nothing at all. That's why I quit the dating game and turned my focus to my work. I haven't regretted it."

"So what about A and B?" she said. "Anything happening there?"

"Sparks." He ran a thumb up her cheek. "Lots of sparks. Dangerous sparks."

"Mmm. A tropical beach and a dashing stranger. I think I'm in trouble."

"*Bwana?*" A deep voice cut into their conversation. "Would you like to buy some shells? or perhaps a newspaper?"

Alexandra turned to find a tall, thin African man holding out a flat tray filled with trinkets. On the top lay a newspaper, its English headline blaring "AMERICAN HEIRESS FOUND IN MOMBASA." The man tapped the paper.

"Perhaps you would like to read this article, madam," he said quietly. "You would find it most interesting."

Alexandra glanced at Grant, who quickly pulled her

close. Then she looked down at the vendor's shoes. Green thongs.

"Yes," she said. "I'll read it."

"Five shillings, please." He held out his hand and added in a murmur, "Please keep your attention on these items in my tray and no other place."

Grant paid him for the paper. "Are we being watched?"

"It is possible, *bwana.*"

Alexandra felt her blood rush to her knees. Was Jones here on the beach? How could he have found her so quickly? The newspaper article, of course. Now everyone in the country knew where she was. She swallowed and forced herself to casually finger the knickknacks in the man's tray.

"You would like to go to another place this afternoon, *bwana?*" the man asked.

"Yes," Grant acknowledged. "I think Miss Prescott would enjoy seeing Fort Jesus. Will that be all right?"

"Fort Jesus is a good place to visit. There are few people and many tall walls and cliffs. The *memsahib* should go alone."

"No," Grant said. "I won't allow that."

"*Bwana,* that is the order I have received. You must comply. And which ring does the *memsahib* like? This silver one is very nice."

Alexandra selected a ring embedded with a sliver of mother-of-pearl. "I like this one. Grant?"

"A trinket for the American heiress," he said, digging into his wallet again. "All right, I'll agree to Fort Jesus. But I'm going with her. I'll leave her alone for a few minutes at a time—and I won't be far away."

"Very good. *Asante sana, bwana!*" Smiling as though the sale had made his day, the man walked backward and called out. "Enjoy the fort!"

"Thank you," Grant said. He turned to Alexandra and slipped the ring over her little finger. "A promise," he said. "I won't let anyone hurt you."

She forced herself to smile. "I know," she whispered. "I trust you."

NINE

Grant held Alexandra's hand as they climbed the broad walkway to the outer gate of the huge Fort Jesus. The bastion, built of carved coral blocks by the Portuguese in the sixteenth century, had weathered countless attacks and sieges. But it wasn't the fort's colorful history that dominated Grant's thoughts.

Back at the bungalow, Mama Hannah had insisted she was feeling fine—*"The Lord is with me,* toto." But she didn't look fine. On changing her bandage, Grant found the entire area swollen and flecked with dry blood. The knife wound snaked from her eyebrow to her ear, dotted with stitches like a row of black gnats. Jones had left his mark, and not even Mama Hannah's beloved nylon head scarf would cover the scar. Grant reminded himself that the guard outside the bungalow would keep a close watch on the old woman while he was away.

Then there was Alexandra. Tall and confident, she walked along beside Grant with her sketch pad under her arm as though this were nothing more than a casual afternoon outing. On the beach, she had seen no one who resembled Nick Jones. All the same, she was determined to lure her stalker into the open as quickly as possible. Grant thought the plan was crazy and more than a little dangerous, and he wasn't about to let her go off alone.

Something about the woman intrigued him. Fascinated him. He felt a powerful need to protect her from the man who threatened her life. The emotion she evoked in him was unsettling. He didn't know what to make of it—and he sure couldn't suppress it.

"Take a look at this, Grant!" she said, pointing out the lengthy inscription inside the long coral tunnel that led into the bastion. "'In 1635 Francisco de Seixas de Cabreira, age twenty-seven years—'"

"'Was made for four years captain of this fort,'" Grant continued. "I can quote the whole thing. When I was a kid, I used to pretend I was Francisco de Cabreira. I subjected all the people along the coast to His Majesty the King of Portugal. I made the African kings of Otondo, Mandra, Luziwa, and Jaca tributaries to the king. I inflicted punishment on the towns of Pate and Sio. I had all the rebel governors and leading citizens of Pemba executed. In short, I was the meanest, baddest Portuguese captain who ever ravaged the coast of East Africa."

"Ooh, I'm scared," Alexandra said.

Grant caught the sparkle of laughter in her blue eyes, and he grinned. "Unfortunately the kings of East Africa—whose real names were Fiona, Jessica, and Tillie—weren't always as cooperative as I would have liked. Sometimes they ganged up and whipped the tar out of me."

"Aw, you poor tyrant." Chuckling, she leaned against him and grazed his cheek with a quick kiss. "You just needed Wonder Woman at your side, didn't you?"

Glad to have her with him now, Grant watched the sunshine gild Alexandra's blonde hair as they emerged from the tunnel into the main courtyard of the fort. When her lips parted and she caught her breath at the sight of the towering battlements, Grant felt his heart stumble. He was smitten—and he didn't know how it had happened.

He had always imagined his heart to be as impenetrable as this fortress. And why not? He had built the walls himself—hewn them out of disappointment, frustration, even rage. But Alexandra Prescott had somehow soared right over those barriers and into the inner sanctum of his very soul.

"There's the ticket office," she said. "Grant, I'm going to give my broker another call. It's still early in New York, but this might be my best chance to catch him."

"Go ahead." He couldn't understand why Alexandra kept making calls to a man who rarely even left her a message in response. But then, he really couldn't imagine money being all that important. He needed financial support, of course, and the thought of losing his funding left him uncomfortable. But not desperate.

Grant paid for the tickets, and then he stood beside Alexandra as she dialed the international operator on the public pay phone. He took the opportunity to study her. In the short time he had known her, Alexandra had changed. Not drastically, but in a subtle, deeply affecting way. She had ceased being glamorous and had become . . . beautiful.

The sleek, chic hairstyle had given way to a casual bob that bounced just below her ears when she walked. Grant had gotten used to seeing her in the tattered dress she was wearing when the Maasai brought her to his camp—or in his own shirt and trousers cinched at the waist with a rope. But with the return of her baggage, this intriguing blue outfit had emerged. The gauzy fabric draped on her tall frame like the gown on a Greek statue. Her designer shoes had been replaced by the tire sandals, which, oddly enough, looked perfect on her slim, pale feet.

Grant turned his focus to the tourists who meandered around Fort Jesus. Was one of them Nick Jones? The two men had met in the darkness once, and Grant could not swear he'd actually seen the man's features.

Alexandra had described her attacker as broad shouldered and brawny. He wore his dark hair combed back into a wave, and he had a gold stud in one ear. The most defining feature was his narrow black mustache.

"James!" Alexandra exclaimed suddenly into the receiver. "Is that really you? It's me—Alexandra Prescott." She laughed in delight. "I know, I know—but I'm OK now. Yeah, I was scared, too. He's some kind of a lunatic, I think. He knows about my family—the business and all. I suspect that's probably what's behind it."

Grant glanced over at Alexandra. She clutched the telephone cord like it was a lifeline to safety. A link to the real world. It was hard to imagine that in a couple of days she would fly out of Grant's life and back into her own. But she would. He'd better get used to the idea.

"How's Lily?" she asked. "The kids? *Harvard!* You're kidding, James! That's great. Give Betsy my congrats, OK? Listen, James, about that weird cablegram I got—" She paused for a long time, listening.

Grant's gaze zeroed in on an African man who wandered up to the ticket counter. Most of the tourists were European or Asian—of the dangling-camera, baggy-shorts species. The African studiously turned the pages of his guidebook as he sauntered past the telephone, his sandals slapping the concrete floor. Green thongs.

"Are you sure everything's all right?" Alexandra asked. "James, you know how important those stocks are to me. If anything is wrong, I want you to tell me." She paused again. "OK, listen, I'm staying in Mombasa. I have a little bungalow on Diani Beach, and I'm doing some touring. Don't worry, OK? I'm safe. The police have posted a guard outside the bungalow at night, and an undercover officer follows me by day. We're actually doing a little sleuthing, trying to lure out the bad guy." She laughed. "I *know* what Daddy would say! But stop worrying, James. You're starting to sound like an old mother hen." Another pause. "All right, I'll call you soon. Even at home. Even if I wake you up. OK, relax, would you? Say hi to everybody for me. I'll be back . . . soon."

Grant shifted from one foot to the other. Already she sounded like she was halfway gone. Alexandra hung up the receiver and let out a breath.

"There was a mix-up at the brokerage while James was away on vacation," she explained. "The notice I got was supposed to go to another client, but his secretary sent it to me instead. One of those glitches."

"So your treasure is safe?"

"Safe and sound."

He pointed in the direction of where they should begin their tour of the fort. "You know what Mama Hannah would say about all this, don't you?" he asked. "There's something in the Bible about treasures on earth that rust and rot . . . and treasures in heaven that nothing can destroy."

She gave him a curious glance. "Quoting Scripture, Professor? I thought you didn't believe in that nonsense."

"The Bible isn't nonsense. It's a very thorough mythology. Origins of the universe. Commandments by which to live. Proverbs. Even poetry. Biblical doctrine provided a strong moral backbone for Western civilization."

"Indeed."

They strolled across the courtyard and paused to inspect a row of long black cannons lined up on the grass. Grant had played around the guns as a child, and he couldn't summon up as much interest as Alexandra. On the other hand, curiosity about *her* plagued him like an itch that demanded to be scratched.

"You're an intelligent woman," he said as he watched her peer into a cannon's iron muzzle. "Do you *really* believe a man walked on water?"

"I believe Jesus Christ did. He was a man, but he was also God." She looked up at him. "That made walking on water a cinch."

"So, you accept the dogma that Jesus was actually conceived in the body of a virgin?"

"Yes, I do." Her blue eyes narrowed as she stood. "Is this some kind of pop quiz? Get any answers wrong and I'm eternally doomed?"

"I suspect that's what you think about me. Grant Thornton, the unrepentant skeptic."

"I think you're a seeker. Nothing wrong with that." The bristles inside Grant softened as she slipped her arm through his and they began walking. He steered them toward the Passage of the Arches, which would lead up to the fort's curtain wall. "You know, the Bible promises that if you seek, you'll find the answers to your questions."

"My years researching mythology haven't led me to the answer you hope I'll find," he said. "Most of the stories in our body of oral and written legends contain similar elements—reluctant heroes, wise old men, even instances of resurrection. The stories also overlap in the morals they're trying to teach. In fact, there's a distinct pattern to myths and to the whole myth cycle. You find the same elements across the board in the world's oldest religions—Shamanism, Hinduism, Buddhism, Islam, Judaism."

"And Christianity."

"That's right. My work with African tribal stories shows that they follow the same patterns as ancient Greek myths and early Native American oral legends. The religious doctrines of the world's great faiths are just highly evolved collections of myths."

Grant cast Alexandra a sideways glance, anticipating a strong reaction to his statement. After all, he'd just blatantly debunked her spirituality. If she was anything like his sisters, she'd probably clobber him. Instead, she was running her fingers along the sides of the pink coral passageway, her concentration on the rough path that led under the arches.

"In all your research," she said softly, "all your study of world religions and mythology, have you ever found a single story you believe is true?"

Grant pondered her question as they climbed the inclined archway path. "Let's see now . . . do I believe the Ganges River arose out of the hair of the Hindu god, Shiva? Or that Muhammad moved a mountain? Or that Moses held out a walking staff and the Red Sea parted?"

"Or that Jesus fed five thousand men with five loaves of bread and two fishes?"

"You've got to admit that's a lot of people. And if I decide to believe the Jesus legend is true, then why shouldn't the others be true, too?"

They turned onto a narrow set of steps that led to the ramparts and gun platforms Grant had explored as a child. He reminded himself to be alert to danger as they approached this vulnerable spot. Their detective in the green thongs was already waiting at the top. All the same, Grant was reluctant to cut off the conversation with Alexandra.

"What makes the biblical miracles authentic?" he asked, taking her elbow to guide her onto the walkway. "And what makes the Maasai stories Kakombe tells me merely fiction?"

Alexandra leaned against the wall that faced the Indian Ocean and let out a sigh. "I think you're looking in the wrong place, Grant." Her voice was soft. "You need to look at Jesus Christ. Learn who he was. Listen to what he said about himself. Study the things he did. His focus wasn't miracles. It was people's hearts."

She opened her sketch pad and turned through the pages. In her drawings, Grant recognized the interplay of paisleys from an Indian sari she must have seen in Nairobi, the blossom of a bougainvillea vine, and the mottled geometrics of a giraffe's hide. Her work was careful and detailed, but it showed a creative flair he would not have expected from the citified lady he had met at the airport.

"Those are good," he said. "You've captured the colors of the giraffe."

She smiled and turned to a clean page. "The colors of the giraffe are part of the reason I'm a believer," she said. "'In the beginning God created the heavens and the earth.' I'm no scientist, but you'll never convince me this world evolved out of some random accident. I don't need proof. I have giraffes."

Flipping open a thin leather case holding a row of colored pencils, she selected a blue one. "If I can believe in the miracle of Creation," she continued, "then I'm open to other miracles, right? And if I accept the presence of a Creator, why not allow him to have the name *God?* Given those two assumptions, I guess that makes me ripe to believe other things I can't prove. Are you with me?"

"More than you realize." Grant watched, bemused, as the colors of ocean began to spill across the white page beneath her hand. He had to admit she made a pretty good case for her beliefs when she saw the hand of God on Kenya. His childhood in the splendor of the African savanna had led him to deep doubts about the theories of a spontaneous formation of the earth and the chance appearance of life-forming DNA. So maybe . . . *maybe* . . . he, too, could say he actually believed in a Creator. Odd he'd never thought of it that way.

"The so-called mythology of Jewish believers," Alexandra went on, "was recorded thousands of years before Christ's birth. But it contains detailed prophecies about the coming of a messiah. Jesus fulfilled all those prophecies."

"You're saying he was the man who made the stories true?"

"He was the Truth." She selected a purple pencil. "Jesus said he was the way, the truth, and the life. No man or woman can come to God except through him. That rules out Buddha and Muhammad and any other deities in the religions you've studied. You can't believe them all. You have to choose. It's Jesus *only* or not at all."

Grant studied the fine line of Alexandra's profile, her straight nose and perfect lips. Her hair shimmered with light in the sinking sun. She was beautiful—but her radiance came from something deeper than bright blue eyes and shiny blonde hair.

"You amaze me," he said.

"I don't know why. Christianity is quite simple really. It's just mind, heart, and life—a conscious decision to believe, an admission of need, and then surrender." She tucked the pencil back into its slot and turned to him. "I figured surrendering control of your life would be the hardest part for a man like you. But if you can ever come to believe without needing all the scientific evidence, you might come around. I hope so."

For some reason Grant couldn't explain, Alexandra's words evoked a pain inside him. It was a physical ache, and it hurt even to swallow. He wanted Christianity to be simple, the way she said it was. He wanted what she and Mama Hannah had—this simplicity of faith, purity of trust. But how? He didn't know how. And he certainly couldn't think why.

"It's time for you to go now, Grant," she said.

"Go?"

"So Nick Jones can get at me, remember? That's why we're here."

"Alexandra, I can't do this. It's crazy. Let's head back to the bungalow. The police will track down Jones one way or another. How hard can it be to find a guy like that in the middle of Africa?"

"Not very hard. He's standing right over there on the rampart."

"Wha——?"

"Don't look!" She caught his arm. "I spotted him a few minutes ago. At first I didn't recognize him. He's changed. But it's him. Grant, I'm scared to death, but I want you to help me with this. Please walk away from me. If he comes over here and tries to touch me, you and the detective can grab him."

Grant regarded the woman, considering her request. What if he couldn't get back to her in time? What if the detective let them down? One shove, and Alexandra would be over the edge, her body crumpled on the rocks below the fort. One quick stab with a knife, and she'd fall dead. Jones had claimed to be able to snap a neck. He had proven with Mama Hannah that he had no heart. And he had over-powered an armed Maasai warrior.

"I've got another idea," he said. "Let's stroll over to the detective, and point out Jones. He can radio in for rein-forcements, and they'll arrest the guy."

"For what? Visiting a tourist monument?"

"For attacking you and Mama Hannah."

"How will I ever prove he did it, Grant?" She lowered her voice. "His hair is blond now, and he shaved off the little mustache. The report I gave the police doesn't match his description anymore. Besides, it was dark when he attacked Mama Hannah and me. Our stories won't hold up in a court. I want him caught red-handed—the way we planned. Grant, please, would you go?"

He took a deep breath. Alexandra was a woman of deep conviction. He had the feeling that once she made up her

mind about anything—from religion to game strategy—
nothing would dissuade her. But what a deadly game.

"All right," he said. "I'll walk down toward the Passage
of Stairs and skirt around so I can keep an eye on you. But
you scream if he so much as looks at you funny. Do you
promise?"

She smiled. "I trust you, remember?"

"I remember." He bent and kissed her cheek. As he
turned his back on her, he wished he had someone other
than himself to place his faith in.

Alexandra's hand was shaking so hard she could barely
control her pencil. Completely alone for the first time since
Jones's attack, she felt vulnerable and fragile. Grant's religion quiz hadn't helped. If this had been the Inquisition, she
would be slowly roasting at the stake right now.

Her answers had been so lame—mumblings about giraffes
and miracles and the creation of the world. The moment
Grant had started his inquiry in the Passage of Arches, she
had prayed that God would speak through her. But what a
jumbled mass of words had poured out. She had no background in myths or world religions. And she certainly
should know better than to reason with a scientist.

Let him go.

The voice was almost audible, echoing somewhere deep
inside her. *Let go, Alexandra. Give all your worries and cares to
God, for he cares about what happens to you.* Trembling, she
clutched her pencil. How could she let go? A man she had
come to care about was slipping through her fingers.

She moistened her lower lip. The detective in the green thongs had vanished. Grant was gone. *Dear God, where are you? Are you with me?*

Determined not to betray her fears, she worked her pencil across the sheet of white paper. Though her focus stayed on the ocean and her sketch pad, she could see the hulking blond man edging across the narrow walkway. She made up her mind to scream the instant he grabbed her. Then Grant would come running, and the detective would appear. And that would be it.

Oh, Father, let it be over soon. Please, Lord!

Jones paused two yards away and leaned on the battlement, his face hidden by the thick wall of the gunport through which he peered. Every nerve ending in Alexandra's body warned her to run. This was her chance to get away. If she stayed, he would attack.

But if she ran, he would find her again. Find her somewhere else. Track her down.

Now was the time.

She sucked in a deep breath and picked out of her case the tiny, single-edged razor blade she used to sharpen her pencils. It wasn't much, but the cold steel between her fingertips gave her some defense. She tilted it, watching the sun glint off the metal.

"We meet again, Miss Prescott." Jones's arm slipped around her shoulders, and a click sent his switchblade skimming across the delicate skin of her throat. "One sound, and you're dead."

Alexandra's voice hung in her throat. She shuddered at the man's touch, his smell. Revulsion rose in her stomach and splashed bitterness into her mouth. Blood hammered through her temples.

"Walk with me nice and slow, baby," he said, holding her firmly against him. "We wouldn't want your boyfriend to get suspicious."

"I'm staying here," Alexandra hissed.

"But I wrote you a poem." He shoved her, and she stumbled forward. "Don't you wanna hear it?

"We walk through the African night.
I hold you so tight.
It feels just right
To keep you in my sight.

"It's almost like a song, huh? I can hear the music. Drums, you know. And maybe a little violin in the background."

Alexandra gripped her tiny razor blade as Jones propelled her along the battlement toward the southern bastion. Where was Grant? What had happened to the detective? Somebody was supposed to rescue her right about now!

"I did *not* like losing you the other night, babe," the thug said against her ear. "But anyway I got a new hairdo out of the deal. Think I look handsome as a blond?"

She squeezed her eyes shut, trying to breathe. "Please move the knife, Nick. I'm going with you."

"Yeah, but your boyfriend might come along. I don't want him to get too close. I got a job to do here."

"Why are you doing this?"

"Aw, if I told you, it might hurt your feelings. You'd be brokenhearted, and I never could stand to see a lady cry."

He moved her past a round turret, up another shallow

flight of stairs, and toward a long, low prison that had been built at the top of the bastion. Alexandra scanned the fortress grounds for Grant. An African—their detective in the green thongs—emerged at the far end of the gun plat-form. Too far! He was much too far away to do her any good.

She stiffened as she realized that Jones was pressing her toward a deeply shadowed gunport beside the prison building. The narrow window had been left unbarred, a view of the old town of Mombasa stretching out from fifty feet below it. The waist-high stone sill gave tourists a measure of protection from the precipitous drop to the ground, but Jones shoved Alexandra hard against it.

"Sit down, pretty lady," he said, forcing her up onto the windowsill. "I'm sorry to say this, Miss Prescott, but you're about to have a very bad fall."

"You won't get my money b-by killing me," Alexandra stammered.

"It's not your money I want."

"Then why are you doing this?"

"I told you not to ask me, baby. Now just relax and lean back." Still holding the knife to her throat, he began to tilt her through the narrow open window, slowly forcing her off balance. "Back, sweetheart. Back, back—"

"No!" Alexandra swiped her razor blade across his bare arm, then down the side of his face. He jerked back in surprise.

"You lousy—" He lunged at her flailing arms. His knife nicked her earlobe and clanged into the bastion wall. "When I get—"

"Let her go!" Grant's fist slammed into Jones's jaw,

smashing his head against the coral. "Alexandra, get out of there!"

"Back off," Jones growled, slashing out at Grant. At the same time, his foot caught Alexandra in the chest, knocking her through the window.

She screamed and grabbed at the rough coral as she tumbled backward. Wedging her knees against the window's sides, she managed to break her momentum. Her shoulders swung in midair, the stone tearing at her knees as her body slid slowly down. Fifty feet below her head, the earth spun in dizzy circles.

A chunk of coral broke loose beneath her and dropped through the air toward the ground. It struck the hard sand, and a puff of white dust drifted away on the wind.

TEN

"Alexandra! Alexandra!"

She recognized Grant's voice. Dangling upside down, braced only by her knees, Alexandra buttressed her hands against the outer wall of the fort. Her fingers dug into the coral as she tried to pull herself onto the windowsill. At her touch, the wall fragmented, pebbles and dust skittering to the sand below.

She grabbed at another chunk of coral. It broke loose beneath her weight. Her hand swung free, and her knees began to give out. "Grant," she groaned. "Help me, Grant!"

A pair of strong hands gripped her ankles. *Jones!* She screamed, shut her eyes, flailed at the coral wall. "Grant! Gra—"

"I've got you, Alexandra!" Grant shouted. "Hang on. You're gonna make it."

Hands—it seemed like a hundred—gripped her ankles and legs, pulling, easing her slowly upward, onto the windowsill. The hands raised her back, her shoulders, then her head. Five frightened faces peered at her as Grant lifted her down from the open window.

"Are you quite all right, madam?" an Englishman inquired, his forehead beaded with perspiration.

"Who was that man?" an African asked. "We thought you would fall from the window!"

Three Japanese tourists stared openmouthed as Grant drew Alexandra into the shelter of his arms. She pressed her head against his chest and fought the tears welling in her eyes.

"Where's Jones?" she whispered.

"The detective went after him."

He got away. She couldn't bring herself to say the words aloud. He had escaped, and he would come after her again. She could hear Grant reassuring the frightened tourists, telling them he would take care of her now, insisting that the detective would catch her assailant.

But he wouldn't. As Alexandra knotted her fists around clumps of Grant's shirt, she knew the truth. Jones would kill her.

"Alexandra?" Grant's hand cupped her head, holding it against his chest as the tourists left. "You're bleeding. Did he cut you?"

"My ear." She couldn't make herself let go of him. "Grant, I'm going to die."

"You're not. The police have seen Jones in action. They know their man, and they'll catch him."

"He's too good. He had already picked out the window. Grant, he knows what he's doing."

"I can't believe he got his hands on you," Grant muttered under his breath. "I couldn't get to you in time. I thought he might . . . I couldn't let him hurt you. It was the knife that held me back. He pulled it on you so fast. He's a pro, all right."

As his words sank in, she lifted her face to his. "Yes . . . he *is* a professional. A hired killer."

Grant's eyes narrowed. "What makes you say that?"

"He told me this was a job. A *job.*" She swallowed. "And the first time . . . under the tree . . . he said he had committed dozens of murders. There was a man in Mexico . . . his only other killing outside the States. Jones said he was a bodyguard in New York, but he knew all about my family, my background. It was like he had a dossier on me. He even knew my travel plans. Grant, I think . . . I think someone hired Nick Jones to murder me."

Falling silent, he brushed the hair away from her ear and neck. His fingers dabbed at the trickle of blood running down her skin. "We ought to wash this off. You might need stitches."

"Grant, did you hear what I said?"

"I heard you. But right now, I don't care why he's after you. I just want him stopped."

"Madam! Madam!" Two African museum guards came racing up the steps of the bastion. "Were you the victim of an attack? The others reported the trouble. We have notified the police!"

Alexandra let out a sigh. It would begin again. The clinic, the police, statements and reports, long hours of sitting in bare offices. "I'll go with these guys to the police station," she told Grant as the officers waited for her. "There's nothing more you can do for me here. I'll stop by the bungalow later to pick up my things and say good-bye. I have to get a plane back to the States and hire some protection. Please go on to Mama Hannah now. Would you do that for me?"

"I'm not leaving you alone, Alexandra." Grant took her

hand. "I don't trust the situation. We'll go to the station together. Once you're under close guard, I'll check on Mama Hannah. Not before."

Without the strength to argue, she walked beside him toward the two officers. She felt like an armed grenade—explosive, dangerous, a threat. At any moment, the people she cared about could lose their lives because of her. And all she wanted to do was rest in the strong embrace of Grant Thornton, a man she had no choice but to leave behind.

Grant stood at the edge of the bungalow verandah and flipped through the pages of Alexandra's sketchbook. After she was placed under the protection of two armed officers at the police headquarters, he had returned to Fort Jesus to look for clues. He had discovered her pad on the walkway near the place where Jones had first accosted her. Her pencil case had been lying open there, some of the pencils scattered and their colored tips broken. Grant had set each one in its slot, running his fingers down the smooth wood, trying to understand what would make anyone want to kill a woman like Alexandra.

Still turning the question over in his mind, he looked through her sketches as if in them he might find a clue. Was she creating something that someone wanted to stop? Was Nick Jones a deranged serial killer and Alexandra just a random target? Or had someone hired him to kill her for another reason—her money, an inheritance, a business deal gone bad?

Who could possibly want Alexandra dead? She was full of

goodness, purity, honesty. Even her artwork showed a unique clarity of vision. Such sensitivity. She had been gifted with a talent few human beings could claim. Who would want to snuff that out?

"She has not returned," Mama Hannah said, joining Grant at the verandah's edge.

He glanced over at her. "What are you doing out here? You're supposed to be in bed."

"Bed, bed." She dismissed the notion with a wave of her gnarled hand. "Do you not remember what wise King Solomon wrote? 'A little extra sleep, a little more slumber, a little folding of the hands to rest—and poverty will pounce on you like a bandit.'"

Grant chuckled. "Now what do you care about poverty, Mama Hannah?"

"I care about you, *toto*. And I want to get out of that bed and talk to you about all of these troubles."

"Would you at least sit down?" He led her to a woven rattan chair. "You're making me nervous tottering around with all those drugs in your system."

"Ehh, I have not taken a pill since you left me. No, do not argue. The pain in my head is not so bad now."

"You're a pain in *my* neck, is what you are."

"Why? Because I will not take elephant pills and lie in bed all day? Or because I was injured and caused you to miss the important Maasai ceremony? Or because my words touch places in your heart?"

"I've resigned myself to missing *Eunoto*." He shut the sketchbook and sat down beside her. "I've already gathered a lot of research on the ceremony. I wanted to see it for myself, but I'm sure I'll manage to write the chapter anyway. No, it's not that. And it's not the medicine either. If you don't want to take your elephant pills, that's fine with me."

"Then it is my words. You know that I speak the truth—even when it is not what you wish to hear."

"I've always enjoyed your stories, Mama Hannah."

"Stories? Do not talk to me of stories and myths, Grant. I speak truth when I speak of a person's need for God—and you know this in your heart."

"Maybe." It was the closest he could come to an admission of the empty place inside him—a void he had long ago filled with his research, his work, his travels. Or tried to fill.

"I also spoke the truth about Alexandra, did I not?" Mama Hannah said. "You love her."

"Love her!" Grant tipped back his head and laughed. "You jump to conclusions faster than anybody I ever met."

"Ehh."

"I don't *love* Alexandra Prescott. I like the woman. I admire her. She's smart and artistic and good-hearted."

"And beautiful."

"Yeah, she's beautiful." He shut his eyes, distracted by the memory of kissing her on the beach that morning. "Soft, too. And she smells good."

"*That* you have noticed? Her scent?" Mama Hannah clucked. "Oh, Grant, this is very serious."

"It's not serious," he said. "It can't be. She thinks this Jones guy is going to kill her if she doesn't get back to the States and hire a bodyguard or something. Alexandra's leaving, Mama Hannah."

"You will let her go?"

"I don't *own* the woman. She's got a life in New York. I

live in a tent out in the African bush. Of course I'm going to let her go. What choice do I have?"

"You could ask her to stay."

He shook his head, constantly amazed at the old woman's naïveté. For all her wisdom, she could be as blind as a bat. "Look at the facts here, Mama Hannah—"

"You should look at your heart instead of facts."

"My heart doesn't matter. The facts say I'm better off as a loner and Alexandra's better off doing her fabric design thing in the big city. She's going to get on a plane, and I'm going back to Mount Kilimanjaro to finish my research."

"And you will never see her again?"

"Maybe one day I'll stop in New York on one of my university speaking tours. I'll drop by the design firm she's planning to build, and we'll reminisce about our adventures. She'll show me pictures of her kids or something. That's how it'll be. That's how it *has* to be."

"Ehh."

"What's that supposed to mean?" Grant jumped up from his chair and strode to the verandah railing again. Frustration poured through his veins at his inability to accept the picture he had painted of his own future. All he had ever wanted to do was live out in the bush among the Africans. Now . . . because of some tall . . . blonde . . . beautiful . . . sweet-smelling . . . wonderful . . .

"Where is she?" he exploded, hammering the rail with his fist. "She should have left that police station hours ago. They already know the whole story. How much more could she give them?"

"You are so certain Alexandra will abandon you," the old

woman said. "Perhaps she already took a taxi to the airport and got on an airplane to Nairobi."

"She wouldn't leave her bags here, would she?" Grant walked over to the bedroom door that opened out onto the verandah. Alexandra's suitcase lay unlatched on the bed, clothing and shoes spilling across the spread. Maybe she *would* leave her stuff here. Why not? She was rich. She could buy more dresses. More shoes.

He pushed open the door, walked to the bed, and began rooting through her things. Feminine things, silky and gauzy things. Alexandra things. Was there anything in the bag to hold her? Anything she couldn't live without?

"Here's her Bible," he called out to Mama Hannah on the verandah. He picked up the little leather-bound volume and slipped it into his shirt pocket. Alexandra might want that one of these days. He could mail it to her.

"She left a lot of socks and shirts and sweaters behind, too," he added. He lifted a cotton blouse and held it to his nose. Alexandra's scent clung to the folds of fabric—something floral and exotic. Where would she keep the bottle? He'd like to know its name. Searching, his fingers stroked over a scattering of black sequins. "Here's some kind of fancy evening dress. Looks expensive. And jeans. She'd need those, wouldn't she?"

"It's a little hot for jeans at the coast," Alexandra said behind him. "What are you doing in my suitcase, Dr. Thornton?"

Grant dropped her blouse and shoved his hands into his pockets. "I thought . . . maybe . . . maybe you left already. Maybe you caught a plane."

"I said I'd come back, didn't I?"

"Well, yeah."

"I told you I'd say good-bye. Didn't you believe me?"

"You were in a hurry."

She shrugged and began to refold her clothes. "They didn't catch Jones," she said in a matter-of-fact voice. "The police are posting a watch at the airports and border crossings."

"Are you all right?"

"My hands are sore." She attempted a smile. "Ear's OK, though. No stitches." She tucked her hair behind her ear to show him the flesh-toned plastic bandage on her lobe.

"How about your knees?"

"Skinned, but stronger than I knew. Thank goodness for that thigh toner I ordered off the shopping network, huh?" she said sarcastically. "You know, somebody ought to put me in a commercial: Are you being stalked? Has someone tried to push you through a . . . through a window?" Her face began to crumple. "Try the Mombasa Squeeze . . . free thirty day . . . thirty day . . . money back . . ."

Grant folded her into his arms. "Alexandra, what did the police tell you after I left? Do they have anything on Jones?"

"Nothing. Nobody knows anything. He vanished. They said maybe . . . maybe there's an accomplice. Maybe it's the Mafia or something."

"It's not the Mafia, is it?"

"I don't know!" She slammed her fists against his chest. "I don't know who Jones is! I don't know why he wants to kill me. If he's not nuts, then somebody wants me to die and is paying him to murder me—and I don't have any idea why!"

Grant rubbed his hand down her back, trying to calm her. "I've been thinking about the money. The bank-account thing."

"It's not the money. He won't get a penny of my money by killing me. Maybe if he kidnapped me and demanded a ransom—"

"Do you have a will? Does someone stand to inherit if you die?"

She sobered. "My father set everything up. If I had children, it would be simple. But no . . . the bulk of the estate goes to a couple of universities, some hospitals, and a dozen or so charities. Daddy told me not to trust anyone. Leave people out of your plans, out of your will if you can. People are greedy. Manipulative. He set the whole thing up with . . . with James. James Cooper."

Grant watched the color drain from her cheeks. "The broker you've been calling?"

"It can't be."

"Did he have a copy of your itinerary?"

"Yes," she whispered.

"Did you tell him where you were when you called from Oloitokitok? Right before Jones attacked Mama Hannah?"

Alexandra nodded, her blue eyes wide with disbelief. "And Mombasa. I called him from . . . from the fort."

"I imagine Jones found you there on his own. But why would this broker want to hurt you?"

"Money," she said simply. "That's all it could be. James has had his hands on the Prescott stocks for years. Maybe he started siphoning off some of the earnings. His wife's been sick a couple of times. His daughter's going to Harvard."

"Didn't you say he takes winter vacations in Arizona?"

"James wouldn't use the money for his own pleasure. My father's money? They were good friends, and my father . . . my father trusted him."

"Sounds like your dad should have followed his own advice."

She groaned. "Grant, maybe that cablegram I got *was* meant for me. What if there's nothing left in those accounts? Could James have bled them dry?"

"How closely did you watch your holdings?"

"He sent me a statement every month. I always glanced at it, of course, but I never gave it much study. That money was for the future."

"Your design firm."

Alexandra looked like she might collapse, and Grant tried to turn her toward the verandah. If they could sit down and analyze the situation, maybe they could make sense of it. But she wasn't into analyzing. She stood rooted to the floor, twisting her fingers together as the emotions racked through her.

"How could James have stolen that money?" she wondered aloud.

"He might have diverted your funds and invested them in dummy accounts. Given a fake name or something. Then when he began to realize he'd managed them badly and lost a lot of money, he got scared."

"The margin call," she whispered. "He must have known it would come, long before I had any wind of a problem."

"Sure. When he found out you'd planned this trip to Kenya, it must have seemed like the perfect opportunity to simply delete his wrongdoing."

"James is the one who suggested the trip." She sank onto

a chair beside the bed. "He took me to dinner one evening just to catch up on things. He's been like . . . like a father to me since my dad died. Old friends, you know. We talked about his kids, his wife, the stock market. I detailed my plans for fabric designs and the firm I wanted to establish. That's when he suggested that I take a research trip. He said I'd be inspired to do something really original. 'Go some- place exotic,' he said. 'Remote.'"

Elbows on her knees, Alexandra lowered her head into her hands. Grant struggled against the urge to hold her again. Soon she'd be gone, and the reality of the woman's absence had caused him enough discomfort already. The more time he spent with her, the harder it became to imagine his life rolling along contentedly without her. He couldn't afford to get tangled. And he knew he had put one foot inside a lethal snare.

"I need to call James," she murmured.

"James Cooper? You're going to call the jerk who probably lost your money and is trying to get you killed?"

"I have to steer him off course so he'll give Jones the wrong information about me. I'll phone him on the pretense of telling him what happened at the fort. Then I'll lead him to believe I'm staying here at the coast for another week or so. I won't lie, but I *will* misdirect him. If I give him the address of the bungalow, you could forward anything that comes in. Would you do that for me?"

She lifted her head, and Grant didn't know when he'd seen anyone so miserable. He couldn't imagine how Alexandra must feel to realize she might have been betrayed by the one person she had trusted all her life. He expected anger. Rage, even. Certainly a drive for revenge.

But in those beautiful blue eyes, he read something altogether different. The spark of faith she had placed in another human being had been extinguished. Hope had vanished. Trust was gone. What he saw in her eyes was death.

"Never mind," she said, standing. "I'll take care of this myself. You've done more than enough."

She threw the rest of her clothing into the suitcase and lowered the lid. As she worked at the zipper and clasps, Grant focused on the moonlit palms outside the window. She was right. He had done more than enough. He'd been chased and knocked around by a hired killer. His mother had been attacked with a knife. He'd lost his chance at the *Eunoto* ceremony. None of it had happened at his own instigation. If Alexandra hadn't come along, he'd be deep into one of his notebooks right now, reviewing his research and crafting his report. And, except for Mama Hannah, he'd be alone.

Alone.

He liked being alone, didn't he? No arguments. No big discussions. No shaving and trying to find matching socks. No need for square meals. Nothing but simple, quiet, empty . . . loneliness.

"My taxi is waiting," Alexandra said. "I reserved a room at a hotel downtown. I figured you and Mama Hannah didn't need Jones breathing down your necks anymore. So—" She heaved a deep breath. "Thanks for your help, Grant. Sorry about the trouble. I'll just say good-bye to Mama Hannah."

She swung her suitcase off the bed and started for the

door. *Let her go,* Grant told himself. *Easier that way. Much easier.*

"Hold it." He'd never taken the easy way out of anything. Taking two strides across the room, he lifted her suitcase from her hand. "You're not going downtown by yourself tonight, Alexandra. That's a sure way to get yourself killed. You'll spend the night right here in this room with Mama Hannah beside you and the guards and me outside the door. In the morning, we'll take the train to Nairobi."

She set her hands on her hips. "Don't tell me what to do, Grant Thornton. I'm through with people ordering me around."

"I'm not ordering you." He slung the suitcase back onto the bed. "You said you trusted me, right? Well, this is what it feels like when someone doesn't let you down."

"Grant, I'm not—"

"My sister Tillie is staying in Nairobi to have her baby. We'll drop by her place. You'll like her."

"I will *not* bring your pregnant sister into this mess!"

"You don't know Tillie. She's kind of into adventure. Besides, it'll do Mama Hannah good to stay with Tillie and her husband while she heals up."

"Jones will follow me to Nairobi. Your family will be in danger."

"We're a tough bunch."

"I don't want your help, Grant. I don't need you. I don't need anybody." She knotted her fists. "I can pray about this and rely on my faith—"

"I'm sure you will. But if there is a God, he didn't throw you onto this earth to spend your days alone. He put me in your life, didn't he? Now, are you going to trust me to help you or not?"

"Grant—"

"Alexandra." He took her shoulders. Speaking slowly, he enunciated words that surprised him with their intensity. "I . . . *will* . . . take care of you."

Her voice was a whisper. "I don't want anybody to take care of me, Grant."

"Yes, you do."

"I'm strong enough alone. I have to be."

He heard his own lifelong theme song in her words and realized how empty it sounded. "You *are* strong enough alone," he said. "But you don't have to be. Let me stand with you."

Holding her arms tight around her middle as though she could lock out the world, she gave an almost imperceptible nod. "All right," she said. "For now."

"I'll pay your taxi. Why don't you come out onto the verandah with Mama Hannah and me? I'll fix a pot of tea, and we can sit and listen to the waves. Kind of take our minds off hit men and account deficits—minor details like that—and focus on what's really important."

Alexandra lifted her head. "What's really important anymore?"

"You," he said. "You're important. And you're alive, which is very important. Me, your belated rescuer. I'm important. And then there was this morning on the beach." He bent and brushed a kiss across her cheek. "I thought that was pretty important."

She stood still for a moment, her eyes still closed from his kiss. "Yes," she whispered. "That was pretty important to me, too."

"The verandah then?"

"Give me ten minutes. I want to take a quick shower."

Grant stroked a hand down her bare arm; then he turned and left the room.

After paying the taxi driver, he went to the kitchen, set a kettle of water on the stove, and took a collection of cups and saucers from the cabinet. He poured a little milk into a jug and placed some sugar cubes in a bowl. As he arranged the tea things, he shook his head.

Carrying the tray to the verandah, he realized he felt curiously light-headed. Odd. Nothing much had changed. Same wicker chairs. Same night watchman lurking in the shadows. Same moon shining down on the same palm trees. Mama Hannah was sitting where he'd left her.

"Alexandra came back," he said, joining the old woman. And he knew that was the reason for his altered mood. Alexandra was back—his again, if only for a few more days. He had managed to defeat her determination to leave and his own instinct to prefer solitude. He had managed, somehow, to keep her.

"Yes, she returned," Mama Hannah said. "But not for the luggage. She came for you."

Grant stretched out his legs and perched his feet on the low rattan table. "You reckon?"

"Certainly."

He sat in the silence, basking in the warm yellow glow of the verandah lamps and in the comfort of Alexandra Prescott's presence in his life. If he could protect her, she was his—to have and to hold, from this day forward . . .

until she left. Until she went back to her own life. New York, that foreign land. A place he could never belong.

He frowned. "Mama Hannah, have you ever heard of something called the home shopping network?"

The old woman shot him a look. "Home shopping network? For what purpose is this thing?"

"I don't know. I guess you can buy things you see on television."

Mama Hannah gave a grunt of dismissal. "Let us speak of Africa and faith and families, *toto*. Let us talk of things we know."

Grant mused a moment. "I wonder what a thigh toner is."

ELEVEN

Alexandra sat on a bench in the Mombasa railway station and stared at the surrealistic scene. Africans clambered up the sides of the steel cars and onto the roofs to tie on produce headed for market—burlap sacks stuffed with charcoal, wicker baskets filled with live chickens, and cardboard boxes brimming with fresh fruits and vegetables. One man shoved a bleating goat into the air while a companion reached down to lift the animal into place. Passengers of the human species elbowed their way through the narrow car doors and crowded onto the seats. Vendors carrying trays filled with everything from grilled corncobs to Chiclets chewing gum hawked their wares at the open train windows.

Two Indian women in bright red and blue silk saris climbed aboard with their black-haired children in tow. A Sikh gentleman in a starched white turban walked by, pausing to glance at the huge gold watch on his wrist. Three children chased a scrawny puppy along the rails, while a gray-suited African businessman mopped his brow.

Oblivious to the array of colors, the babble of cries and chatter, and the swirling smells of ocean air and crushing humanity, Mama Hannah sat beside Alexandra on the bench and read her Bible. "Here the wise King Solomon has written a very interesting thing," she said, looking up.

"'The wicked run away when no one is chasing them, but the godly are as bold as lions.' Do you think this means it would be good for us to be bold and to hunt down the wicked man who tries to kill you?"

Alexandra let out a breath. "I don't know what it means."

"Jesus told his followers, 'God blesses those who are merciful, for they will be shown mercy.' So, shall we be bold, as King Solomon said? Or shall we show mercy to this wicked man, as our Lord commanded? Perhaps it is bold to be merciful. What do you think?"

Trying to concentrate, Alexandra shifted on the bench. "I'm not really sure."

"Of what are you sure, *toto?*"

"Not much these days. I just hope Grant gets here with the tickets pretty soon. That train is jammed."

Mama Hannah folded her hands around her Bible. "I do not believe you are thinking about the train. What fills your mind, *toto?*"

Alexandra shrugged. "I guess I'm wondering what's happening to my money, and I'm trying to figure out how that's going to affect my life. If the message I got at the lodge was accurate, I may not have any money to wonder about."

"Ehh."

"I'm also thinking about what it's going to feel like when Jones finally kills me."

Mama Hannah clucked in sympathy. "Death comes in many forms. It is good that you and I have the promise of eternal life."

"Somehow I can't make the thought of heaven seem

very comforting right now. I'm not ready to die, Mama Hannah. I want to do things. I have plans. Dreams."

"Oh, yes indeed. You are young. The young forget so quickly that no one knows what tomorrow may bring. Hope in the Lord, *toto.*"

Alexandra reached over and patted the old woman's folded hands. How could Mama Hannah know the impact of losing more money than she had ever imagined? How could she possibly understand what it meant to be betrayed by the only person you truly trusted? How could she relate to the aura of impending death that hung over Alexandra's head like a black cloud—a constant threat that followed her everywhere, lurking, waiting, seeking out her vulnerability.

"Tickets," Grant announced as he strode toward the bench. "First class. No one ever said that Thornton can't treat two lovely ladies to the elegance they deserve."

Alexandra glanced at the train with more than a measure of skepticism. Elegance? She'd have to see that to believe it.

Grant loaded her bags onto a luggage cart and set off toward the train. Alexandra and Mama Hannah followed more slowly, making their way past vendors eager to sell them a packet of cashews or a few ripe tangerines. Every touch on her arm made Alexandra's spine prickle. Twice, when someone brushed against her, she jumped. Sensing someone following, she kept turning to scan the crowd behind her. But she never saw anyone resembling the hulking Nick Jones.

"This way, ladies," Grant said, offering a hand to Mama Hannah first and then to Alexandra as they climbed aboard the first-class car.

Sure enough, it was nearly as full of passengers as the rest of the train, the floor under the narrow leather seats cluttered with bags, baskets, and cardboard boxes. Grant picked his way down the crowded aisle to their designated seats. He offered Mama Hannah and Alexandra the two adjoining seats, but the older woman deferred.

"I will sit there," she said, indicating the empty seat beside a dignified elderly man wearing the traditional embroidered white Muslim cap and ankle-length caftan. She leaned against Alexandra. "If not, I am afraid Grant will bother the poor gentleman with requests for stories and legends of Muhammad. No one should have to endure such a thing for nine hours." She tugged at Grant's sleeve. "And do not disturb Miss Prescott either. Today she is considering important subjects. She is thinking of money and dying."

"Money and dying?" Grant gave Alexandra a curious glance. "You want to explain that one?"

She groaned inwardly as he stepped aside to allow her the window seat. "Forget it," she said. "I'm not in the mood to talk."

Grant slid down into his seat, his knees touching the seat in front. "Fine with me." He gave a yawn and dug around in his jeans pocket. "I don't want to talk about money and dying. Two of the most desolate subjects I know. Care for a lemon drop?"

He held out a couple of cellophane-wrapped candies dusted with lint. Afraid to ask how long they'd been in his pocket, Alexandra took one, blew off the lint, and unwrapped it. Savoring its sweet-sour flavor, she relaxed against the seat and closed her eyes.

"Money," Grant said, "is overrated. True, you've got to have it to get by in the modern world. But nobody *needs* it."

Alexandra opened one eye. "Give me a break."

"I'm serious. It's not a basic need—like shelter, food and water, meaningful work."

"How do you get shelter and food without money? And what kind of meaningful work is there that doesn't pay wages or a salary?"

"Anthropology."

"If you want to live in a tent and eat bananas."

"Sounds good to me."

"I'm sure it does. Excuse me, I'm going to take a nap now." She shut her eyes again as the train began to roll out of the station. "No matter what kind of skewed logic you try to use on me, I'll always think money is important. I need it to give my life significance."

"Supposing that stockbroker has bled you dry. Are you saying your life has no meaning?"

"I don't know."

"What do you mean you don't know? *You* are not your money. *You* are *you:* Alexandra Prescott."

"I've never been Alexandra Prescott without money. I don't know who that is."

"I'll tell you who she is. She's one smart, talented, beautiful woman."

"And what good are any of those things without money?"

Irritated in spite of his compliment, Alexandra edged up in her seat and leaned one elbow on the window. The passing scenery only served to remind her how completely off-kilter her world had become. Unlike the commuter railway on which she watched New York's skyscrapers give way to small Westchester County towns composed of brick stores and tidy houses, this rickety train chugged past square, red-mud huts and swaying palm trees. How on earth had she ended up here?

"When you get back to New York," Grant asked, "are you going to start living in a subway station and pushing all your belongings around in a shopping cart?"

"Of course not. I earn a decent living from my fabrics. I'll survive. I just won't be . . . the same. I won't be able to start my design firm, for one thing. And the little stuff I've always counted on will be much more difficult. You know—going out on the town for a nice Chinese dinner or enjoying front-row seats at a Broadway theater on opening night or dropping into Macy's for a pair of designer shoes." She looked down at her comfortable rubber-tire sandals. "Oh, forget it. You wouldn't understand."

Grant studied her shoes for a moment. "You have a problem with the footwear I bought you?"

"They're OK."

"You don't like what I've been feeding you?"

"I've eaten well enough. It's just that—"

"You don't like sitting on a verandah with front-row seats to the sound of ocean waves?"

Alexandra reflected on the previous evening she had spent with Grant and Mama Hannah. The three had sipped hot tea while sea breezes played in the dried fronds of the thatched roof. Silent, they had listened to the rush of waves on the sand and the gentle creaking of the palm trees. It had been relaxing, peaceful, perfect.

"It was a wonderful evening," she acknowledged.

"Didn't cost a thing."

"Nothing's free in New York."

"Maybe you ought to change your address."

Alexandra gave him a frown. "Are you suggesting I move to Kenya and live in a tent or something?"

"No." He shook his head. "Absolutely not."

"Why not?"

"You'd be terrible at it. No electricity for your hair dryer."

"I resent that. What makes you such an expert? I could live in a tent if I wanted to, Grant Thornton."

"No way. You are a woman accustomed to the finer things in life. You need your designer clothes and satin sheets."

"I don't have satin sheets."

"And your sketches. You definitely need a studio with a telephone, fax machine, computer—"

"Oh, what do you know about my work?" She crossed her arms. "I can design anywhere I want. If I had to, I could sketch and paint in Timbuktu."

"Timbuktu. Now there's a brilliant thought. You'll have to talk to my sister Tillie about it. Maybe she can put you up at her place when she gets back to Mali."

"There's not really a city called Timbuktu, is there?"

"Sure. And now that you've decided you don't need money after all—at least not to live in a decent place and keep doing the work you love—maybe you'd like to move there." He gave her a smug grin.

Unfortunately, the morning light that filtered through the train window made the man's devastating gray blue eyes actually sparkle. Otherwise, Alexandra would have been tempted to wipe the smirk off his mouth. As it was, she felt sorely tempted to kiss it. The mouth, not the smirk—

although Grant Thornton did have a pretty cute smirk. The creases that crinkled at the corners of his eyes only added to his charm, and when a curl drifted down onto his forehead, Alexandra had to look away.

"I'm not moving to Timbuktu," she said.

"But you could. That's the point. You don't *need* your money." He let out a breath. "Now that we've resolved the issue of money, let's move on to the subject of death."

"You're driving me nuts. Look, I just want to take a nap, OK? Could you possibly allow me to have a few minutes of uninterrupted silence?"

"You're not going to die anytime soon."

"Shh."

She closed her eyes and did her best to feign sleep. Grant had somehow managed to argue her into a corner about the stocks. It was true she'd been making ends meet without her father's money, and she could survive if James Cooper had destroyed her inheritance. She wouldn't want to, but she could.

If she lived that long.

Grant had no business pontificating about the fact that she could be killed. *He* hadn't been attacked under a thorn tree. *He* hadn't nearly been pushed out a fifty-foot-high window. And he certainly didn't know how it felt to be stalked by a hired killer.

"If Jones has any sense," Grant spoke up, "the logical thing for him to do would be to lie low and then slip out of Kenya before they can arrest him."

"Logic doesn't have anything to do with this," she mumbled.

"But *I* do. Even though Jones came close at Fort Jesus, he

didn't succeed. I wasn't there as fast as I wish I'd been, but I got to you in time to run him off. I told you I wouldn't let anything happen to you." He took her hand. "There's my ring right on your finger. My promise of protection."

Alexandra opened her eyes as Grant threaded his fingers through hers and pressed her hand against his chest. For some reason his simple gesture sent a flood of warmth into her chilled heart. She had known a lot of men in her life. But not one of them had Grant Thornton's assurance, intelligence, and wit. Certainly none shared his obvious concern for her.

That was the oddest thing. Grant cared about *her*. It wasn't her money or her family name or even her designing ability that had caused him to take her hand and promise to protect her. Such details didn't matter to him. *She* mattered.

Alexandra leaned toward him and laid her head on his shoulder. "Thanks," she said. "For the ring."

He kissed her forehead and began to stroke her hair with his fingertips. She had never felt anything better in her life.

The longer Alexandra slept, the more uncomfortable Grant became. And it didn't have anything to do with the fact that she was resting against him with her head on his shoulder. It was simply her: Alexandra. The reality that she would be gone soon. Too soon. The leaden stone of dismay that settled in the pit of Grant's stomach grew heavier each time he looked at the woman.

Her blonde hair lay like threads of silk scattered on his shirt as she napped all morning and right through the lunch hour.

Several times he couldn't resist touching the soft strands, sifting them through his fingers and marveling at the way they caught the brilliant sunlight. He'd always been partial to long hair, maybe because his sisters had worn theirs at waist length in girlish pigtails and braids. But Alexandra's short, bouncy style was just right for her. More important, it smelled good, and the pleasure of brushing his cheek against her head reminded him of the scent of a frangipani blossom. Exquisite, exotic, alluring.

Though he had never been a drinking man, Grant felt intoxicated in the woman's presence. Alexandra's hair had besotted him, and her face held him in trancelike fascination. He studied the way her eyelashes cast long, dark shadows across her cheeks. Perfect lashes, curved like a pair of satin fans. Perfect cheeks, the skin now rosy and soft, healed from her sunburn. He memorized her mouth. Perfect lips, a pair of damp pink petals. How quickly he had seen her mouth alter from a pout of frustration to a tense line of fear to the wide exaltation of her laughter.

How am I going to forget her mouth when she goes?

He would never forget it—and that was the trouble. Grant knew Alexandra was going to be impossible to put out of his mind. He'd gotten used to the sound of her voice. He knew exactly the touch of her hand. Like the professor in the play he'd watched on Broadway years ago, Grant had "grown accustomed to her face."

But his fair lady was an educated career woman with a life of her own. And she intended to get on with it.

Grant thought about his small campsite, his two tents, his old Land Rover, and his battered gas cookstove. Instead of comforting him with their familiarity and the promise of interesting work they provided, the images sent a wave of discontent through him. No matter what Alexandra claimed about her ability to live anywhere, she wouldn't want to spend the rest of her life on a permanent camp-out. Not many people would—which was why Grant had made up his mind to be a bachelor. Busy, contented, challenged, alone.

He looked out the train window and studied the passing scenery. Wide-open savanna grasslands stretched to the horizon. The occasional baobab tree lifted long bare limbs toward a cloudless blue sky. Scrappy acacias provided scant shade for a small herd of gazelles or a lone bull elephant. *Africa*. No matter how lonely he might get, Grant could never give it up for paved streets and skyscrapers.

And so he would go on back to his tents and his Land Rover. He would fall asleep to the sound of lions grunting in the darkness, and he'd wake to the patter of vervet monkeys on his canvas roof. Alexandra would fly away to New York's glass-sided buildings and clattering subways. She would sleep with the honk of passing cars, and she'd rise with the drone of street-sweeper machines and the cries of newsboys.

Grant looked down at her sun-kissed cheeks and golden hair. The leaden stone in his stomach turned over, and he swallowed against the gritty lump that had somehow lodged in his throat. That's how it would be. That's how it had to be.

Sultan Hamud. Konza. Ulu. The strange names of towns hardly larger than a train platform danced in Alexandra's head as she peeled a banana. The fresh scent of the ripe fruit was like nothing she had ever smelled in a grocery store or supermarket. And the taste—the sweet white pulp melted in her mouth like butter.

"Most of this land we're passing through once belonged to British colonists," Grant said. His arm around her shoulder, he leaned forward to watch the passing landscape. "Traditionally, it's a no-man's-land between two enemy tribes—the Wakamba and the Maasai. The British took it over at the turn of the century. They had concocted the idea of establishing huge ostrich ranches."

"For meat?"

"Feathers. You know those fancy hats women used to wear?" He swirled his fingers around his head indicating the huge, ostrich-plumed hats favored by late-Victorian and Edwardian society. "But two things conspired against the intrepid ranchers. First, lions discovered how easy it was to raid the ostrich pens and decimate the flocks."

"Fast food?" Alexandra said.

Grant chuckled. "Carnivore style. The second problem the ranchers faced—and what really defeated them— occurred back in Europe. The automobile was invented, and its low roof made the fancy hats impractical. So that was the end of ostrich farming."

"Did the British pack up and leave?" Alexandra peeled a second banana. She was enjoying Grant's tales of the African countryside. In fact, with a good rest and a little food in her stomach, she had started to feel more optimistic.

"Hardly," Grant said. "The colonists turned to cattle ranching and dairy farming. They hired Wakamba tribes-men to guard their herds against lions and against their enemies, the Maasai. See, the Maasai believe that *Engai*—

their name for God—originally gave their tribe all the cattle in the world. Logically then, anyone else who owns cattle must have stolen them from a Maasai."

Alexandra laughed. "How convenient. So if a Maasai raids a Wakamba's or an Englishman's herd, he's not really stealing. He's just taking back what rightfully belongs to him."

"Exactly. The only problem with your statement is the linguistics. One member of the Wakamba tribe is called a Mkamba. See, in Swahili, we have what we call the M-Wa class. The 'people' class. Wakamba is plural, Mkamba is singular." He paused and reflected a moment. "I guess you don't need to know that."

Surprised at the sudden change in his tone, Alexandra glanced over at him. He was right, of course. She didn't need to know any of it—the history, the tribal names and legends, the intricacies of the language. In Nairobi she would book a flight to New York. Within a day or two, she'd be gone.

Strange. Not too long ago she would have left this country without a second thought. In fact, she would have been thankful to see the last of it. Now, the idea of leaving sent a pang of dismay through her stomach. But it wasn't the loss of Kenya that grieved her, even though she was learning to appreciate the spacious vistas and the eternal sunshine. What pained her was the prospect of leaving this man.

Did he feel the same about her? Or was she just another diversion, an interesting anomaly he could study and analyze? Did he care at all that she'd soon be gone, or was he anticipating the peace and solitude she would leave in her wake?

"You could teach me a little Swahili," she offered, trying to gauge the response in his eyes. "Languages fascinate me."

"We should have started you on a crash course sooner."

"Well, I might not leave Kenya right away. For a few days, anyway. I mean, I'll have to find a flight with empty seats."

"You'll find one."

She looked away. "I guess so. I hate to let Jones run me off. After all, I had scheduled a whole excursion, and I don't have as many sketches for my designs as I'd hoped to do."

"Maybe you'll come back after you get Jones put away."

"Maybe." She thought about the chances. Slim. She wasn't even sure she'd have the money to make it from one month to the next, let alone to buy an expensive ticket back to Kenya.

"I guess you'll be pretty busy," Grant said. "Your work and all that."

"Yeah." She swallowed. "How about you? When will your project be finished?"

"A few months. Maybe a year."

"So, what will you do after that? Take a vacation?"

"I might."

"Do you ever get to the States?"

He stared at the seat in front. "Not often. Every four or five years maybe. I have to track down grants and endorsements. Usually I hit a few universities and do some speaking. Sometimes I get a magazine assignment, or I'm asked to contribute to a textbook. At that point I might need to meet with the publisher."

"Why don't you come to New York on your next trip?"

she tossed out, as though she'd just thought of it. "I'll show you the sights."

He met her eyes. For a moment he said nothing, holding her gaze. Then he let out a breath. "The only sight I'd care to see in New York City is you."

A ripple of delight ran up her spine. It was just as quickly squelched by the fact that he turned away and dropped his head back against the seat. She could see the muscle in his jaw flicker with tension.

"Grant," she said softly. "We can always—"

"No, we can't. You know it. I know it. Anybody with half a brain in his skull knows it. The facts just don't add up. You're there, I'm here. You're big city, I'm Africa. You want money, I want freedom. You're wrapped up in religion, I'm a doubter."

"Yes, and you're analyzing again."

"What am I supposed to do?"

"Feel. Listen to your heart."

"Feelings are for artists. I'm a scientist, Alexandra. I want to figure things out."

"But that's not what's happening between us, Grant. It's something in here." She laid her open palm on his chest. "Isn't it?"

He covered her hand with his and shut his eyes. "I don't trust my heart."

"Somehow," she said, struggling to contain the emotion welling inside her as she felt his heartbeat hammering against her palm, "somehow, you taught me to trust *you*, Grant. At a time when people I've counted on have let me down, when I could so easily choose to shut the door of my heart to everybody, you walked in. Into my heart. I don't know how you managed it, and I don't pretend to understand what's going to happen. Sure, my brain is telling me the same facts yours is telling you, and I'll listen to it, of course. But I'm not going to shut off my heart. I can't."

He studied her, the gray in his eyes reflecting the turmoil inside him. "Does the human heart give honest answers, Alexandra? Can emotion ever lead to truth?"

"Yes," she said firmly. "You don't have to understand everything, Grant. You don't always need proof. Sometimes you just have to trust."

As she turned back to the window and the sight of Nairobi's approaching skyline, she heard her own heart whisper words of truth: *"For I know the one in whom I trust, and I am sure that he is able to guard what I have entrusted to him until the day of his return."*

Her thoughts tumbled out in the form of a prayer. *Lord, my life belongs to you. My faith and my hope lie in you. I entrust you with Grant Thornton now. Open him. Fill him. And teach me how to give you this terrible . . . unbearable . . . ache I feel inside whenever I look into his eyes.*

TWELVE

"Grant!" A woman with billowing long blonde hair and a bulge the size of a baby elephant under her dress waved from the far end of the platform at the Nairobi railway station. "Hey, Grant! It's me, Tillie!"

Tillie? Grant stopped stock-still and stared. This beautiful, vivacious, and incredibly maternal-looking woman was his scrawny little sister? And who was the big guy beside her? Not the renegade who'd taken her on a wild-goose chase up the Niger River and then married her. Not him . . . Tillie's husband . . .

Every protective big-brother instinct surged to the forefront of Grant's being as the woman who claimed to be his sister hurried toward him as fast as her swaying gait would take her. The guy had better be good to Tillie. He'd better be faithful. He'd better be employed and hardworking and—

"Grant!" Tillie threw her arms around his neck. "Oh, Grant, it's so good to see you! You look great. Such a handsome devil!" She detached herself and whirled away. "Mama Hannah!" she exclaimed, clasping the older woman. "I heard what happened to you. Oh, let me see your head."

With the women chattering to one side, Grant sized up his approaching brother-in-law. At least the guy wasn't some knock-kneed kid. His hair was too long. Too black. He looked like a rugby player or something.

"Dr. Thornton?" the man said, extending a hand. "I'm Graeme McLeod. Tillie's husband."

Grant gave the man's hand a firm shake. Not a bad grip, anyway. "Call me Grant."

"Oh, Grant and Graeme!" Tillie swung around. "I'm so glad you two are finally meeting. Graeme's a writer, too, Grant. He's working on a biography of the explorer Joseph Thomson, so it worked out great for us to fly over to Nairobi so he can do research and I can have the baby. Perfect timing, huh? And now you're here! I was afraid you'd be dug in with your Maasai." She turned to Alexandra. "And is this your . . . ?"

"This is Alexandra Prescott," Grant said. Alexandra had hung back by the luggage during the greetings. Now she walked forward and shook Tillie's hand.

"When Grant phoned us this morning to say he was coming, he told me you'd had quite a time in Kenya." Tillie's bright eyes registered concern. "Then Graeme showed me an article in the newspaper. Some lunatic attacked you while you were staying at the lodge in Amboseli? And then he tried to push you out a window at Fort Jesus?"

Alexandra nodded. "That's it so far. Your brother's been very helpful."

"Grant?" Tillie turned to him in mock surprise. *"Helpful?"*

"What's the big deal?" Grant said, squaring his shoulders. "I can be helpful."

"My big brother has never been helpful a day in his life,"

Tillie confided, linking arms with Alexandra. "He's a pest. He used to con Fiona and Jessie and me into doing his chores for him. He always talked us into sewing on his buttons and hemming his jeans. When Mama Hannah told us it was time to put away our toys and clean up our rooms, Grant would suddenly vanish. Half an hour later we'd find him up the pepper tree in our front yard."

"Lies," Grant barked. "All lies. Alexandra, don't listen to a word she says."

"Ha! I bet your place looks like a shrine to bachelorhood, Grant Thornton—no food in the fridge, dishes in the sink, clothes piled on chairs. Am I right, Alexandra?"

"He lives in a tent," she said.

"A tent!" Tillie crossed her arms over her bulging stomach. "Oh, Grant, that's pathetic. It really is. What about that house you bought in Nairobi? Do you ever even visit it?"

"You own a *house,* Grant?" Alexandra asked.

"I guess so." He rubbed a hand around the back of his neck. He felt about as uncomfortable as he had the day a pair of charging rhinos chased him up a tree. "I bought some property a few years ago. I had extra money from a book contract, and I didn't want to put it in the bank. Inflation can eat you up in Kenya. So, I bought a house. At least, I think I did," he concluded, winking at Graeme.

Tillie rolled her eyes at Alexandra. "I bet he never even looked at the place before he put down his money," she said. "My brother is the most wonderful, loyal, good-hearted man in the world. But he's in bad need of a good woman."

Grant groaned. "Tillie, give it a rest."

"Don't you agree, Mama Hannah?" Tillie asked.

The older woman nodded. "For his dinner, your brother eats chocolate candy bars."

"Kit Kat bars, I bet," Tillie said. "Something has to be done about this. Mama Hannah, are you with me? And, Alexandra, how about you? Are you willing to tackle my big brother's case of bacheloritis?"

"I've been working on it already," Alexandra said, and Grant caught the unmistakable sparkle in her blue eyes. "I don't know, though. He's pretty set in his ways."

"Stodgy." Tillie nodded, throwing an arm around Mama Hannah's shoulders. "I know exactly what you mean. Come on, ladies, let's head over to the apartment for a cup of tea. Maybe we could talk Jessie into flying up from Zanzibar for a few days. And then there's Fiona. Nah, she's as bad as Grant is. But with a little work . . ."

Grant stood by the luggage cart and studied the three musketeers who had made it their quest to reform him. They could not be an odder bunch. Tall, lithe Alexandra strolled arm in arm with waddling Tillie, who had her other arm around tiny, wizened Mama Hannah.

"A formidable trio," Graeme said, coming to stand by him. "Are you sure you're up to the fray?"

Grant couldn't hide his grin. "I'd say the odds are against me."

"Would you like an ally in the battle for male freedom?"

"Looks like you surrendered a long time ago, pal."

"And glad of it. Tillie's great." Graeme rubbed his chin. "On the other hand, I waged my own war against the civilizing forces of the female gender for a good many years. I'd hate to see a fine soldier like you fall into one of their snares. Unless, of course, it was worth it." He hooked Alexandra's flowered tapestry cosmetics bag with a forefinger and dangled it in front of Grant. "Would it be worth it?"

Grant smiled. "It might be, you know. It just might be."

The two-bedroom apartment Tillie and Graeme had rented in the Westlands area of Nairobi was exactly what Grant would have expected of his sister. Tidy and clean, it contained little furniture and about a hundred plants. Clay pots sprouting green vegetation lined up along the windowsills. More pots hung suspended by twine from the curtain rods. Still others nestled in the corners of the living room and marched down the kitchen counters.

"How long have you been living here, anyway?" Grant asked, peering between the leaves of a philodendron at the city lights outside.

"A couple of months." Tillie sprawled Buddha-like on the sofa and peered over her stomach as the others cleared the evening meal. "I've been collecting every plant I can get my hands on. I'm going to take them back to Mali and find out if they'll grow. You should fly up and take a look at my experimental substation, Grant. The government finally awarded me a big stretch of land up north near the desert around Timbuktu. It's been rough, but my trees are hanging on."

"Mama Hannah said the tribespeople up there gave you a hard time," Grant said, joining his sister on the sofa. "Some warrior chieftain kidnapped you?"

"Actually, *Graeme* kidnapped me." Tillie laughed at his expression. "Don't get your feathers ruffled, big brother. It worked out, didn't it?"

"Did it?" Grant eyed the dark-haired man in the kitchen; then he studied his sister. "Are you happy, Tillie-Willie?"

She smiled at his use of her childhood nickname. "I'm more than happy," she said softly. "I'm blessed. Graeme and I have seen God's hand in our lives in such a powerful way. We've both grown so much."

"I can see that," he said, cocking an eyebrow at her stomach.

"That's not what I meant, doofus." She flicked him on the shoulder. "Give me your hand. Come on, now. Put it right there on the baby. Wait a minute. Wait . . . wait . . ."

Surprised at the firmness of her stomach, Grant held his breath and stared at the solid mound. Suddenly something moved under his palm—like a marble rolling under a sheet. He jerked his hand away. "Wow, what was that?"

Tillie gave a deep laugh. "That was your nephew's elbow. Or your niece's big toe."

"No kidding?" He placed his hand on her stomach again. "When are you due?"

"Another month—and I'm about to go nuts waiting. Graeme's been wonderful, though. He's as excited as I am about the whole thing." She giggled as Grant laid his ear against her belly. "You're not going to hear anything but my stomach gurgling."

"Whoa! He kicked me!"

"Tell me about it. The kid's going to make a great soccer player one of these days." She feathered her fingers through her brother's hair. "How about you, Grant? Don't you want to be a daddy someday? Aren't you curious about all this stuff? I mean, *family*. The Thornton kids didn't exactly grow up in the normal way, you know. Don't you want to try it out for yourself?"

Grant straightened and wrapped his arms around his sister, pulling her close. "You know me pretty well, Tillie. Think I'd be any good at the husband and dad routine?"

"With the right woman by your side, you would." She tugged on one of his curls. "I like Alexandra a lot."

"I do, too." He focused on the tall blonde as she stacked plates in a cabinet. "But she lives in New York."

"Mmm."

"She's an artist."

"Uh-huh."

"She's rich."

"Ooh."

"And she's religious. Christian."

"You'd better marry her quick."

Grant laughed. "Come on, Tillie. You know I couldn't live in a big city like New York any better than you could. I'd be a fish out of water."

"I don't see that as much of a problem. It's the religion thing that's going to doom you. If Alexandra is really a believer, she's not going to want to be yoked to a pagan like you."

"I'm not a *pagan*."

"What are you, then?"

"I'm a scientist. I need proof before I believe something exists."

Tillie took his hand and laid it on the moving mound of her stomach. "Feel this, and tell me there's not a God, Grant. This baby is your proof. And Mama Hannah is your proof. After Mom died, Dad could have hired any number of women to look after us kids. He chose *her*. Don't tell me that was an accident."

"I know, but—"

"Alexandra is your proof, too. You don't think gorgeous blondes come walking into the lives of renegade anthropologists every day, do you? God has a plan for you, Grant Thornton. He wants your love. He wants your surrender. If you'd just take off your blinders, maybe you'd see him as clearly as Alexandra does."

She leaned over and kissed his cheek. Then she heaved herself off the sofa and padded into the kitchen. "Hey, everybody," she said. "Let's divvy up the rooms and hit the hay. I'm bushed."

Before Grant could put in his two cents' worth, his little sister had assigned him the living-room couch and plopped a pile of blankets and pillows on a nearby chair. Alexandra and Mama Hannah disappeared into the spare room, while Tillie made a beeline for her own bed. Graeme remained for a moment, switching off lights and checking the water level in some of his wife's plants.

"Need anything?" he asked, pausing beside the couch.

Grant gave a little chuckle. Yeah, he needed a lot. Explanations. Reasons. Answers.

"Not unless you're smarter than I am," he said finally.

Graeme's dark brows lifted. "Maybe I am, maybe not. At least I was smart enough to know a good thing when I saw it. And I married her."

"Treat my little sister right, buddy."

"I do." He smiled. "She loves you a lot, you know. Not a day goes by that Tillie doesn't mention you in her prayers."

"You listen to her praying?"

"Sure. We pray together. The first time we did it, I felt pretty ridiculous down on my knees on the living-room floor talking out loud to God. Now, my day doesn't go right without it." He shrugged. "Prayer is part of the bond between Tillie and me. Our faith is our foundation, you know?"

No, I don't know, Grant wanted to say. *And what's an intelligent guy like you doing down on his knees talking to some nebulous entity? And how can faith be a foundation when you can't even put your finger on it?*

"Whatever," Grant said.

Graeme glanced down the hall. "Looks like the bathroom's all yours." He started for his bedroom. "Tomorrow, then."

"Tomorrow."

Grant stood, picked up his bag, and rooted around for his toothbrush, hoping somebody had left a tube of toothpaste in the bathroom. Down in the bag, his hand brushed the little Bible he had found in Alexandra's suitcase and put into his pocket. He'd intended to return the book to her, but he hadn't gotten around to it.

Picking it up now, he opened the burgundy-leather cover and turned through the pages. His eye scanned familiar names, familiar stories, familiar words. How many hours had he spent on Mama Hannah's lap listening to her read from her own little Bible? He had loved those times. Perhaps they had even been the spark that led to his fascination with the study of ancient oral myths.

But *truth?* Could truth really be hidden somewhere in the black printed words of the Bible? Alexandra had said she believed that Jesus Christ himself was Truth. Grant flipped to the concordance in the back of the little book. In a moment, he had sunk onto the couch again and was riffling through the thin, crinkly pages.

In the Gospel written by Jesus' disciple John he found an intriguing verse. "While Jesus was teaching in the Temple, he called out, 'Yes, you know me, and you know where I come from. But I represent one you don't know, and he is true. I know him because I have come from him, and he sent me to you.'"

Grant studied the words a moment. Like the people in the temple, he didn't know the truth Jesus claimed to represent. Mama Hannah wouldn't like it, but her *toto* was probably as great a doubter as the worst traitors in the Bible.

He scanned through further chapters, searching for a character who might represent himself in this elaborate mythology. What about Pontius Pilate, the governor of Judea? At the trial of Jesus, Pilate was as full of questions as Grant would have been. Are you the king of the Jews? Why have you been brought here? What have you done? Are you an earthly king, then?

And finally the biggie. "'What is truth?' Pilate asked."

Jesus didn't answer that question, probably because he'd already given Pilate a sort of explanation. "I came to bring truth to the world. All who love the truth recognize that what I say is true." Grant pondered the enigmatic response. He loved the truth. So why didn't he recognize Jesus' words as true?

Blinders. Tillie had accused him of wearing blinders. But how could a man in obvious pursuit of knowledge be wearing blinders? Maybe because he was looking with his mind instead of with his heart, as Alexandra had insisted he must.

Grant stared down at the Bible, his eyes unfocused as he searched inside himself. "I want to know the truth," he whispered. His own words startled him—they sounded uncomfortably like a prayer. *A prayer?* Whoa!

Could a man like him really pray? Grant wiped a hand across his brow. Why not? Tillie, Mama Hannah, Alexandra, and even Graeme prayed. Kakombe prayed. Every Maasai he knew prayed.

"Creator," he murmured, starting at the only place in the morass of his own doubt that he could pin down. "Creator, I want to know the truth. Show me. Do you exist? Do you care about us down here? About me? Do you . . . do you *love* me?"

For some reason a knot formed in his throat. When he spoke again, his whispered voice was husky with emotion. "I want to know the truth. Was Jesus the Nazarene who he claimed to be? Was God sent to earth in human form? Did he really die and rise again in order to bring forgiveness and the promise of life after death?" He swallowed. "Is Jesus the Truth I'm looking for?"

Grant lifted his head. Feeling foolish, he dropped the Bible back into his bag and took out his toothbrush. But before he could stand, a wave of emotion swept through him. Powerful, tormenting, it washed open the black hole inside his soul. He bent over and knotted his fists.

"Tell me!" he ground out, his eyes finally brimming. "I need to know! I'm tired . . . so tired . . . of searching. Give me the *truth.*"

Struggling to cover again the gaping hole inside, the

vacuum he had denied so long, he shook his head in misery. Where were the brave, shining trophies he had always used to fill it? Education. Intellect. Logic. Reason. Like little grains of salt, they rolled around inside the raw, empty wound. What could heal him?

"Alexandra." He whispered the name that haunted him. No, that was wrong. She wouldn't fill the emptiness. Couldn't. But maybe she could help him. Teach him. Show him the way.

"If you're out there, God," he mouthed, "don't let Alexandra go. Not yet. I've got to have time. I've got to find my heart . . . and then . . . I've got to find a way to heal it."

"You cannot leave Kenya for the time being, Miss Prescott." The official at the United States consulate in Nairobi shook his head. "I'm sorry."

Seated in the man's tidy, sterile office the following morning, Alexandra felt her blood rise clear to the tips of her ears. "What do you mean I *can't leave?* I came to this country on a working vacation, and I've decided my business is done. I need to get back to the States immediately. My financial situation—"

"I understand your predicament, ma'am. You've explained yourself clearly. If it's any comfort to you, the Kenya immigration authorities believe the man who attacked you may have left the country traveling under a different name than the one he gave you. They reported to us here at the consulate that an unaccompanied American male departed on a flight to New York right after the Fort Jesus incident."

He leaned across his desk and continued in a low voice. "If you want to know the truth, Miss Prescott, we think the guy is long gone."

"What makes you say that?"

"He blew his cover at Fort Jesus. The police are onto him now. Every border crossing and every airport is on the alert. Unless he's very clever—or very stupid—he hotfooted it out of this country."

"Then why do *I* have to stay?"

"Unfortunately, the government will not allow you to exit the country until the case is resolved. They want confirmation that the man did indeed leave Kenya, and they need your help to prove it. You're the primary witness to two brutal attacks—"

"Witness! Try *participant*. That maniac has tried to kill me twice."

"Believe me, your well-being is of utmost importance. The Kenya police have assured us that you'll be protected to the best of their ability." The official lowered his voice again. "Look, I'll be frank, Miss Prescott. This is not really about you. It's about tourism."

"Tourism?" Alexandra gripped the arms of the chair. "I can't leave Kenya because of *tourism?*"

"Tourism accounts for a large part of this country's economy. Unfortunately, every time a report of violence leaks out—especially violence toward an American—the tourism industry here takes a nosedive. Kenya can't *afford* to let you go. They've got to prove that the perpetrator left the country, or they've got to catch him, put him behind bars, and then show you off to the world as a happy camper. A happy, safe camper."

Alexandra looked down at the passport, tickets, and official documents lying in her lap. At a travel agency that morning, she had been told she couldn't get a flight out for another two days unless she was willing to wait at the airport as a standby passenger. But when the travel agent examined her visa, she recognized Alexandra's name. Following the agent's suggestion to take her case to the consulate, Alexandra had wound up with this big, fat *no*.

"Are you telling me that if I tried to leave the airport, I'd be stopped?"

"I'm telling you that you cannot leave Kenya without government permission. You'll need an exit visa stamped into your passport—and you're not going to be issued one. If you try to leave, you won't get past the airport-security people."

"But I haven't done anything wrong. Look, I'm an American citizen. I insist that you get me out of this mess."

"As I said before, I'll do everything I can to help you, Miss Prescott. Believe me, the last thing we want is an incident. When you disappeared from that lodge, we thought we had a huge problem on our hands. Now that we know you're all right and we think the perpetrator has fled, we'd like to keep the damage to a minimum. I'll talk with the authorities again and see if I can explain the urgency of your situation. I'm afraid that's the best I can offer you right now."

"So, what am I supposed to do? Just sit around and twiddle my thumbs?"

"You were on a tour. Why don't you resume your vacation?"

Alexandra dug into her purse and pulled out her wrinkled itinerary. "This is how I got into trouble in the first place.

Do you think I really want to go trekking around in the wilderness again?"

The bureaucrat heaved a sigh. "It really doesn't matter to us what you choose to do with your free time, Miss Prescott. Just stay in contact with us and with the police. As soon as we have approval for your exit visa, we'll let you know."

Fuming, Alexandra stood. "I'll be in touch."

She walked out into the lobby feeling as helpless as she'd ever felt in her life. How could they *force* her to stay here? Jones had victimized her. Now the Kenya government was doing the same thing.

Emerging into the bright sunlight of the afternoon, she searched the parking spaces for the car Grant had rented. He had told her he was going to run a few errands, but he'd be waiting when she came out of the consulate. He wasn't.

Great. She leaned against the side of the building and shut her eyes in frustration. How could this all be happening to her? How could God let her fall into such a mess?

Lifting her head, she stared up at the blue sky and the flag fluttering overhead. *Is there a reason for this, Lord? Are you trying to teach me something? Do you have a plan here? Because if you do, I sure wish you'd let me in on it.*

"The old red, white, and blue," Grant said, appearing beside her. "So, how'd it go?"

Alexandra shook her head. "You won't believe this. I'm not allowed to leave the country. I'm stuck here."

"Stuck?" Grant's suntanned face blanched a clammy-looking white. "You're *not* leaving?"

"That's what I said. The police think Jones fled the country after the Fort Jesus incident, but they want me to hang around anyway. Evidently my problem has threatened the entire economy of Kenya."

"How do you figure that?"

"Tourism," she said. "My story needs a happy ending so the press can spread the word and keep vacationers coming."

"So, you're staying?"

"I just *said* that!" She glared at him, unable to contain her frustration. "Don't worry, I won't keep bugging you. I'll get a hotel room somewhere in Nairobi and just . . . I don't know . . . I'll just chill out. You can go on back to your research, OK?"

"I didn't realize I was such a pain to have around."

"Huh?"

"Hey, if I'm not too much trouble, I'll hang out with you. Keep my eye on you."

"Don't think you have to protect me, Grant. I can take care of myself." She wriggled the ring off her finger. "Here. I release you."

He took her hand. "Alexandra." Before she could protest, he slipped the ring back over her knuckle. "Wear it. I don't know how this happened. . . . I don't understand it . . . but somehow . . . somehow . . . you're not leaving Kenya. That's really . . . odd."

"Odd?" She had never seen Grant tongue-tied before. In a way, it was endearing. A measure of the frustration inside her began to ebb. *"I'm* odd? Or my not leaving is odd?"

He laughed. "You're not odd; you're beautiful. And I'm glad you're staying. If Jones is no longer a threat, why don't you come back to the camp with me? You could work on your sketches."

Alexandra looked into his eyes, wishing she could read

him better. Did he want her to stay? Did he want to be with her? The idea that Grant Thornton's feelings for her might mirror her own growing attraction to him sent a wave of trepidation through her. She couldn't care about him. He couldn't want her. They didn't belong. Didn't match.

"Well, uh . . . I thought . . ." She fumbled for a moment before seizing on an escape route. Reaching into her purse, she brought out her travel schedule. "I thought I might go back to my original plan. Take up my old itinerary."

"I see." He glanced down at the paper. "So, where are you headed?"

Alexandra studied the schedule for a moment. "Well, it looks like I'm . . . I'm . . ." She looked up at Grant and grinned. "I'm supposed to be headed for the slopes of Mount Kilimanjaro."

THIRTEEN

"Welcome home!" Tillie sang out, lifting her arms high.

Grant climbed out of the car and blinked. This was not a tent. Those were not acacia trees. This could not be his home.

"*When* did you say you bought this place?" Alexandra asked as she passed him and started up the graveled walkway to the large stone structure in the distance. "Either things were cheaper back then or you had more money than you knew."

Grant couldn't make an answer emerge. He owned *this?* The empty house stood on a large lot in the Karen suburb of Nairobi—an area named for author Karen Blixen, who had immortalized Kenya in her book *Out of Africa*. Twelve-foot-tall evergreen hedges rimmed the property. They badly needed pruning. So did the lawn, an expanse of shaggy grass overgrown with a tumble of lantana and vines.

The house itself sat back on the lot like an aging gray elder, content to survey life as it passed by. Curtainless windows revealed empty rooms, and a scarlet bougainvillea plant threatened to pull down the verandah's sagging roof. As Grant approached the house, a half-dozen small brown lizards scattered from their sunny spot on the flagstone porch into the tangle of shrubbery.

"This house is beautiful," Alexandra said, stepping up onto the verandah. "It has so much character."

"It's rotting," Grant snorted. He walked over to the door and inserted the key he had retrieved from a lockbox at a downtown bank that morning. "Everybody stand back. This may be the fall of the house of Usher."

He pushed open the door. It swung into a large, sun-filled foyer with a parquet floor and white-painted walls. A long staircase with a wooden banister curved upward to the second floor. Grant entered, glanced around, and then beckoned everyone inside.

"Whoa, big brother," Tillie said as she stepped into the foyer. "This is pretty incredible."

"I can't believe you've never even seen your house," Alexandra murmured as she began roaming the perimeter, peering out the windows and peeking into rooms. "Do you have any furniture?"

"A house of your own, *toto,*" Mama Hannah said softly. "Now, like a baobab tree, you have roots."

Grant swallowed. Twin emotions rose inside him like a pair of rival warlords. On the one hand, he felt a sense of satisfaction. Yes, he mentally asserted, he owned this house. Of course he did. He was a responsible, hardworking man who knew how to invest well. He was a fine and upstanding member of society. An emblem of the landed gentry. A man of foresight, wisdom, and shrewd financial instinct.

Roots? the other half of him bellowed. *Roots!* Grant Thornton had never wanted roots in his life. He was a vagabond, a restless sojourner on the tossing seas of existence. He was a gypsy. Freedom sang through his veins. Adventure was his middle name. Roots would choke and strangle and tie a man to his own grave.

He'd sell the house immediately. Get rid of it, like a drowning man with a millstone tied around his neck. Cut it loose. Set himself free. Breathe again.

"You amaze me," Alexandra said, stepping again into the foyer. The golden afternoon sunlight lit up her hair and danced on her bronzed skin. "A man of many secrets. So what else have you got tucked away in your pocket, Grant? A Rolls-Royce in the garage? A membership in the cricket club?"

He shoved his hands into his pockets and discovered what he *did* have tucked away—the Maasai wedding chain. He fingered the silver links as he watched Alexandra stroll into the living room and move to the long bank of windows that opened onto the backyard. *Give it to her,* the responsible gentleman inside him commanded. *Give her the chain, the house . . . your heart. Commit. Do it now.*

"It's strange, you know," Alexandra said. As he approached, she leaned toward the dusty panes and gazed out at the tangle of greenery. "You're the man who doesn't want to own anything except his two tents and seven socks. But suddenly your sister forces you to face the reality that you own an estate. I'm the woman who thinks she needs the millions her father left her, but suddenly I'm facing a future of financial ruin. Maybe even bankruptcy. It's like we've traded identities."

She tucked a strand of hair behind her ear. Grant studied her posture, trying to read it. The woman mesmerized him. He wanted to understand her, even though at times like this it seemed impossible. Traded identities? He couldn't fathom it. How would it feel to be rich? To value wealth? To *need* money?

And how would it feel to lose that bulwark of security?

"You know what's even odder?" Alexandra said, turning to him. "I'm sort of getting used to the whole idea of not having money. I'm thinking I'll just be a regular person from now on. Average. I'll shop at outlet malls, and I'll buy bedsheets stamped *irregular,* and I'll get my hair done at one of those places where you don't need an appointment. I'll be like everybody else and buy frozen dinners . . . and . . . and drugstore sunglasses . . . and . . ."

Her shoulders slumped. She sank down onto the wide windowsill and stared at the parquet floor. "You don't want things," she whispered, "and I can't imagine life without them. The picture looks so . . . bleak."

Grant walked over to her and knelt at her side. He took her hand and spread her fingers across his, palm to palm. "Things can't fill a life," he said. "Not my life anyway. People can."

She shook her head. "I told you I don't trust people. My father—"

"Your father was wrong, Alexandra. I'm sure he was a good guy, great businessman, made lots of money. But he was wrong about people. If you keep following his advice, you're going to find out what emptiness really means."

He paused a moment and studied the miracle of her hand pressing against his. By all logic and common sense, Alexandra should be on a plane to New York right now. But she was here—warm, real, alive. Again, Grant's anguished prayer of the night before echoed back through his thoughts.

Had that prayer breathed in torment actually been heard? Was this moment his answer?

"Take Jesus," he murmured. "Alexandra, you talk about him as though he's real to you. It's like he's a force in your life—someone even more important than your father. But his teachings, his stories, his life weren't about things. They were all about *people.*"

"But Jesus knew that people would let him down, Grant. One of his own inner circle betrayed him to the authorities. Even Peter couldn't come through for his master. When a serving girl asked Peter if he knew Jesus, Peter denied him three times. Everybody failed Jesus, Grant. Everybody."

"Yeah, and he died for them anyway." He let out a low laugh. "I've got no business preaching to you, but even a guy like me can see that Jesus had his focus in the right place. Sure, people let him down. They betrayed him. Some of them eventually killed him. But he loved them all, Alexandra. He loved them so much he was willing to die for them. Wasn't he?"

Her blue eyes fastened on him. "Sometimes you scare me to death, Grant Thornton."

"Likewise."

Tillie's laughter filtered through the cavernous house. "There's stuff in the attic, Grant! Oops!" She came to a halt just inside the living-room door. "Sorry, didn't mean to interrupt."

"Whoa," Graeme said, peering around his wife at the couple by the window. "Leave a tender moment alone, Tillie-girl."

Mama Hannah's dark face peeped out from behind

Graeme's broad shoulder. "We will go outside and look at the garden," she said.

"It's all right." Grant stood and brushed off the knees of his jeans. "I want to get back to Tillie's apartment and arrange transportation to my camp. It's time I headed home."

"But, Grant," Tillie exclaimed, "you should at least take a look in your attic! It's full of things. All kinds of great stuff!"

Grant looked at Alexandra and cocked an eyebrow. "Things? Stuff? Miss Prescott, I believe that's your territory."

She laughed. *"Au contraire.* I'm a woman under conviction." She held out her elbow. "Dr. Thornton, please take me away from this earthly paradise before I fall any further under its spell."

"This way, my dear." He linked his arm through hers and escorted her toward the door.

Behind them, Tillie gave an exasperated sigh. "You guys are weird, you know that? Really weird."

"A perfect duo," Graeme said.

"Ehh," added Mama Hannah.

Through a dusty bus window, Alexandra watched Mount Kilimanjaro slowly rise to dominate the landscape. After a restless night struggling with her fears and worries, she had awakened with the firm decision to accompany Grant back to his campsite. From there, she planned to join a walking safari—part of her original itinerary. If nothing else, the activity would keep her mind off her concerns.

Earlier that morning she had telephoned the police, who

agreed to turn her protection over to Grant Thornton—though they wanted her to check in with them on a regular basis. Then she called the United States consulate and the travel agency. When everything was in order, she and Grant said reluctant good-byes to the McLeods and Mama Hannah. Then they took a taxi to the Nairobi bus terminal.

Alexandra had thought the train was crowded, but after interminable hours on the jam-packed bus, she doubted she would ever get the kinks out of her back and stand up straight. "How much longer?" she asked over the muffled roar of the engine.

"The bus stop is just ahead. We'll have to walk to camp." Grant brushed at the powdery red dust that had settled on her cheeks and nose. "Think you're up to a hike?"

"The last time I walked to your camp it was a grueling marathon in blistering heat."

"Only a couple of miles this time." He glanced down at her rubber sandals. "And now you've got those great shoes."

"I call these my Firestones. You know, 'Where the rubber meets the road.'" At his blank look, she giggled. "Boy, are you out of it, Grant. That's an old tire slogan. I mean really old."

"I guess I'm a regular Rip van Winkle. You could probably carry on an entire monologue, and I wouldn't have a clue what you were talking about. Home shopping network. Thigh toners. It's a foreign language."

The bus pulled to a stop, and their fellow riders made way as Grant and Alexandra struggled down the aisle with their baggage. They stepped out into the searing late afternoon, and Grant gave the driver a wave.

"*Asante sana, bwana,*" he called. "*Tutaonana.*"

"*Kwaheri daktari na bibi!*" The driver grinned as he shifted the bus into gear. "*Mungu akubariki!*"

When the bus pulled away in a cloud of red dust, Alexandra shouldered the single satchel into which she had condensed her luggage. "Hey," she spoke up as she started down the path, "who's speaking in a foreign language now? Thigh toners won't do me a lot of good out here, but Mungu-angu-bangu sure has been popular."

"*Mungu akubariki.* It means God bless you."

"*Mungu a-ku-bar-i-ki.* God bless you." As relief at escaping the confines of the bus surged through her, she threw back her head and whirled around in the sunshine. "*Mungu akubariki!*" she called up into the brilliant blue sky. "Hellooo, Africa! It's me, Alexandra. *Mungu akubariki,* everybody!"

Grant gave her a questioning look, but she didn't care how silly she appeared to him. It felt great to be off that bus. Great to be back in the open air. Great to be free of the constant threat of attack, to be rid of ever-lurking guards and police reports, to be with Grant. She paused and glanced at the man who was striding along the path like some modern-day David Livingstone.

Grant was the best part of all.

Thank you, God, her heart sang out. *I don't understand why I'm still in Africa . . . or what I'm supposed to do next . . . or what plans you have for me. But thank you! Thank you for this moment. Thank you for Grant Thornton.*

"There ought to be a song about that mountain," she said as she appraised the snowy peak. "I'm going to make one up and shout it at the top of my lungs."

"No fears about Jones jumping out of the bushes?"

She sobered for a moment. "Jones. Do you think he really did leave Kenya?"

"I hope so. But I'm not letting down my guard, just in case he's still in the country."

"Well, tough beans if he is." She swung around again. "At this moment, I feel like I could haul off and knock that jerk straight to kingdom come. Just let him set a foot on this path, and he'll regret it."

Chuckling, Grant scratched his chin. "All right then, get set to shout. There's already a Swahili song about Mount Kilimanjaro, and here it goes. Are you ready?"

"Let us go to heaven," she said, repeating Mama Hannah's phrase.

Grant taught her the chant, a trilling cry echoed by a low-pitched response. By the time they spotted the campsite in the distance, they were singing so loudly even the flies were reluctant to bother them.

"Kili!" Alexandra shouted.

"Kilimanjaro," Grant echoed in a deep bass.

"*Mlima!*"

"*Mrefu.*"

"*Mlima.*"

"*Mrefu.*"

And they sang together on the grand finale—"*Katika Africa!*"

"Now I know three Swahili words," Alexandra said as they sauntered the last few yards toward the tents. "*Mlima* means 'mountain.' *Mrefu* means 'tall.' And *katika* means 'in.' And that doesn't even include *Mungu akubariki,* 'God bless you.'"

"I award you an A-plus on your first lesson." He squinted toward the campsite. "Hold up a second—who's that?"

Alexandra stiffened, fear knifing through her. In the long afternoon shadows cast by the acacia trees, she couldn't distinguish anything unusual. "Where?"

"Beside my tent." He stepped protectively in front of her. "Who's there? *A-ing'ai o-ewuo?*"

"*Nanu kewan*—Kakombe."

"It's Kakombe," Grant said, relief evident in his voice. "My buddy from the *kraal.*"

He slung an arm around Alexandra's shoulders and strode toward the tents. The lanky young Maasai man emerged from the gloom to greet them with outstretched hands. He and Grant spoke quickly. Alexandra recognized the mention of Mama Hannah, and she noted the discussion of the missed *Eunoto,* but she could make neither head nor tail of the rhythmic Maasai dialect.

Instead, she studied the body language of the two men. They chatted rapidly and with eager animation, their words overlapping as they finished each other's sentences. Kakombe often touched Grant on the arm or hand, a gentle gesture that expressed total confidence in their relationship. Grant laughed easily, now and then laying a hand on his friend's shoulder. Though the men were as comfortable together as brothers, they could not have been more opposite in appearance.

Grant wore his Levi's and chambray shirt like a second skin. His sun-streaked brown hair clustered at his collar in a rumple of loose curls, and his only adornment was a ball-point pen stuck in his pocket. The tanned arm that hung over Alexandra's shoulder glistened with pale, coarse hair, and a utilitarian watch glinted at his wrist.

Kakombe—a dark mocha to Grant's paler latte—was draped in bead necklaces, chokers, and earrings. Chalky paint, elaborately streaked to reveal the dark skin beneath, covered his arms and legs. His hair had been parted from ear to ear and then tightly cornrowed to create a magnificent ocher-plastered headdress. In his right hand he carried his six-foot spear and a long peeled stick. With his left, he pointed repeatedly in the direction of the *kraal*.

"Alexandra, you won't believe this!" Grant exclaimed suddenly. "The elders decided to postpone the *Eunoto.*"

"Really? That's great!"

"No, that's *unbelievable*. Maasai warriors have been gathering at the *kraal* for some time. The ceremony was set to go off as scheduled. But when I left for Mombasa with you and Mama Hannah, they decided to put the whole thing on hold. In fact, they're not going to start anything until after the next rainfall."

"Grant, they're showing you the greatest respect."

"Kakombe says the elders want me to record the ceremony. With many of the Maasai children attending school now, and more and more men going to Nairobi to work, they're afraid the traditions might be forgotten."

"So you're more than a friend to them. You're their historian."

"Kind of an intimidating thought." He gave her a warm smile. "I'm glad they waited—you're going to be knocked out by the ceremony. You'll see things no white woman has ever seen before. You won't believe how detailed—"

"Grant." She stopped him by stepping out of his

embrace. "I'm probably . . . well, you know I might be gone by then."

"*Kaji negol?*" Kakombe asked, motioning to his friend for an explanation.

Grant's eyes narrowed as he translated Alexandra's words. At their conclusion, Kakombe let out a universal expression of disgust. He pointed at Alexandra, then at Grant as he uttered a lengthy response to the news that she would be leaving Kenya soon.

"Kakombe tells me that Sambeke Ole Kereya and the other elders have issued you a formal invitation to the *Eunoto,*" Grant explained to Alexandra. "They liked your song about Zacchaeus and the way you came to Mama Hannah's rescue the night of the attack. The elders are insisting on your presence at the ceremony. Kakombe doesn't think they'll understand your hurry to leave."

"Please tell them my home is in New York," Alexandra said. "I have a job at a design firm in the city. I have to work."

Grant translated for Kakombe. At the African's response, he gave a slow grin. "Kakombe says a woman's work is to milk cows and plaster the house after a hard rain. He wants to know how many cows in New York are demanding your attention."

Alexandra shrugged and let her satchel sink into the long dry grass. "Just tell him that if I'm still in Kenya at the time of the next rainfall, I will be honored to attend the *Eunoto.*"

She dragged the heavy bag toward the tent that she and Mama Hannah had shared. In spite of the joy she had felt at returning to this place with Grant, she could taste the uncertainty of her situation like a bitter lemon in her mouth. She lifted the tent flap and ducked into the shielding shadows.

Evidently the Maasai had tried to reassemble Grant's camp after Jones's attack. The cots were back in place, the blankets spread, and the pillows stacked. Alexandra searched the tent in the dim light until she found a lantern and a box of matches. After lighting the wick, she sat on her cot and tugged off her sandals.

Images of past days flashed into her thoughts. With them came questions that flapped at her like dark-winged bats. Nick Jones—*die by a knife or a rope?* Mama Hannah—*be bold or give the Lord control?* James Cooper—*be rich or poor?* Kakombe—*design fabric or milk cows?* Grant Thornton—*stay in Kenya or go back to New York?*

No, that last dilemma was a figment of her imagination. Grant had never asked her to stay. He enjoyed her company, and he seemed pleased that she had returned with him to the bush. And he had made a vow to protect her.

Alexandra twisted the simple band on her finger, considering Grant's gift. No, she shouldn't read more into the ring than was intended. Grant wasn't the kind of man to make a permanent commitment to anyone or anything—except his work. Even the house he owned in Nairobi sat on its weedy lot like an orphaned child. He didn't want the rootedness it stood for—just as he would never seek the obligations of love.

Love? The word flashed at Alexandra like a neon sign. Did she love Grant Thornton? Startled at the unexpected image—and the terrifying appeal it held—she gripped the aluminum cot frame. No, she didn't love him. Surely not.

They were too different, worlds apart—work, lifestyle, interests. They didn't even believe in the same God.

"Oh, Lord!" Alexandra slipped off the cot and sank to her knees in prayer. "Lord, I'm so scared. I've never known anyone like Grant. I've never cared about a man the way I care about him. Why is this happening to me? Are you trying to teach me something? Father, don't let me love Grant. Please keep my heart safe."

She clasped her hands together, knitting her fingers so tightly the blood stopped. "You know I've worked hard to do the right things, Lord," she murmured. "But I'm so confused. I worked at my art so I wouldn't rely on my father's wealth and end up putting my faith in his money. I wanted to use the money for something good, and I thought you were leading me to build the design firm. But now it's gone. Why did you take that away from me?"

She paused, waiting in the silence of the tent. Then she went on. "I tried to trust people, Lord—and I ended up with Nick Jones. Then I tried not to trust—and I wound up with Grant."

She swallowed hard. "No, I haven't wound up with Grant, have I? I think you're asking me to let go of that money and to let go of Grant. Is that it, Father? Is that what you're asking of me? To stop trying so hard . . . to stop wanting so much . . . and to just surrender?"

For a long time, she listened to the wind rustling through the acacia leaves in the trees overhead. *Be silent,* the whispered voice drifted through her. *Be silent, and know that I am God.*

As Grant stacked wood in the outdoor stone hearth, he studied the silhouette inside Alexandra's lamplit tent. She was praying—*on her knees*. Did people really do that?

The way her clenched hands pointed upward sent a surge of emotion through his chest. Alexandra's shoulders slumped; her posture showed anguish that echoed his own that night in Tillie's apartment. What was she saying? What troubled her so deeply that she had fallen to her knees to express it?

He struck a match and lit the dried kindling beneath the logs. As the bits of grass and bark crackled into flame, he settled back on his haunches and pondered the woman inside the tent. Alexandra was praying—not just as a release of tension, not as a gesture of habit, not even as a form of meditation—but because she *believed someone was listening*.

He lifted his focus to the stars overhead. Odd. In spite of his years of doubt and his reams of research, Grant had a growing sense that Alexandra was right. Someone *was* listening.

Odder still, someone had actually heard Grant's own prayer. In the old Jewish writings, that someone called himself *I AM*. In Christian Scripture, he was the Alpha and the Omega, the beginning and the end. He was the Creator, always present, always listening, always caring. God.

Grant stood and gave the snapping fire a prod with his boot. Sparks shot up into the blackness. Oddest of all— every time Grant acknowledged the presence of God, that aching place inside him felt a little less empty. Not full, not healed, not even comfortable. Just a tiny bit easier.

Pondering the significance of this realization, he walked to his tent and rummaged around for a cooking pot and some plates. Too bad Mama Hannah had decided to stay with Tillie and Graeme. Alexandra would have to make do with canned soup instead of the savory stew that was Mama Hannah's specialty. On the other hand, Grant thought as he loaded his arms with supplies, Mama Hannah had suffered a pretty bad wound to the head. She needed to rest, and Tillie could use her help when the baby came.

When Grant stepped out of his tent, he saw Alexandra standing beside the fire. She had pulled on a long skirt that nearly touched her ankles. Its hem fluttered in the breeze that drifted down from Mount Kilimanjaro, and she had drawn a sweater around her shoulders to keep off the chill.

As he approached Alexandra—this woman God had somehow permitted to remain in his life—a knot like a fist lodged in Grant's throat. Hearing his footsteps, she turned, and her skirt swirled softly at her calves. A smile lit her face.

"The chef emerges," she said.

He tried to find a lighthearted response. Instead, he set the pots and cans on the ground. Then he straightened and pulled her into his arms.

"Alexandra," he managed. "What can I say to make you stay?"

"Oh, Grant." Tentatively, Alexandra's arms slipped around the broad chest of the man who held her. She laid her head against his shoulder. "Grant, please don't ask me to stay here. Don't make this hard."

"It's already hard."

"It's impossible. We have to think of our meeting as a kind of bump in time. An event that happened to teach us something."

"What have you learned?" he asked, stroking her hair with his hand. "Tell me, Alexandra, because I'm more mixed-up right now than I've ever been in my life."

She closed her eyes, trembling at the sensations rocketing through her. Just to be in his arms . . . to hear his voice against her ear . . . to know the touch of his fingertips . . . How could she blithely fly away and pretend she had felt nothing for this man?

"I'm confused, too," she admitted.

"Then stay. Stay until we've worked it out."

"What are you asking from me, Grant? You know I can't live at this camp with you in some sort of indefinite relationship. I won't walk away from the moral standards I follow— no matter how tempted I might feel."

"That's not what I'm asking from you, Alexandra. I don't want you that way." He swallowed hard. "That's a lie. I *do* want you—in every way a man can want a woman. But I haven't had time to examine and define how we can make this thing between us work. I don't yet know how we can blend our lives, our jobs, our beliefs. I'm just asking you to stay until I figure it out."

"Until you have us analyzed?" She fingered the curl that drifted against his forehead. "Scientific deduction won't help you on this problem, Grant. There's too much separating us. I've done a lot of thinking about this, and I've come to realize it's not really our jobs or our backgrounds that put such a space between us. It's the heart stuff."

"I don't know that I'd agree with you. My heart has been feeling pretty active these days."

She smiled and touched his chest. "I knew you had one in there someplace."

"I've been trying to listen to it."

"I listen to mine all the time, and, Grant, the truth I hear is so clear I can't deny it no matter how much I might want to." She took a deep breath, praying she could speak with grace the words she knew had to be said. "My heart doesn't belong to me, Grant. I gave it to Christ a long time ago. I'm not a paragon of faith by any means, but I do know that I can never be happy with a man who doesn't choose to walk the same path I travel. You can't be happy that way either, trust me."

Before her emotions could spin out of control, Alexandra stepped away from Grant and picked up one of the cooking pots. She opened a can of soup and poured out the contents. After adding water from the jug he had set out, she placed the pot on a flat, hot hearthstone. Then she knelt by the fire and began to stir.

"Tillie warned me about this," Grant said finally. "She told me the religion thing would hold you back."

"She understands."

"Yeah, well, I don't." He flipped a twig into the fire, and a tiny tongue of flame flared up. "What is it with this Jesus Christ, anyway? I wish somebody would explain it to me because the whole thing makes no sense. No sense at all."

Alexandra stirred the soup, her focus on the flames licking the sides of the metal pot. No, it didn't make sense. It couldn't be analyzed or figured out or proved. Understand-ing Jesus Christ took faith—and she didn't have a clue how to explain that to Dr. Grant Thornton.

FOURTEEN

Alexandra woke to the thump of monkeys playing tag on the canvas roof of her tent. In the early sunlight, she watched their scampering silhouettes as they chased and leapfrogged and danced around each other. A soft green light filtered across the tent floor and cast an emerald glow on Alexandra's satchel and sandals.

Oz, she thought. *This is my emerald city. Somehow I've landed in Oz, where everything is different. The essence of wickedness is after me, and it's going to take more than a bucket of water to defeat him. I've met a man with a brain—a man who's badly in need of a softer heart. But where's the yellow-brick road? And how will I ever figure out how to click my heels and find my way back home?*

"Alexandra?" Grant's shadow fell across the tent wall. "You OK in there?"

"I'm fine."

"Sleep all right?"

"Not really." She had stayed up sketching by the fire for hours after they ate, and later in the tent her thoughts had been too tormented to permit much sleep. "How about you?"

"No." He was silent for a moment. "Listen, I'm going to walk over to the *kraal* in a few minutes. I don't want to leave you here alone. Will you come with me?"

She considered his request. Fear of the possibility that Jones still lurked warned her to stay close to Grant and the protection he offered. Fear of Grant—and the effect he was having on her heart—cautioned her to steer clear of the man. The itinerary in her purse gave her one day before the start of her scheduled walking climb of Mount Kilimanjaro. Should she hide for twenty-four hours in her green cocoon? Or should she venture out into Grant's world?

"Still in there?" he called, tapping on the tent wall.

"I'll come with you."

"OK. Ten minutes."

In New York ten minutes would barely have given Alexandra time to start her morning routine—treadmill, shower, blow-dry, dress, makeup, breakfast, train. Inside her emerald Oz, she dressed in a loose skirt, tank top, and sandals, ran a brush through her hair, and was ready to go in seven minutes flat. Grant was waiting with a pair of bananas and a tall glass of water.

"You really ought to get a refrigerator," Alexandra said, taking one of the bananas and the lukewarm water. "In this heat, ice cubes would be a big plus."

"Electricity's a little tough to come by out here."

"I guess so."

"Yep." Falling silent, he started in the direction of the *kraal*. Alexandra walked along beside him, chewing a bite of banana as she tried to absorb the textures of Grant's life in the bush. He had given up things like electricity and running water in exchange for acacia trees, windswept savanna grasslands, herds of zebra and wildebeest, and his precious work. Was the trade-off worth the sacrifice?

Grant strode purposefully, as if oblivious to his companion. The early-morning sunlight cast golden glints in his hair and turned his skin a deep bronze. The mountain breeze blew open his collar, tugged at the sleeves of his loose cotton shirt, and played in his long, loose curls. As a contented expression settled at the corners of his mouth, he drank in a deep breath.

This was sacrifice? No, Grant Thornton didn't need a refrigerator, Alexandra admitted. He was as much a part of this natural land as the baobab trees and the graceful giraffe. Here, in the wild bush country, his roots grew deep. No refrigerator or house—*or woman*—could ever bind him more firmly.

"I found your sketch pad by the fire this morning. I brought it along," he said, indicating the backpack slung over one shoulder. "Thought you might like to draw."

"Thanks." His thoughtfulness touched her. "My creativity's been a little blocked lately."

"Really? I think your designs are good. You captured the country better than I figured you would."

"The country captured me."

He glanced over at her, the blue in his eyes intense. "Has it?"

"More than I thought possible."

She could see the *kraal* in the distance. Two half-naked little boys were leading a herd of goats through the opening in the thorn fence. A spear glinted in the sun. The sound of singing drifted across the open countryside.

"I'm glad you like it," Grant said.

"But I'm not comfortable here in the same way you are. It feels foreign to me. This morning in my tent, I thought of myself as Dorothy in Oz. I'm out of place and out of time. Nothing makes much sense to me. Take the *kraal*, for example. I mean, the houses are made out of cow dung, Grant. The people drink blood. They ream huge holes in their ears. It's all so . . . weird."

He nodded. "And they think *we're* weird. Our women teeter around on high heels, we chew gum for hours on end without swallowing it or filling our stomachs, and we erect multistoried office buildings out of breakable glass."

"Well, I guess—"

"Plus, they think we stink."

"Stink! But we bathe."

"With flowery soap and spicy shampoos. You should hear what they say about that. You wouldn't be flattered." He shrugged. "It's all a matter of perspective."

"If they think we're so strange, then why do they accept *you?*"

"We trust each other." He lifted a hand in greeting as Kakombe and three other warriors emerged through the *kraal* entrance. "Trust goes a long way toward building bridges, you know. You might give it a try sometime."

He left her and strode forward to meet his friends. Alexandra's urge to respond to his comment subsided as she watched Grant lay a hand on Kakombe's shoulder and begin to chat with the men.

Then the truth in his words swept over her and was followed immediately by a wave of remorse. Instead of building bridges, she had built an island—with herself at its protected center. Distrust, wariness, even vanity filled the moat that kept people at a safe distance.

But it was frightening to reach out. She had been warned against it, and experience had taught her the dangers. Even

Grant, who had promised her his protection, somehow had become a threat. He wanted to build a bridge across the moat and enter the island she had created for herself. He wanted her *in every way that a man wants a woman.* How easy it would be to surrender. But if she gave in to her own desires, the results would be disastrous.

Lord, she prayed as she approached the group of men, *how can I love people as you want me to? Show me how to trust the way Grant trusts. Teach me to let down my barriers. And most of all—protect me, Father! Protect my heart!*

"The elders have asked to talk to me," Grant said. "Kakombe thinks they want to try to initiate me during the *Eunoto* ceremony even though I'm not a part of the warrior age set."

Alexandra smiled at the image. "I'd call you a warrior. Or maybe a crusader."

"I haven't killed any lions or raided any villages lately."

You've raided my stronghold, she wanted to say. *You've robbed my peace. You've stormed through my life in a way no other man could.* But she looked away.

"I guess I'll see if I can find Sambeke Ole Kereya," she said. "At least I can talk to him in English."

Grant dug her sketch pad out of his bag. "Use this to communicate. You won't need words." He handed it to her along with her pencil case. "But don't draw the people. The Maasai hate being photographed, and a sketch wouldn't be much better."

Alexandra tucked the pad and pencils under her arm. As she entered the opening in the thorny fence, the earthy odor of cow dung hit her like an ocean wave. Flies settled on her arms and darted around her mouth and eyes. Wood smoke, thick and cloying, drifted into her nostrils. She nearly choked.

A group of children scampered toward her. Half of them were clad in nothing more than a beaded string around the waist, and the other half wore loose, mud-colored togas. Most of the children had runny noses. Flies seeking moisture rimmed their eyes and mouths. A festering wound dribbled pus down one boy's leg.

Dear God, I can't do this, Alexandra thought, glancing behind her for a way of escape. *I'm sorry. I have to get out of here.*

"Um, excuse me," she muttered, swinging around. Determined to make a beeline for the gate, she was stopped by a firm tug on her skirt. When she turned, the boy who had saved her from the wild dogs was gazing up at her with liquid brown eyes.

"Alinkanda," he said, giving her a shy smile.

She swallowed. "Mayani. How are you?"

"Hawayoo," he repeated.

"I'm fine."

Mayani squared his shoulders. "Amfine."

The other children giggled. "Amfine, amfine!" they shouted until Mayani scolded them and gave them a set of severe instructions in the Maasai language.

Then one by one the children obediently presented themselves to Alexandra, heads bowed to receive the blessing of her hand's touch. As she laid her palm on each round, walnut-brown head, the child murmured, *"Na kitok."*

Hoping she wouldn't arouse more laughter, Alexandra tried the greeting she remembered. *"Iko."*

The children made their way through the line in respect-ful submission. But the moment the formal greeting was complete, they rushed to begin a bold exploration of her clothing. They pulled out and snapped the knit fabric of her tank top. They lifted her skirt to peer at her calves. They poked the belt buckle around her waist. One child reached up to touch the ends of her hair. Another prodded a small freckle on her arm. A third counted her toes.

"I'm just a regular person," she said. "Like your mother or your sister."

Mayani gaped at her, clearly not understanding a word she'd said. Wishing she had a translator, Alexandra searched for old Sambeke. She discovered him amid the group of elders clustered around Grant. There would be no help from that quarter, she realized.

"*I-lotu,* Alinkanda," Mayani said, taking her hand and pulling her toward one of the low plastered huts. In the scant shade of a scraggly acacia tree sat a group of Maasai women, their legs stretched straight out in front of them, bare feet crossed at the ankles. While stitching intricate patterns of beads onto leather, they chatted, laughed, and kept a watchful eye on their children. Alexandra tried to remember the proper greeting from one woman to another, but nothing came.

"*Mungu akubariki,*" she said finally.

The women laughed in delight, and Alexandra found herself grinning widely. She had spoken in Swahili, but they understood! Feeling as victorious as she had the day she'd sold her first line of fabric designs, she seated herself among the women in a space they created for her.

Two of the toddlers crawled into their mothers' laps.

Despite the flies, the women cooed and babbled in universal "mommy" language and kissed their little ones on the cheeks. Mayani crouched beside Alexandra, nestling as close to her as he could. After rubbing the golden hairs on her arm with his small, dark fingers, he laid his shaved head against her shoulder.

"*I-saen,*" an elderly woman said to Alexandra. She held out a handful of beads—red, white, blue, orange, green.

"*I-saen,*" Alexandra repeated. "Beads."

The women chuckled with pleasure at her efforts to speak their language. Shyly, but with obvious pride, they began to display their handiwork. Alexandra could hardly believe the fabulous patterns these women had worked onto stiff cowhide. One young woman showed a belt she had beaded in primary reds and blues with a hint of green for contrast. Reminiscent of Native American handicrafts, the belt incorporated geometric designs in a rich, primitive pattern.

"It's beautiful," Alexandra said, half forgetting in her amazement that they couldn't understand her. "This belt would be wonderful to wear. I can picture it on a great-looking denim dress accented by a pair of tooled-leather western boots. You know who would love to put your belt on one of his runway models? Ralph Lauren."

The woman giggled. "Rafloren."

Alexandra laughed. "That's right. Ralph Lauren."

Another woman held up a choker she was beading. Again, the bold design astonished Alexandra. She examined the ostrich-eggshell central medallion from which hung a short silver chain and arrowhead. "This is amazing," she said. "It's very good."

"Rafloren?" the woman asked.

"Very Ralph Lauren."

As the Maasai women handed her their delicate earrings, bracelets, and necklaces, she shook her head in wonder. Not only had they incorporated beads, they also had added cowrie shells, bone, snipped tin, chain, and wire. "This is more than a craft, you know," Alexandra said. "This is art. You are artists."

The women stared at her unblinking, uncomprehending. Finally, they took back their beadwork and resumed stitching. But the elderly woman who first had spoken with Alexandra pointed at her sketch pad. *"A-inyoo enda?"* she asked.

More wary than she'd ever felt at displaying her portfolio to a clothing designer, Alexandra began to turn through the pages. What would these women think? Would they laugh at her splotches of color and her attempts to capture the essence of their land?

She pointed out the hues of the ocean, the sunset, the dappled green leaves on the tent canvas. Brows drawn together in concentration, the women scrutinized Alexandra's work. They touched the bold colors and then examined their fingertips. They discussed the sketches among themselves and, shaking their heads, seemed to come to the conclusion that their guest's book was a mystery.

Resigned, Alexandra turned to the picture she had been working on the night before. She had sketched the big acacia that grew between Grant's two tents, a huge, yellow-barked fever tree with spreading branches and spiky thorns. It rose umbrella-like across the white page in a detailed execution of each color, line, and shadow nuance.

"Ol-tarara!" the old woman cackled, pointing to a similar tree that grew inside the kraal. *"Ninye* Rafloren!"

"Rafloren!" the other women agreed as they took the sketchbook and passed the picture around. "Rafloren!"

Alexandra laughed. "Thank you very much. Would you like me to draw something for you? How about those beads?"

Opening her pencil box, she focused on one of the flat beaded collars around the elderly woman's neck. She selected the bright primary colors and began to draw. Within moments, the women were exclaiming with delight as the necklace appeared on the white paper. When it was finished, Alexandra tore off the page and gave it to the woman.

"Ashe nalang!" she said in thanks.

Another woman handed over the armband she was beading. Alexandra spent the rest of the morning sketching page after page of beadwork. Some women wanted to keep the reproductions, but others turned shyly from the gift. As they beaded and chatted, Alexandra worked to capture in her sketchbook the patterns of their bright red togas and the beautiful chocolate shades of their skin.

By the time Grant wandered over, she had all but forgotten the pungent odor of her surroundings. She was even oblivious to the flies that settled on her white paper to rub their front legs and air out their wings. In fact, Alexandra almost felt as if she'd stepped into one of her mother's tea parties—ladies sitting around doing needlework and exchanging the latest gossip. Despite the morning heat, she and her congenial hostesses had been sipping tin mugs of fragrant amber tea thickened with milk and sugar. Alexandra had decided its smoky flavor topped any tea she'd ever tasted.

Mayani was curled up against her side, a piece of sketching paper on his bare thigh as he tried out her colored pencils. He had copied her detail of some of the beadwork, and now he was attempting to draw her rubber sandal.

"*Noo kokoo,*" Grant said, greeting the older women.

"*Iko.*"

"Alexandra, this is Kakombe's mother." He introduced the elderly Maasai who had first displayed her beads. "*Ng'oto* Kakombe."

"*Pa-oing'oni,*" she said.

"What did she call you?" Alexandra asked. "Was it that *he of the white behind* thing?"

He chuckled. "Unfortunately, I acquired another nickname by giving her a gift one time. It's a Maasai tradition to refer to people by the name of the animal they offered you."

"So what did you give her?"

"A bull."

"Bull, huh?" Alexandra said, the corners of her mouth twitching.

"No wisecracks, please." He hunkered down beside her. "So, what have you been up to while I was getting roped into the initiation ceremony?"

"Art." She pointed out the beadwork and sketches. "These women are so talented. They're wonderful."

"You're wonderful with them."

Blushing in spite of herself, Alexandra held up Mayani's drawing. "Look at this. He reproduced my shoe on paper. It's not perfect, but he's getting the idea."

"Mayani's crazy about you."

"He's so comfortable with me. I'm sort of amazed. And you know what? I'm comfortable, too."

"You fit, Alexandra."

"Maybe."

"So stay."

She gripped the pencil in her hand. "Grant, please."

"Please stay."

Dismayed at the intensity in his words, she searched his eyes. *Yes,* her heart answered him. *Yes, I'll stay. I'll stay here forever if it means I can look into your face and listen to the sound of your voice.*

But such an act would be rash. Impossible. She glanced around at the circle of women as if their strength could lend her support. Their dark eyes flashed back and forth between the young couple. *Yes,* the women seemed to be urging her. *Do this. Give your life to this man.*

"I'm . . . um . . . I'm thinking about getting back to the camp," she fumbled. "I'd like to rest up for the climb tomorrow."

"All right." Grant stood and stretched, easing the tension of the moment. "The elders have offered lunch, but I'm guessing you'll want to pass."

"Actually, a banana sounds pretty good right now." Alexandra rose and looked around at the assembled group. The children were coming to their feet, ready to accompany the visitors to the gate. Alexandra scanned their faces. "Grant, what happened to that little boy's leg? The wound is infected."

"Thorn," Grant said. "It's been getting worse by the day."

"Why don't you do something? You should take him to a doctor."

"I never interfere in their lives."

"This wouldn't be interference. It would be *intervention.*"

"I'll help when they ask, but they probably won't say anything until it's too late." His face grew somber. "The boy's father died last year, and his mother is blind. She has very few cattle and no money. She'd never be able to afford medicine."

"But that's exactly why the child needs your help. Look, I'll donate the money for medicine. What would it take— a few dollars? The boy could lose his leg if somebody doesn't do something."

"Go ahead."

"Why won't you get involved, Grant? These are *your* people, not mine."

"Why aren't they yours?"

"I hardly know them, for one thing. And I don't speak their language. I'm not . . . I'm . . ."

She glanced around at the faces, women who had welcomed her so warmly, children who already accepted her. Maybe they weren't her people, but they belonged to God. *"He made us, and we are his."* Wasn't that what the Bible said?

"I'll get the money as soon as we're back in camp," she said. "But I still don't understand why you won't do anything to help. That doesn't fit with what I know about you."

He said nothing as they left the women and waved fare-well to the elders. But when they had stepped outside the *kraal,* Grant turned a harsh glare on Alexandra. "What do you really know about me and the way I live my life?" he demanded. "Tell me."

"You've said a hundred times how much you care about these people." Alexandra jammed her hands into the pockets of her skirt. "If you really cared, you wouldn't stand around and watch them die."

"That's the way it works. Dying is part of living."

"But look at the way they live! They have absolutely no sanitation. No running water. No sewage system. Do they even have soap? I doubt it. The flies are crawling all over the children's eyes—and you can be sure those exact same flies have just been walking around in cow dung. No wonder the boy's mother is blind. I'm surprised they're not all blind. This is appalling, and something ought to be done about it."

"So do something."

"Why don't *you?*"

"Why should I? I'm an observer, a recorder. I'm not here to change things. In making a record of Maasai stories, I've learned to appreciate their way of life. They have a culture—a civilization—that works. It's worked for centuries. Sure, some of them die of injury and disease. And I mourn with them. But I didn't come to upset the delicate balance of their lives."

"Soap would upset the balance? Antibiotics would upset the balance? Come on, Grant. Don't bury your head in the sand like some ignorant ostrich."

"Ostriches don't bury their heads in sand. That's a legend that has no basis in fact."

She stopped, sure that steam was coming out her ears. "OK, maybe I don't know Africa as well as you do, Dr. Thornton. But that little boy shouldn't have to die just because you're a scientist and don't want to get involved. If there's medicine out there that could help him, he should have it. And he will because I'll give it to him."

"When did you start caring so much about people, Alexandra?"

She gulped down the hurt his words evoked. "When I realized they were *God's* people."

"So you're going to throw your money at them? Big wads of American bucks. You think that'll help?"

"Can it hurt?"

"Has all your money ever done you any good?"

As they entered the campsite, Grant left Alexandra's side and set off toward his tent. Frustrated, she kicked at a pebble and sent it skittering across the beaten ground. It bounced into a tin rain barrel with a ping that echoed across the open space.

Grant turned. "Do you really want to help that little boy?"

Breathing hard, she glared at him. "Of course I do."

"Then give yourself to his mother." He strode toward her again, his finger pointed in a challenge. "Live inside her darkened world. Teach her how to make a better life for herself."

"Not everyone can exist out in the bush like you do, Grant. Not everyone can give *themselves* to the Maasai. Some of us have to figure out ways to help from a distance."

"Yeah, but not you. Not you, Alexandra." He stopped a pace away. "You can give yourself."

"Stop trying to make me stay here."

"Stop running away."

"You don't believe I'm trying to escape the Maasai. You think I'm running from *you.*"

"Are you?"

She looked away. "Yes."

"Why?"

"You're the scientist. Surely you can see that the two of us don't compute."

"Alexandra." He lifted a hand and ran his finger down the side of her neck. "What's your *heart* telling you?"

She clamped her hand over his. "Grant," she whispered, "please stop using my words against me."

"You told me to listen to my heart, and it's been getting louder and clearer by the minute. I'm waking up to ideas I've never thought before. Emotions I never knew I could feel. Dreams I didn't know existed inside my head."

"You're scaring me."

"You think *you're* scared?" He drew her close. "Alexandra, last night I couldn't sleep thinking about this thing that's happening between us. I'm going up the mountain with you tomorrow."

"Grant, you can't leave your work again." She shook her head as he pulled her against him. "I'll be with a group. I'll be safe. Safer without you . . . because I can't . . . shouldn't . . ."

Against her intent, she rose into his kiss. Warm, pliant, his lips covered hers, seeking out her response. She slipped her arms around him and drifted in the magic of the moment. His strength enfolded her, a promise of protection. His tenderness seeped through her, a budding blossom of honor. As his fingers slid into her hair and his mouth moved across her ear, she could do nothing but hold him tighter still.

Lord, don't make me leave this man! The prayer escaped her breaking heart. *Take my money. Take my goals and aspirations.*

Take everything but him. Oh, Father, please allow me this love . . . this gentle, beckoning love.

A tear squeezed from the corner of her eye and started down her cheek. His kisses found it, moving from her temple to her eyelid and again to her lips. "Don't cry," he murmured. "Alexandra, I never meant to hurt you."

"I know," she said. "But it hurts. It all hurts."

"Yeah, it hurts." Holding her close, he let out a deep breath. Then he gave a low chuckle. "That word makes me think of Mama Hannah. When I was a kid and I had a cut or a scrape, she'd say, 'If you are hurt, you should pray, *toto*. God will take your hurt, and he will bear it for you.'"

Alexandra dabbed her eye, wishing she could hold back the emotion that had lodged in her throat and tangled her tongue. "I can't pray," she managed. "Can't even talk."

Grant was silent a moment. "I can," he said. "I'll pray." When he began again, his voice was strong, firm, assured. "God, it's me, Grant. I'm talking to you again—and that's something. So, here's the thing. Alexandra and I . . . we could use a little help here. How about it? Could you work this out somehow? We think you can, or we wouldn't ask. That's it."

Alexandra buried her head against his shoulder. "Amen," she whispered.

FIFTEEN

"This is not going to be a leisurely stroll, you know," Grant said as he and Alexandra set off up the gravel road with her tour group just after dawn the next day. He felt more than a small measure of concern for his traveling companion's well-being. "The altitude is over nineteen thousand feet at the top of that thing."

"That thing," she retorted with playful disgust, "is called Mount Kilimanjaro, and I know how high it is. I signed up for this tour, didn't I? I read all the brochures, and I've been using my treadmill and thigh toner faithfully in preparation for this climb."

Thigh toner. Grant grinned to himself as he tried to imagine any exercise contraption that could prepare a person for a hike up Mount Kilimanjaro. Sure, Alexandra had prepared the paperwork details of the climb. In fact, she and Grant had spent the previous afternoon in Oloitokitok meeting her tour leader, arranging visas to cross into Tanzania, paying necessary fees, and obtaining permits to scale the mountain.

But Grant had made the ascent of Kilimanjaro three times in his life, and he knew it was a grueling trek that could challenge even the fittest athlete. The first day required a climb of two thousand vertical feet to an altitude of nine thousand feet. The second day would take the climbers to thirteen thousand feet. But it was the climb from that point on that had defeated many an intrepid mountaineer.

Grant didn't have high hopes for the success of the group of gawking tourists that made up Alexandra's expedition. One of the three men chain-smoked his way through the tropical forest, dropping cigarette butts onto the path. Another appeared to be at least ten years into retirement. Though he was fragile, his white-haired wife plunged ahead with all the enthusiasm of a teenager. Her friend, a plump lady with platinum hair, snapped photographs of everything from Grant's Land Rover to a warthog that trotted across the road.

Alexandra was the youngest and fittest of the group, and her energy buoyed the others. In the time he'd known her, Grant had never seen her so elated. He knew part of her confidence came from the certainty that if Jones still lurked, he could never make it through the border crossing into Tanzania without capture. The guards were on the alert, carefully checking every passport and visa. So she was free—truly free.

Swinging her arms, Alexandra strode up the thickly forested incline. Just ahead of Grant on the narrowing path, she pointed out bright birds, monkeys, and trees overgrown with vines. Every time she spotted the volcanic peak of Mount Kilimanjaro, she exclaimed in delight. "There it is! Look, Grant! There it is!"

Grant preferred the view closer at hand. Alexandra's blonde hair swung at her neckline, bouncing in time with her jaunty walk. Her waist narrowed into the belt of her khaki shorts, and her long, tanned legs were bare except for the thick socks bunched at her ankles. She had traded her tire sandals for a pair of sturdy hiking boots, but they did little to detract from the overall portrait.

"Lunchtime!" Alexandra sang out as the tour leader headed the group off the main path and up a trail to an icy stream. As they emerged into a clearing, Alexandra linked her arm through Grant's. "You know what?" she said. "This is the best thing I've done since I came to Africa."

"Lunch?"

She swatted him. "No, this climb. I feel like I'm back on track now. This is where I was supposed to be, what I had planned to do all along. Jones is like a bad dream."

"Oh yeah? Then what am I?"

Her blue eyes sparkled. "A good dream."

Unsure of the correct response to that comment, Grant seated himself on a fallen log and opened the box lunch provided by the tour. Alexandra dug out a boiled egg and began peeling. He studied her slender fingers as he bit into his chicken sandwich. Chewing, he pondered her words.

"I don't want to be a dream," he said finally. "Dreams vanish."

She leaned against his shoulder and nibbled on her egg. "I think my money was a dream, and I have the oddest intuition that it's all gone now. Somehow James Cooper has managed to sell off Daddy's stocks. Either that or someone else has invaded the portfolio. I think I'm broke. But you know what's really weird? I feel free."

He wished he could share in her elation. "I still don't like being lumped in with the dream of Jones and your vanished money."

"Don't you get it? I've surrendered, Grant. That money was such a weight, such a responsibility. In a way, it hung around my neck like a millstone. I felt like I had to find some means of honoring my father's memory by investing his legacy in the best possible manner. Now I can honor him with the way I live my life—with the choices I make."

Grant downed the last of his bread crust. What choices would Alexandra make? If she had surrendered her money, had she also given up her goal of founding a big design firm? Did that freedom she felt include the independence to make a new life in a different land? And could she ever commit herself to a man she considered an illusion, a temporary mirage?

He didn't get his answers. The tour guide roused the sleepy group, and they set off again. Almost immediately the groans began. "I can't breathe," the smoker complained. "Can we slow down a little?" the portly lady puffed. And it went on. "My legs hurt." "I have a headache." "Are we nearly there?" "How much longer?"

Grant's lungs felt as if they were bursting from the strain of breathing the thin air. His calves complained, and the soles of his feet ached. Alexandra stopped swinging her arms. Her hair no longer bounced. She sucked in deep breaths, pausing gratefully with the rest of the group every few hundred feet.

When the expedition reached the first camp—a simple stone building at the edge of the rain forest—everyone collapsed to the ground gasping. Grant tried to cover his amusement as he helped the tour guide and porters carry sleeping bags and backpacks into the hut. After a supper of hot soup, which the hikers devoured like ravenous hyenas, the whole group crawled gratefully into separate bunks.

Grant lay awake listening to the snores. Even in their

sleep, these folks couldn't breathe worth a flip. He doubted the chain-smoker would last through the next day. Alexandra slept in a lower bunk across the room. He studied her profile lit by the single gas lantern, and he fell asleep wondering how it would feel to lie beside such a woman every night of his life.

The next day everyone rose with the sun, ate quickly, and began the trek up a narrow, slippery path through dense forest. The four-thousand-vertical-foot hike demanded caution and vigilance. Grant pushed himself upward, occasionally using branches and vines for leverage. Sucking in deep breaths, Alexandra fell completely silent as she made her way over roots that stuck out into the muddy path.

When a cold, misty rain began to fall, the whole group turned somber. Anoraks and sweaters grew wet and heavy. Mud clung to boots, weighing everyone down and making the climb even more tedious. The few glimpses of the peak the thick forest had allowed vanished as a wreath of gray clouds enveloped the mountain.

Just when Grant was sure a mutiny was about to break out in the ranks, the forest ended. The timberline looked as if it had been drawn with a ruler. As the sodden group stumbled out onto a wide-open grassland traversed by crystalline streams, the sun peeped through the clouds and began to burn off the steam.

The tired travelers found a new spurt of energy. But in the oxygen-deprived atmosphere, their enthusiasm didn't last long. When they stopped for lunch, Alexandra flopped out on a rock and shut her eyes.

"The terrain is alpine at this stage," Grant said, hunkering down beside her and popping open a can of sausages.

"That's the amazing thing about East Africa. You can go from sea level to savanna to rainforest in a matter of miles. On the mountains, you can experience alpine terrain, and there's tundra up ahead. When we get to the stony scree near the summit, you'll think you're on the moon."

Her eyes slid open. "Wonderful."

He grinned. "Air up there's almost as thin as the moon's. Everyone will be throwing up. You'll think you're going to die—or wish you were already dead. But, hey, why am I telling you all this? You read the brochure."

She groaned and curled into a ball. "Shut up, Grant."

"Weenie?" he asked, offering his fork. When she squeezed her eyes tight and shook her head, he chuckled. "Alexandra, you're amazing. And you know what I've been thinking?"

"What?" she mumbled.

"I've been thinking about that prayer of mine. Maybe there's been a plan for us all along. Look how things have worked out. You've realized you don't need your money, and you've given it up. I've admitted science doesn't have all the answers, and I've come to believe there really is a God. We've discovered a sort of compromise, a happy meeting place. And up here on Mount Kilimanjaro, we're finding the real treasure we've both been looking for all our lives. Each other."

Drinking in a breath, Alexandra pushed herself up into a sitting position. Tucking her hair behind her ears, she regarded him with sapphire eyes. "Grant," she said, and her voice sounded too much like a teacher's to make him comfortable about what was to follow. "Grant, admitting there's a God isn't enough."

"Why not?" That had been a monumental step for him to take. What more could she want? "I said I believe, Alexandra. I *believe*."

"Even the demons believe there's a God . . . and they tremble in terror." She stretched out her legs and rested her forehead on her bent knees. "Oh, Grant, you have to go a step beyond belief. You have to surrender."

"What do you mean, surrender?"

"Admit your mistakes. Your sins. Ask for forgiveness. Give up trying to run your own life. Turn around, start traveling a different road."

He prodded the sausages with his fork. That *was* a step beyond belief. A big step. Was he willing to take it?

"There's more to this than just acknowledging God," Alexandra said. Her cheek lay against her knees, and her blue eyes searched his face. "Lots of people talk about a higher power—Hindus, Muslims, New Agers. But I've given my heart to Jesus Christ, God the Father, the Holy Spirit. My faith is not general. It's specific. And I have a strong feeling that you and I . . . that we . . . we're not together, Grant."

He tossed his empty can into the cardboard lunch box. "I need more time. Time to sort it out."

She nodded, but the fading light in her eyes said more than her words ever could. There wasn't enough time, enough faith, enough hope to bridge the gap between them.

Maybe there wasn't even enough love.

"Add miracles to the list of things in which I now believe," Grant said as he and Alexandra sat beside a tiny campfire at two o'clock on the morning of their fourth day on Mount Kilimanjaro.

After trekking across the alpine grassland, they had spent their second night in a tin-walled hut at thirteen thousand feet. The next day the party clambered up and over rock-falls, through dry streambeds, and across prickly scrub grass. Frigid air nipped their aching lungs. At midafternoon, they reached the saddle between Kilimanjaro's two peaks, Mawenzi and Kibo.

Although the saddle was flatter and the climbing easier, the stony scree made for rough going. Gasping for oxygen, the climbers followed a rhythmic pattern—struggle forward a few feet, pause panting, rest ten minutes, stand and totter a few more feet before collapsing to the ground again. Despite nausea and headaches, everyone managed to make it to the last hut at sixteen thousand feet.

"Did you notice Hubert yesterday?" Grant whispered to Alexandra beside the fire. She was sipping a cup of luke-warm coffee as she shivered beneath a blanket. "I bet he threw up fifteen times."

She covered his mouth with her hand. "Please, Grant. I'm barely keeping this coffee down as it is."

"But the guy's been smoking two packs a day, and he's still with us. It's a miracle, Alexandra."

"So, now you believe in God *and* in miracles. Will wonders never cease?"

He chuckled. "Maybe not."

Grant knew the best part of the climb was yet to come, and he was looking forward to spending it with Alexandra. She, too, had amazed him. Though her face turned pale and she couldn't sleep at night, and her fingers were too cold and cramped to sketch, she marched doggedly onward. Long ago Grant had realized the woman was tougher than she looked. But this was conclusive evidence of the stubborn determination and sheer willpower that had brought her through two encounters with Nick Jones.

"You know something?" he said. "You're gritty."

"What did you expect?" she retorted. "I haven't had a bath in days. Neither have you, for that matter."

He laughed. "I mean you're strong. Determined. I like that."

"I get my mule-headedness from my father." She lifted her focus to the moonlit sky. "Daddy wasn't a quitter. When things got tough, he got tougher. That's part of the reason he was such a success."

"Grit is a good legacy to leave. Better than money."

She nodded. "You're right, Grant. I thank God for my father and the things he taught me." She paused a moment, and her voice was wistful when she spoke again. "But he was wrong about people. I was wrong about them. Somehow . . . I want to be more open. Even though it might hurt, I want to trust. I just wish . . ."

"What, Alexandra? What do you wish?"

"I wish you could be around to help me work on that. You do it so well."

"Stay with me."

She shut her eyes, and the muscles in her face tightened. "Grant, you don't know how hard this is."

"Guess again. I'm dying inside, and it doesn't have anything to do with the altitude."

He took her hand as the tour guide began to round up the weary travelers for the final ascent. Abandoning their packs and sleeping bags at the third hut, the group donned parkas, gloves, mufflers. As they started forward, their destination emerged. Ahead in the moonlight a cinder cone, an impossibly steep slab of solid black, rose two thousand feet into the night sky.

"Wait a minute," Hubert, the chain-smoker, panted, coming to a halt. "We're not climbing *that*, are we?"

"Don't worry," Grant said. "The path zigzags."

The man turned toward him, his eyes dull. "I'm not going."

"Sure you are, buddy. All you have to do is walk twenty feet one way, turn, and walk twenty feet the other way. Then do it again. It's not a problem."

"No," the man said firmly. "I . . . can't . . . breathe."

"None of us can." Grant slipped his arm under Hubert's. "Come on, we'll make this a team effort."

Alexandra hesitated only a moment before taking the man's other arm. "You can do it, Hubert."

Coughing, he took a tentative step forward. Then another. Grant had forgotten how terrifying the cinder cone could be. It was so steep, so dizzying, that one look down could send a person reeling with vertigo.

Gasping, panting, sucking in one chilly breath after another, the travelers ascended the zigzag trail. By the time they were halfway up, Grant considered each footstep a major victory. Hubert dragged his feet over a stony rock, then through a patch of snow.

"Snow in Africa," Alexandra mumbled.

"Another miracle," Grant managed.

Her smile carried him forward the next half mile. With each labored footstep, he played Alexandra's words over and over in his mind.

You have to go one step beyond belief. You have to surrender.

One step beyond belief. To surrender.

One step beyond.

Surrender.

Surrender.

How to surrender? What to surrender? Grant studied his boots as they crunched down on black cinder. *Surrender the things that stand in the way. Pride. Self-reliance. Intellect. Arrogant doubt. You stand in the way, Grant. You depend on yourself. Depend on Christ. Surrender.*

Why?

For Alexandra? To make her stay.

No. That couldn't be the right reason.

Grant's lungs were bursting with the effort to breathe. He could hardly hold onto Hubert. Gritting his teeth, he took another step. Everything inside him ached. Most of all, his heart ached.

That was why he must surrender. To fill his heart. To heal the wounded emptiness. To bring hope into the wasteland.

A hot tear trickled down his frigid cheek. *Yes, God. I want to surrender. I will surrender.*

I do surrender.

Grant reached the last switchback and turned to start up the final few yards. *Turn onto a new road,* Alexandra had said.

As his feet took the final steps to the peak, his resistance broke. *Jesus Christ, I surrender. Guide my feet on this new road.*

And then they were there—all of them—standing at the summit and staring down into the wind-whipped crater of the dormant volcano, Mount Kilimanjaro. Hubert burst into tears. Alexandra hugged him. Everyone shook hands. Cameras snapped. The tour guide passed around a flask of coffee. Then everyone sank to the ground to await the sun.

Alexandra snuggled down next to Grant, a little apart from the others, and kissed his cheek. "Miracles," she whispered.

Grant had the strangest sensation he was floating. But it wasn't the altitude. It wasn't even the woman beside him, though he took her hand and folded it within his own. He had expected surrender to bring darkness. He had anticipated a heavy depression at the death of what he had treasured most—the well-integrated sense of himself. The baring of his heart and soul should have brought despair. Instead, he soared.

The stars faded. The moon slipped away. Pink light filtered across the eastern sky, banishing the blackness. An orange hue washed in behind the rose. And then the sun emerged—brilliant rays of burning gold. The snow turned to diamonds.

Grant stared, transfixed. Awed. Humbled. His own significance paled in the glory of God's majesty. Tears streamed down, and he couldn't make them stop. Didn't care.

"I love you." Alexandra's words barely registered.

God loved him. At this moment nothing more mattered to

Grant. He understood; his vision was clear; he saw the road ahead.

"I don't know what to do about it," she murmured into the wind. "I can't figure out how to make my feelings for you OK, but I need to tell you. Grant, I love you."

He bent and kissed the chilly wool of her mitten. How could he speak? How could he convey what was in his heart—for her and for his Lord and even for himself? Wrapping his arms around her, he buried his face in her hair.

Alexandra had said she loved him. Another miracle. A miracle so rare, so precious, the words of response failed to form on his tongue. He kissed the silky strands of gold and held her so tightly she could probably feel the beating of his heart.

"Alexandra," he tried. "I need . . . need to say . . ."

Whoops of celebration shattered the moment as a second group of climbers emerged at the crest. Grant fell silent, observing the repeat of tears, photographs, and hugs. One of the newcomers, a burly fellow in a heavy parka and ski mask, pumped his fists and managed to do a modified victory tango. Grabbing a female climber, he swung her around twice and gave her a big kiss.

Grant smiled, his own heart brimming with joy. "Alexandra, something happened to me," he began again. "Climbing the mountain, I . . . saw . . . I understood . . . the reason—"

"Look, everybody!" their tour guide shouted. "The clouds!"

Grant and Alexandra scrambled to their feet. The thick mist that had wreathed the mountain had begun disintegrating rapidly in the early sunlight. As the clouds parted, a sweeping vista unrolled like a carpet. Greens, browns, and golds wove into rich brocade patterns. Villages nestled among patchwork fields of corn and beans. Like thin silver threads, distant roads crisscrossed and then forked into channels of rust red dirt. As far as the eye could see, this majestic Eden rippled on and on, finally fading into distant shades of olive, blue, and purple.

"Where's my camera?" someone cried.

The stunned awe vanished as suddenly as it had come. Climbers began vying for the best and highest spots from which to photograph the scenery. Not far from Grant and Alexandra, the burly fellow dug around in his backpack and began fitting pieces of his camera together.

Standing behind Alexandra, Grant held her close, sheltering her from the chill wind whipping across the mountaintop. He had to tell her what had happened to him, had to find the words. For a man whose life had been consumed with choosing the right phrases to convey folktales of mystery and wonderment, he was at a loss to explain the puzzling miracle that had just occurred in his own life.

Paradoxical phrases tumbled around, tangling his tongue. *Surrender had brought victory. Death had led to new life. Sacrifice had allowed healing. Darkness had transformed into light.* Ironic. Confusing. The experience of transformation defied analysis and explanation, yet it demanded revelation.

Grant took a deep breath.

"It's about God," he said. "Jesus Christ. Alexandra, a few minutes ago . . . while we were on the last few steps of the cinder cone . . . I finally understood."

"Understood what?" She lifted her head. "Grant, what are you trying to tell me?"

"Surrender. I know what it means. I get it now." Still searching for the right way to explain, he focused on the other climbers in the distance. The burly man had assembled his camera. Now he lifted it and swung it into position.

"I saw my own life for what it was," Grant continued. "The emptiness overwhelmed me and I knew—"

A muffled pop cut off his words. Alexandra jerked backward in Grant's arms. Then she cried out in pain and slumped against him. He turned toward the sound.

A nine-inch silver barrel gleamed in the early light. *It was not a camera.* The burly man held a gun. *Jones*. Recognition dawned slowly in Grant's stunned mind. Too slowly. The metal slide on the semiautomatic pistol slipped back to click in another round.

As Jones squeezed the trigger a second time, Grant shoved Alexandra toward the ground. The bullet slammed into her arm, and she lurched. Grant pushed her down and threw himself over her.

Amid a chorus of shrieks, the shooter whirled and fired into the group of terrified onlookers. *Pop, pop, pop.* The climbers began running. Falling to the ground. Diving for cover. Someone sobbed. *Pop, pop, pop.*

Beneath Grant, Alexandra moaned. He shifted, searching for a weapon. Looking for protection. His hand closed on a stone. He lifted it and hurled. But Jones was already scrambling back down the cinder cone, his feet skittering on the loose scree.

"Go after him!" someone shouted.

Another cry. "Somebody help me!"

"I'm dying!"

"Catch that man!"

Grant rolled off Alexandra and scrambled to his feet. *Get him. Get him.* Alone, he started down the wind-whipped cone in pursuit of the gunman.

"Jones!" he shouted.

The hit man swung around and took aim. *Pop, pop.*

Cinders sprayed upward at Grant's feet. He slid to the ground. *Catch him! Get him!* How many more rounds in the pistol? Crawling on hands and knees, he watched Jones race down the slope. In moments the man would disappear into the trees. Impossible to catch him.

An image of Alexandra slumped against him hit Grant full force. He rose unsteadily. Alexandra! Sucking air into his aching lungs, he scrambled back up the cinder cone. No time for the zigzag path. He had to get to her. Had to save her.

At the summit he found a scene of complete chaos. Moaning, crying, the wounded climbers huddled in agony. The uninjured stumbled from one victim to another attempting to help. Grant clawed his way across the loose cinders to the place where Alexandra lay. On her side, she had curled into a fetal ball. Her breath escaped in shallow, wheezing bubbles.

Grant cupped her white face between his hands. "Alexandra, it's me. Talk to me."

"Can't . . . breathe." Her blue eyes slid open. "Help me."

He rolled her over to examine her wound, but what he saw made him draw back in disbelief. The bullet had entered her chest, torn through her lung, and exited her back. Bright blood seeped through the dark hole in her jacket in a widening stain.

Gurgling, she clutched at him. "Grant . . ."

He staggered to his feet. "I need help over here!"

Hubert looked up from the climber whose leg he was wrapping. "What's wrong?"

"Lung!" Grant shouted.

White-faced, his lips an ugly shade of gray blue, Hubert lugged a first-aid kit across the cone. "I was a medic," he puffed, falling to his knees beside Alexandra. "Vietnam. Find me some plastic. Get Vaseline."

Grant tore through his pockets, locating the sandwich bag that held a chocolate candy bar and banana he'd planned to snack on. He shook them out onto the ground and tore open the plastic. In the first-aid kit, he found a tube of petroleum jelly.

"Gotta cover the chest with plastic," Hubert panted as he smeared gauze with the sticky jelly and began packing it into the wound. "Lung is collapsing."

"Grant?" Alexandra gripped his hand, her eyes filled with terror. Pale as snow, her skin was already turning clammy. "Sm . . . smothering!"

"Keep her warm," Hubert muttered. "She goes into shock, we've got real trouble. Body shuts down to keep blood in the heart and head. Wrap her up."

"What about the bleeding?" Grant demanded. "Should I put pressure on her chest?"

"Not the lung. Can't use pressure there. Clamp down on her arm. She's been hit there, too."

Grant grabbed Alexandra's arm. Already her eyes were glazing over. He wrapped a wool mitten around the wound and pressed it tightly. She winced. "Hurts. Can't . . . can't breathe."

"It's your ribs," Hubert said as he worked. "Bone chips in the wound. Punctured the lung tissue. I've packed the bullet hole, and I'm putting the plastic on now."

"Gra . . . ," she mumbled. "Not the blue . . . it's daddy . . . but . . ."

"Don't let her go into shock!" Hubert shouted at Grant. "Get her a blanket. Hold her. Keep her warm. Alert." He pushed himself to his feet. "Five others wounded. Gotta help."

As Hubert staggered away, Grant lifted Alexandra into his lap. Eyes glassy, she moved her lips in random, meaningless messages.

"Ice cre . . . that bell . . . but I don't . . ."

"Alexandra," Grant said. Sick with disbelief, he kissed her icy cheeks and lips. "Alexandra, stay with me. Please be all right." He threw back his head and shouted into the howling wind. "God, let her be all right!"

Sixteen

Alexandra was sure she had died. She knew she had because, first of all, she couldn't breathe. Second, she couldn't hear. Third, she couldn't see. But most significant, she felt no pain.

Floating in a liquid world of soft, translucent bubbles, she knew the certainty of God all around her. Yes, she had been shot in the chest. That truth was evident but completely unimportant. How could such a thing matter? It was nothing at all when compared to the overwhelming sense of glory that surrounded and suffused her.

God held her in his arms, bathed her in his protection, warmed her with his love. In the golden light of the Father's presence, Alexandra felt the power of his Son and knew the holy comfort of his Spirit. Immeasurable joy flooded her body and lifted her soul.

And then she realized she could see again. Distant, beyond a shimmering curtain, she recognized someone waiting for her. More than one. Her mother stood on the shore of a gleaming river. Daddy was there, too. And Grandma Prescott. Was that Uncle Zeke, the ranch hand she had idolized when she was a child?

Hi, Uncle Zeke! Hi, Daddy! Wait for me, OK? I'm coming.

"Alexandra, stay with me."

Who said that? She tried to locate the source of the voice. Someone precious and beloved had spoken those words. All the same, she didn't want to stay. She wanted to go on. She ached to slip through the curtain and cross that shining river in the distance.

Let me go, Lord, she pleaded.

"Alexandra, please. Please don't go."

The words compelled her, but she didn't want to obey them. Joy awaited her on the other side. Peace. Eternity in the Father's presence.

Let me go, Lord. I want to cross over now.

"Alexandra, I love you. I need you. Please . . . please . . ."

Torn, she again searched for the source of the voice. It was a treasure. An earthly treasure, to be sure, but that voice was valuable to her all the same. Wanting it made her tremble inside.

But, oh, Lord, I want to go on with you even more. Please allow me to cross the river.

In response to her plea, a voice that was beautiful, powerful, dear, and intimately known echoed through her soul. *Not yet, my beloved child. In time I will welcome you into my arms . . . but not yet.*

"Alexandra. Alexandra."

No, Father, don't send me back! She reached for the shimmering curtain, trying to hold onto it. But it faded to a gray mist that lifted before her eyes. Acacia trees formed a canopy over her head. White clouds like puffs of cotton hung in the thorny branches.

"Alexandra? Are you awake?" Grant Thornton's face appeared where the trees had been. Eyes filled with unspeakable torment, he gazed down at her. "Are you here with me?"

At his words, pain rushed in a torrent through Alexandra's body. She convulsed in agony and grasped again for the blissful curtain. Instead, Grant gathered her close, his strength enveloping her.

"Don't go, Alexandra," he murmured in a ragged voice. "You have to stay with me until we can get you to a hospital. Can you hear me, my love?"

Oh, Grant, she tried to say. *You don't know where I've been! If you had seen that river, you wouldn't beg me to stay. If you had felt the arms of God as I did, you'd never want to leave them.*

"Everything's going to be all right now," he was saying, as though he hadn't heard her. "The tour guide radioed Amboseli for a plane. We're not far from my campsite, and the plane should be here any minute. We got you and the others down the mountain about half an hour ago. Six of you were wounded. You were hurt the worst, but you're going to be OK, Alexandra. Can you hear me? You're going to be all right."

The searing pain in her chest and shoulder belied his words. She *wasn't* all right. Somehow she had been forced to leave that golden place and return to the ache and fear and uncertainty of this life. Why? Why was she here—and how could she bear the agony?

"We'll be flying into Nairobi," Grant said. "The hospital already knows about you. In an hour or so, you'll be in surgery."

Surgery? Alexandra opened her eyes again. *But I just want to rest, Grant. Let me sleep, OK?*

"I called Mama Hannah and Tillie from Oloitokitok,"

he went on. "They'll meet us at the hospital. We'll take care of you. You'll be fine."

The last of his words were drowned by the throb of propellers beating the air, the roar of an engine, and the shouts of welcome. Grant settled Alexandra on a sleeping bag beneath the acacia tree and vanished from her side.

She couldn't take much air into her lungs, and every breath hurt beyond belief. She thought about not bothering with the effort. If she could just rest completely, just stop the trouble of breathing altogether, she might be able to get back to the shining river.

But Grant appeared again, and with him were several people she didn't recognize. They all spoke at once, giving each other directions, pushing on her, lifting. In a blaze of white pain, she moved through space until she was hauled up a flight of steps and loaded like an old carpet into the belly of the airplane.

Someone moved over her in the dim light. Was it Hubert? She tried to smile, but he was squeezing on her arm and pushing at her chest—which didn't seem very kind considering how much it hurt. And then he stuck a needle into her hip. *Oh, Hubert, did you have to do that?*

"Listen, Alexandra," Grant said, suddenly appearing above her. "The pilot just told me there's not enough room for me on the plane. It's already overloaded with the six injured, and we want to send Hubert to keep an eye on everybody."

His warm hand touched her cheek. "Gra . . . ," she managed.

"Shh. It's OK." Struggling for control, Grant bent down

and gently kissed her lips. "Tillie and Mama Hannah will meet you at the hospital in Nairobi. And I'll get there as soon as I can. I love you, Alexandra."

Oh yes, she wanted to say. *Now I understand why it wasn't time. Now I remember why I came back. For you. I want to live this earthly life with you. I love you, Grant.*

But he was gone. The airplane door shut, the engines rattled to life; the plane shuddered as it moved down the bumpy roadway.

"We're going up now." Hubert took her hand and patted it. "We're flying. Before long, you'll feel good again—maybe better than you've ever felt."

Alexandra stared up at the row of narrow lights on the airplane's ceiling, and she thought about that shimmering curtain. One day—maybe very soon—she'd go back there. And that would be the best place of all.

Grant knotted his fists and choked back a cry of rage. The tiny airplane skimmed toward the clouds, fading to a mere whine in the distance. Around him, the uninjured climbers were getting back into the waiting Land Rovers. Subdued, nervous, they hardly spoke. Grant couldn't blame them. The group had endured shock, unexpected terror, and helplessness.

"*Ol-oibor siadi.*"

The voice behind Grant startled him. A dark hand gripped his shoulder as he jumped and swung around.

"Kakombe? Oh . . . . it's you."

"*E-miureishoyu*," Kakombe said, reassuring his friend that there was no need to be afraid.

"How did you find me here?" Grant asked in the Maasai tongue. Once the two groups of climbers had made it on foot down to Oloitokitok, they had driven to the meeting place designated for the airplane sent from Amboseli. The pilot had known of a stretch of deserted roadway flat enough to accommodate a landing and takeoff.

"In the *kraal,* we learn of many things." Kakombe stood at Grant's side to watch the Land Rovers pulling away from the landing area. "She of the long legs was injured?"

Grant nodded. Wrestling with his memories, he pictured the moment when Jones had pulled the trigger. From that instant—through countless hours as the climbers labored to bring the victims to safety—until this moment, Grant had not allowed himself time to think or even to feel. Now his anger flooded in.

"Her enemy shot her," he ground out. "The man who attacked my camp many days ago."

Kakombe leaned on his spear. "And how was this enemy killed?"

"He wasn't killed. He escaped."

Kakombe let out a whistle of disbelief. "Then we must find him, my friend. We must put him to death."

Grant rubbed the back of his neck. There was nothing he'd like better than to see Jones get his just deserts. But his focus was not revenge.

"I have to go to Oloitokitok again and speak to my sister on the telephone," he said. "I want to make sure Alexandra is safely in the hospital. Then I must drive to Nairobi. She needs me."

"This is good. I believe you have given Alinkanda the silver chain. She will be your wife."

Grant shoved his hand down into his pocket and touched the chain. "I don't know what will happen about these future matters, Kakombe. I know only one thing. I promised to protect Alexandra, and I failed her. I have to go and be with her now."

The Maasai warrior regarded the plumes of red dust rising from the road as the Land Rovers threaded their way toward the main highway. "Night comes soon," he said. "That wicked man will try to make his escape from the forests of Kilimanjaro soon. Will you permit your enemy to flee?"

"My first responsibility is to Alexandra."

"Yes, you wear her blood on your hands and your shirt. Your love for her is great. It is for this reason you must destroy her enemy. Only then will you truly protect her. Only then will she welcome you to the doorpost of her hut."

Grant let out a hot breath. How could he tell his friend what had happened to him as he climbed to the summit of Mount Kilimanjaro? How could he explain the treasure he had found there? Unexpected peace in the face of turmoil now filled his heart—and it lessened his need for vengeance. Sure, he was angry. Enraged. But his focus was on Alexandra. On a new life and a new path.

"Here is a good plan," Kakombe said. "Go to your camp and fetch the things you need for your journey. I will return to the *kraal* and summon the warriors. We will all drive up to Oloitokitok. There—at the edge of the forest—we will begin our search for the enemy of your woman. We will track him like a rogue bull elephant. And we will find him."

"Kakombe, I must drive to Nairobi tonight."

The Maasai frowned. "This evil man cannot be allowed to go free. Like a mad elephant who attacks a *kraal,* he has touched many lives with his wicked actions. Do you not know that this man shamed all Maasai people when he tied the great warrior Loomali to the tree in your camp? You are our friend, the adopted son of our tribe. Do you not know that your enemy attacked *us* when he attacked your mother? Do you not know that he wounded *us* when he injured your beloved woman, Alinkanda? Yes, we warriors have discussed this dangerous man. We have decided he must taste the bitter medicine of justice."

Grant understood enough about the Maasai way of thinking to know Kakombe spoke in deadly earnest. But he had to think of Alexandra. Had to get to her as soon as he could.

"Will you permit that enemy to track down your woman once again?" Kakombe asked. "Will you permit him to kill Alinkanda?"

"I will never allow that. But, Kakombe . . ." Grant paused, searching for the words to explain himself to his friend. "Today, on Mount Kilimanjaro, I met God—the one, true God. I heard his voice, and I asked his Son, Jesus Christ, to enter my heart and direct the path of my feet. So, how can I take the death of another man into my own hands? Justice must be brought by God."

A broad grin spread across Kakombe's face. "Oh, my friend! This is the way my father has also chosen—a worthy path indeed. But now you must go to your camp. I will return to the *kraal* and summon the warriors. We will meet soon and drive to Oloitokitok. Perhaps there the justice of God himself will rain down upon the wickedness of our enemy."

Grant lifted a hand in farewell as his friend loped away. Filled with a sense of mission, the young warrior would not rest until the honor of Loomali had been restored and the attack on "Alinkanda" had been avenged. As much as Grant loved the Maasai, he knew he would never fully understand their ways. Nor they his.

All the same, one God had created them both. One God loved them both.

"God," Grant said aloud, "please keep her alive. Don't let Alexandra die!"

A small brown face materialized above Alexandra. Sharp brown eyes sparkled amid a wreath of wrinkles. A bright scarf in a pattern of lemon yellow and blue provided a jaunty contrast to the scar that ran along one cheekbone.

"They have not permitted me to return the blood you gave me," the old woman said solemnly.

"Mama Hannah?" A warm tingle ran down Alexandra's spine. "Is it you?"

"Do you know another who looks as I do?"

Alexandra tried to smile. "No, it's just . . . where am I?"

"In the Nairobi hospital." Tillie McLeod's face appeared beside that of Mama Hannah. "You've just come out of the recovery room. You arrived here earlier this evening. They had you in surgery for a while, trying to stabilize you. How are you feeling?"

"I can breathe better."

"They reinflated your lung. By the time you got here on the plane, the whole thing had collapsed."

Alexandra shut her eyes, remembering the pain and panic of suffocation. "Where's Grant?"

"He's at his camp. I'll talk to him when I get back to the apartment. He said he'd call me later."

Alexandra tried to process the information. Grant wasn't with her. He hadn't come. Why not? She loved him. She wanted him beside her. But maybe he didn't feel the same way.

"Is he coming here?" she asked.

"I'm not sure. There really wouldn't be much point." Tillie glanced at Mama Hannah. "Alexandra, the surgeon who stabilized you wants to evacuate you to the States immediately. He's working right now on setting you up with a pulmonary specialist in Dallas."

"Dallas? But I'm . . . I live in New York."

"Alexandra, the bullet caused a lot of damage. You're going to need more surgery and the best care available. We just can't provide that in Nairobi. But you're going to be OK. Really."

"Jones?"

Again, Tillie looked at Mama Hannah. "That man has not been captured," the older woman said, laying a warm brown hand on Alexandra's cheek. "But do not fear. He will be far from you."

"An official from the U.S. consulate is sitting out in the waiting room," Tillie went on. "He's cleared all the paperwork to get you on the first flight out. In fact, there's already a plane scheduled for you. An ambulance will take you to the airport in a few minutes."

Alexandra searched the two worried faces that hovered over her. Jones didn't concern her much. Even her own health seemed oddly unimportant. But Grant . . . What about Grant?

"You'll be happy to hear this," Tillie said. "The consulate got word from the FBI that your stockbroker has been apprehended."

"James Cooper."

"That's the guy. They nabbed him on some kind of embezzlement charges. Right now, they don't have any solid evidence that he hired Jones to kill you, but they think they can show he was messing around with your stocks."

"The money of which you like to think," Mama Hannah said.

"I don't care about that money anymore," Alexandra whispered. "I surrendered it."

"Ehh, this is of God. And the dying of which you also think?"

Alexandra shut her eyes. "I used to be so afraid of death, Mama Hannah. I wasn't afraid to be dead—I knew I'd be in heaven. But I was frightened of the actual *process* of dying. I didn't want to go through it." She opened her eyes and held the old woman in her focus. "I'm not afraid anymore."

"You have found peace."

"Surrender."

"A difficult thing," she said. "Yet, such joy it brings when we surrender all to Jesus. All, my dear Alexandra. *All.*"

Mama Hannah's benevolent face was replaced by that of a

frowning African in a pale green cap. "Miss Prescott, I'm Dr. Karanja, your surgeon. How are you feeling?"

"I've felt better."

"Indeed." The flicker of a smile crossed his lips. "You will be escorted to the airport by a gentleman from the United States consulate. He will accompany you to Dallas, Texas, where you are scheduled for further surgery. A former instructor of mine will perform the surgical reconstruction necessary and will see that you obtain the finest medical care and therapies available. Do you have any questions, Miss Prescott?"

Grant, she wanted to ask. *Where is Grant? When will I see him again? What's to become of this ache in my heart?*

"Very good, then," the doctor said. "The airplane cabin will be fully pressurized, of course, but you may continue to experience some pain in your lung. I do not anticipate any further collapse of the organ. The wound in your arm also may give you a measure of discomfort. I suggest you attempt to rest as much as possible during the flight. I've prescribed some pain-relieving medications to be transmitted to you through your IV. Should these prove insufficient, you must inform the consulate representative. He has my instructions to assist you in all matters."

"Thank you," she managed.

"My best wishes to you, Miss Prescott," he said. "And I hope you will not hold our country responsible for the misfortunes you have endured during your visit."

"No . . . of course not." She was still speaking as the gurney on which she lay began to roll.

As the doctor vanished, Mama Hannah's face appeared

again for a moment. "Good-bye, Alexandra. May God hold you in the palm of his hand."

And then Tillie. "Get well, Alexandra! We'll miss you."

As she approached the doorway, another face materialized. "Get better, Alexandra," Hubert said, his eyes filling with tears. "Thanks for helping me up that mountain. You and Grant are the best. The best."

You and Grant. You and Grant. Alexandra saw the starry sky unroll over her head before she was lifted into the back of a waiting ambulance. As the sirens began to whistle and the lights flashed on and off, she watched the stars of the Southern Cross gradually fade in the pink light of dawn.

"What do you mean she flew to the States?" Grant bellowed into the telephone.

"Stop shouting at me, Grant Thornton!" Tillie hollered back. "What's so hard to understand about what I said? She flew to the States. She needs more surgery in Dallas."

"Dallas!" he roared.

"I'm going to hang up in two seconds, big brother."

"OK, I'm sorry. Just tell me what happened." Grant shoved his free hand into his pocket and knotted the silver chain in his fist. "Start at the beginning."

Tillie recounted the events from Alexandra's arrival on the small plane, through the time of her surgery and recovery, to her departure at dawn. "I haven't slept all night, Grant," his sister said, "and I've been having these annoying contractions—"

"Contractions!"

"Stop shouting!"

"Where are you? Are you still at the hospital?"

"I'm at the apartment, Grant. *You* called *me,* remember?"

"Does Graeme know about the contractions?"

"Will you just calm down?"

"You're about to have a baby!"

There was a long silence on the other end of the line. Finally Tillie's voice began again, this time soft and almost fearful. "I'm . . . I'm, uh . . . sort of losing some water all of a sudden. I didn't think it was . . . I mean, I've had contractions before . . . but . . . but . . ."

"Tillie? Are you there?"

"We're having a baby!" Graeme shouted into the line. "We're having a baby!"

A clunk sounded at the other end. Grant raked a hand through his hair. "Tillie!" he demanded. "Graeme—what's going on?"

"Good-bye, *toto,*" Mama Hannah's voice came on suddenly. "We will go to the hospital again. You must pray for your sister. And be sure to eat a good breakfast today. No Kit Kat bars."

The line went dead. His heart racing, Grant set the receiver on its cradle. Outside the shop where he had used the telephone, a group of Maasai warriors awaited him. Standing straight and tall, their spears upright, they stared at him. Kakombe stepped forward.

"Come out now, brother," he said in the Maasai tongue. "Tell us the news of Alinkanda."

Grant stepped into the pearly light. "She has returned to America."

Kakombe's eyes narrowed. "She has left you because you allowed her enemy to injure her."

"No, she went for treatment of her wounds."

"Wounds can be treated in Nairobi. There is strong medicine in that place."

"There is stronger medicine in America."

Kakombe looked highly skeptical of this news. It was clear he regarded Alexandra's disappearance as a direct result of Grant's failure to perform his role as warrior and guardian. "If the elders learn of this," Kakombe said, "it is possible they will not permit you to enter the *kraal* at the time of *Eunoto*. You must prove your worthiness by capturing the enemy of Alinkanda and returning her to your camp."

Grant shook his head. "My sister is giving birth now. I must go to Nairobi to be with her."

At this, the men in the group began to whistle their disapproval. "A man should never go into the hut of a woman who is giving birth," Loomali said, stepping forward. "That place is for women only. I believe you give us an excuse in order to avoid the true task of a warrior."

"Our customs are different from yours," Grant began. How could he explain to these men his need to be near his sister and his mother? He wanted Mama Hannah's wisdom. He needed Tillie's love. Even the companionship of Graeme McLeod would be welcome as he began walking the new path onto which he had stepped.

"Our friend speaks truth," Kakombe said. "His ways are different. But his ways are also the same. Would not any of us wish to be near his family at a difficult time? As elders, we will be called upon to examine many such problems. Let us look at the situation of our friend. Three things have entered his life. His sister will have a baby on this day. His beloved Alinkanda has gone away to America. And he has met God on the top of Kilimanjaro. Shall we also force him to march with us in our quest for justice? I say no. We shall respect his desire for peace."

Loomali and the other warriors began to confer. Grant stifled his irritation. If they were practicing for elderhood, the debate could last all day. He was about to head back into the shop for supplies when Loomali suddenly tapped the butt of his spear on the ground.

"The choice will be yours, my brother," the Maasai said to Grant. "Will you go away to Nairobi? Or will you go with us?"

"I would ask you to leave this matter to the government," Grant said.

"Never. The honor of our tribe is at stake." Loomali laid a hand on Grant's shoulder. "My brother—go to your people? Or remain one of us?"

Grant searched his heart, trying to pray for an answer. He felt he had just barely turned away from his old beliefs and onto this new road. How could he know the right decision about such a choice?

Was it a choice between forgiveness and revenge? Not really. The Maasai would go after Jones whether he was with them or not. In fact, his presence might serve to temper their anger if they found the gunman. Maybe he could persuade them to hold back their spears and turn Jones over to the police.

So what was the choice? *Go to your people, or remain one of us,* Loomali had said. How easy it would be to rush to Nairobi and the comfort of his family. Without blinking an eye, he could give up this life he had built. Go to Nairobi. Go to the house he owned. Go all the way to America.

Or stay. Live in the bush. Eat poorly. Sleep in a tent. Be alone. Alone.

"The problem you present is like the story of Engipika in the deserted *kraal,*" Grant said, summoning for them the illustration of a man caught in an impossible dilemma.

The Maasai nodded in understanding. Kakombe spoke. "Only you, who know the stories of our people, can bring us understanding—and only you can help us to bridge the river of confusion that surrounds us. Come, my brother, make your decision."

Grant turned inward, trying again to form a prayer. But the answer echoed in the words of his friend—*only you, who know the stories . . . only you . . . my brother . . .*

"I will go with you, my family," Grant said, once again surrendering. "Come."

Kakombe lifted his spear. "We go!" he shouted. "And with our running legs, we sing a prayer for our brother!"

The warriors loped up the dusty road toward the forest. With each step of their feet, they beat out a song.

The one who is prayed for and I also pray.
God of the thunder and the rain,
Thee I always pray.
Morning star which rises,
Thee I always pray.
The Indescribable Color . . .

Grant joined them on the final line. "Thee I always pray."

SEVENTEEN

In New York City Nick Jones might have vanished from the scene of his crime without a trace. But on the slopes of Mount Kilimanjaro, he left a trail as vivid as a series of neon signs. The Maasai warriors found this fact highly amusing.

"Here he walks like a hippopotamus through the mud!" Kakombe cried out at the edge of a clear stream of melted snow that trickled down the mountain. "Our fearsome enemy is nothing more than a fat, waddling hippopotamus."

He threw back his head and blew a spray of saliva into the air in imitation of a hippo spewing water through its nostrils. The other warriors laughed and joined him in mocking their prey. Spears glinting, they began to dance around the obvious boot prints in the sticky black mud.

From the moment Loomali had located the discarded woolen ski mask at the edge of the forest earlier that morning, the Maasai warriors had been onto Jones's every move. The gunman had wandered around for a while at the edge of the forest. During that time, he had left behind a chewing-gum wrapper, a wad of used gum, an unspent round from his pistol, and an empty airline whiskey bottle.

Once he left the forest—which Kakombe decided must have been sometime in the middle of the night—Jones had tripped over a fallen limb and dropped a pen and a small notepad scribbled with bad poetry. He had lost a shoestring in the tangle of a scrub thornbush. And he had tossed a second gum wrapper.

Now the footprints.

"Here he drinks water!" Loomali exclaimed, pointing out marks the man's knees had left at the stream's edge. "But he will be thirsty again soon."

"And hungry," Grant said. "If all he's got on him is chewing gum and candy, he's probably going to head for some kind of a kiosk."

"I cannot believe he will show himself to people after such a terrible attack as that on the mountain," Kakombe said. "I think he will try to travel all the way to Nairobi."

Grant agreed. "He would be more comfortable in a city. He's used to that."

Loomali and the others shook their heads, chuckling in amusement at the notion that such a hopeless bumbler could survive a journey across the plains to Nairobi. After taking judicious sips from their calabashes filled with milk and blood, the Maasai warriors set off again in pursuit of their prey.

As the men loped down onto the open grassland, Grant jogged alongside Kakombe. He was tired from the sleepless night, but the mission to find Jones had begun to consume him as wholly as it filled the chests of his companions. He had not protected Alexandra from injury. He doubted he had even won her heart. But *this* he could do for her. He could capture her enemy. He could save her from any further attacks. With God's help, he would join his brother warriors and bring justice to the wicked.

Equally important, he now understood the incredible

value of human life. Christ loved even scumbags like Nick Jones enough to die on a cross in an offer of salvation from sin. What right did Grant have to cut short any life that might one day claim that offer?

As much as he despised what Jones had done to Alexandra, Grant knew he had chosen to follow the Lord of love. He loved his African brothers enough to join them in their quest. Now Grant had to love his enemy enough to prevent Jones's death at the hands of the Maasai.

"We should be quiet," Grant said. "If he hears us, he'll hide."

Loomali sneered. "Where would he hide that we could not find him? The man is more obvious than Mount Kilimanjaro."

"Maybe so, but he has a gun. He will not hesitate to use it."

"Our brother is right," Kakombe said. "Although the hippopotamus is a fool, he is dangerous. We must take him by surprise."

Loomali conceded, and the men fell silent. As they followed Kakombe through the grass, noting broken blades and footprints in the dust, Grant breathed up a prayer of thanks. A warrior's sense of bravado could outweigh his caution, and if one of these men fell victim to Jones, it would be unbearable.

When Kakombe held out his spear in a horizontal line, the men stopped. Motioning in silence, the warrior pointed in the direction of a cluster of acacia trees. Sitting calmly in the shade, his hair dyed a bright orange, was their hippopotamus.

Nick Jones.

The warriors crouched in the long grass like lionesses on the hunt. "See how he takes off his shirt," Loomali whispered, "like a snake sheds its skin."

Kakombe nodded. "He is hot and hungry. Probably thirsty."

"Shall we wait for him to sleep?" Loomali asked.

Grant had seen Maasai warriors creep up to a dozing Cape buffalo—the most belligerent animal in Africa—and lay a pebble on its back without disturbing the creature. This strategy seemed like a good one when facing an armed man. But Kakombe shook his head.

"He is a fool. He sleeps even when he is awake. We will come upon him from the rear."

"And then we will slit his throat," Loomali said.

"Wait a minute." Grant held up a hand. "I have told Kakombe of my decision to follow Jesus Christ, a man of love. I love you, my brothers, and . . . and I care for the future of my enemy's heart. I cannot allow you to kill him. Besides, if one among us kills the hippopotamus, we will have to explain the action to the district commissioner. The government will not be happy at the death of an American—even such a wicked man as this."

"How will the district commissioner know who killed the hippopotamus?"

"Who but a brave Maasai warrior could track and slaughter an armed man?"

Loomali gave a proud grin. "This is true."

"We must capture him and take him to the district commissioner ourselves," Grant said. "I will be the man to take his weapon."

The warriors studied their white friend, clearly assessing

his ability to perform this most difficult of tasks. "Good," Kakombe announced. "By this deed, you will prove your worth for the *Eunoto*. You will be our leader in this attack."

With one accord, the men began creeping silently through the grass toward the cluster of acacia trees. Heart hammering, Grant led them single file behind the tree under which the bare-chested Jones sat. The man's dyed orange hair was matted with sweat. Flies danced around his face. The pistol lay cradled in his lap.

Grant selected a round stone. Rising to his knees, he heaved it beyond the tree. When it thumped into the grass, Jones jerked upright.

"Who's there?" he called in the direction of the fallen stone. He lifted his gun into position.

Grant tossed a second stone, this time causing it to land about ten feet to the side of the first. Jones leapt to his feet, swung the pistol and fired off three rounds. *Pop, pop, pop.*

Grant glanced over his shoulder to find the Maasai warriors covering their ears in pain at the loud report. Frowning, he beckoned them. Certain they would follow, he charged out from behind the tree and plowed into Jones. The man yelped in surprise as he tumbled to the ground. Grant grabbed for the gun.

Pop, pop, pop. Bullets sprayed harmlessly into the air. Grant smashed his fist into his enemy's nose. They wrestled for control of the weapon as Jones struggled to aim it at Grant. *Pop, pop.* A bullet knocked a chunk out of the thorn-tree trunk.

And then a spear sliced through the air and into Jones's biceps, pinning his arm to the ground. A second spear tore through his pant leg. He let out a scream. Grant jerked the handgun from the man's clutches.

"Take the weapon, Kakombe!" Grant shouted, handing over the gun. "Now talk to me, man. Who are you working for?"

"Get this spear out of my—" He let off a string of cursing.

Grant jerked the spear tip from the man's arm. Instantly Jones rolled to his side and leaped to his feet, tearing open the leg of his trousers. Blood streaming, he took off running.

The warriors let out a whoop of delight and started after their prey. Grant caught up with the group just as the Maasai surrounded their quarry, spears pointed at his chest. Backed against a towering red anthill, Jones had grabbed his arm and was sputtering a string of invective. Spotting Grant, he moved as if to run, and four spears sliced neatly into him—two pinning his arms to the anthill and two immobilizing his legs.

"Get these maniacs away from me!" he thundered at Grant. "They're savages! They're gonna kill me!"

Grant cocked his hands at his waist. "You're the savage, Jones."

"What are they—cannibals or something?"

Grant's translation for the warriors led to a round of guffaws. Loomali opened his calabash and splashed a little of the bloody milk mixture into Jones's face. The man bellowed in terror, writhing against the blades that pinned him to the anthill.

"Look," he blubbered. "I'm just a guy trying to make a living, you know? I write poetry—ask Miss Prescott."

"You don't deserve to speak her name," Grant growled.

"Hey, I didn't have nothing against the lady. I was just doing my job."

"Who paid you to kill her?"

"I don't know his name. Honest."

Grant knew the man would not hold out long. "I guess you realize your predicament here," he said. "All we have to do is walk away and leave you impaled on this anthill."

"Anthill?" Jones's eyes bulged. "You mean like in the movies? Where the ants come out and . . . and . . ."

Grant considered informing the man that these ants were harmless termites and wouldn't be interested in his fleshy hide. They were nothing like the voracious safari ants that moved in long, black columns over dead birds and picked them clean to the bone. Termites were more interested in wood. But already Jones's imagination had taken over, and he began to writhe in terror.

"What's that?" he screeched. "Is there one on my neck? I feel something crawling down my collar!"

Grant inspected the fly that had lit on the gunman's sweaty flesh. "You've got trouble there, for sure," he said in a grim tone. "Won't be much longer until they start to swarm. It could get pretty uncomfortable for you before the end. But, hey, if you don't want to talk—"

"James Cooper," he blurted. "The guy's a stockbroker in New York. He was pulling down some kind of scam on the lady—putting her money into a phony account or something. Ow! The ant bit me! Look, you gotta get me off this hill!"

Grant plucked a termite from the mound and dangled it between Jones's eyes. "So James Cooper contacted you?"

"Not him." He was sobbing now. "He knew a guy who

knew me. I got half the money up front—plus the plane tickets and expenses. But I don't care about the rest of the dough. It don't matter to me. Just get me out of this godforsaken country."

"This is a God-*blessed* country, and don't forget it. Now tell me your real name."

"Sam. Sam Jones."

"That's not what Alexandra called you." Grant lowered the termite. "Full name."

"Frank Jones."

Grant let out a breath. "You give me your name or you die." He placed the termite on the man's eyelid.

"Ow! Ow! OK, OK—it's John Franklin. I swear that's my name. Look, take out my driver's license. My passport. That's my name, OK? Get that ant off me!"

Grant brushed the hapless termite to the ground and dug in the man's pocket for his wallet. Without bothering to check data that he knew could be fake, he slipped it into his own pocket.

"Well, Franklin, or whoever you are," Grant said, "I'm thinking I'll just leave you here. You deserve to have jackals tear you to pieces and vultures pluck out your eyes. Did you know a lion's tongue can lick the skin right off your body—while you're still alive? But they prefer to go for the throat. One bite will crush your windpipe—"

"Don't do that to me! I swear I'll spill the beans on Cooper and everybody in the deal. You'll get everything you need to know. Just let me go! I'm bleeding to death here already!"

Grant pondered for a moment. Then he turned to the warriors and spoke in Maasai. "Set free the hippopotamus."

Loomali stepped forward. "This man shamed me. Brother, permit me to slit his throat."

"If you kill him, he will not be able to speak the truth about those who wanted to kill Alexandra. God forbids me to kill—and because I love you, I cannot allow you to make such a mistake. What other form of justice will satisfy you, my friend?"

"In Maasai tradition, this man would owe me many bullocks."

"How many?"

Loomali considered. "Forty-nine."

"Forty-nine is the payment for murder."

The warrior smiled. "You know our ways too well. Thirty bullocks will satisfy me."

Grant took out his captive's wallet and removed enough money to pay for the cattle. Jones wailed that he was being robbed, blubbered about the ants he was certain were swarming to devour him, and mumbled at the disastrous turn of events.

"I shoulda stayed in New York," he groaned as the warriors pulled their spears from his arms and tied his hands behind his back. "Why'd I ever come here?"

Grant tore strips from one of the warriors' togas and tied them around his captive's wounds. "We will take the hippopotamus to the lodge at Amboseli," he said. "It is not far from this place."

"Africa," Jones muttered as Loomali and Kakombe prodded him forward with their spears. "What a terrible place."

Grant raked his fingers through his damp hair and started walking. How could Alexandra feel any different about the country in which she had experienced such pain and fear?

How could she think kindly toward a continent that had permitted three encounters with death?

Alexandra would never return to Africa, Grant realized as he sipped from Kakombe's calabash. And how could he ever leave?

Alexandra stretched out in the hammock that swung between a couple of big Texas pecan trees and tried to sleep. Two weeks had passed since her surgery at the hospital in Dallas. As she recuperated on the Prescott family ranch south of the metropolis, she did her best to put the past behind her.

"Do you want the newspaper, Miz Prescott?" Uncle Zeke's son now managed the small spread. Carrying a pile of mail in his arms, Pete ambled toward the hammock. "And you got a bunch of them padded envelopes from New York, too. You want me to put 'em in the house?"

Alexandra sighed. "I'll take them here."

"Okeydoke." Pete set the mail beside her and flipped open the Dallas paper. "You want me to read you the weather again?"

"No. It's OK." She paused, struggling. "Well . . . just tell me if it rained yet."

"It's seventy-six degrees in Nairobi," he said. "And sunny."

Alexandra stared up at the leafy pecan branches. She had to get past this compulsion to read the world's weather listings every day. It would rain in Kenya one of these days. The *Eunoto* would take place. Grant Thornton would attend. Life was going on there without her.

"That weather over there in Africa sure troubles you, Miz Prescott," Pete said, pushing back his straw hat and scratching his forehead. "Them folks havin' a drought or somethin'?"

"No, it's just that rain is necessary to them. . . . See, I've been thinking about this little boy with a bad leg. . . . I met a wonderful old lady I might never see again . . . and there was this man who . . . oh, never mind." She swallowed hard and tried to force a smile. "Thanks, Pete."

"Sure." He jammed his hands down into the pockets of his jeans. "Miz Prescott, I don't mean to pry into your bidness or nothin', but Josefina's been goin' half crazy over all them telephone calls comin' into the house. She's threatenin' to quit, and the hands ain't too happy about losin' such a good cook. I was just wonderin' if you'd mind talkin' to some of them New York folk that's been callin' here day and night. I mean, you got messages from doctors, lawyers—you name it. The mail's been pilin' up, too, and all you got the gumption to do is ask me to read the Africa weather report." He sucked in a breath that swelled his chest. "Well, I'm just wonderin' if you might ought to pay your doctor another visit. You got the blues badder'n I ever saw 'em."

Alexandra shut her eyes and struggled to hold back the emotion. "I'm just so . . . lonely."

"Aw, Miz Prescott, I bet you are."

"I never knew how it felt to be connected to people. I miss . . . everybody."

"Why don't you give 'em a call? There's folk up in New York just about to go crazy to talk to you. From the messages Josefina's been takin' down, looks like they caught the feller that plugged you. And they got the snake that hired him to do it. I reckon every lawyer in the big city wants to handle your case. And there's some lady askin' for your artwork, too. She's been pitchin' a downright hissy-fit to get her hands on some designs she says you promised her. Shoot, you got enough people wantin' a piece of you to fill up this whole ranch."

They all wanted a piece of her, Alexandra acknowledged. That was right. They didn't love her for who she was—as had Sambeke, Mayani, Mama Hannah, Grant . . .

Had Grant ever truly loved her? Alexandra studied the cowboy whose brown eyes reflected his concern. Of all the calls and letters that had come in, none had been from Grant. Even if he had loved her—just a little—it hadn't been enough to forge an unbreakable bond between them. He had let her go back to the world in which she had insisted she belonged. And he had stayed in his world.

She had surrendered her need for her money. She had worked through her fear of death. Now she must submit to the Lord her aching passion for Grant Thornton.

"Just let me know what I can do for you, Miz Prescott," Pete said. "You want Josefina to bring you some lemonade—nice and cold?"

Alexandra shook her head. "Thanks anyway, Pete. Tell Josefina I'll come to the house in a while and start answering those messages."

The rancher smiled. "Sure thing, ma'am."

As he sauntered away, she leaned back in the hammock. *Father God,* she prayed, *I give you my love for Grant Thornton. Teach me how to live without him.*

Eighteen

"Fabulous! Absolutely marvelous!" Barbara Stein spread her long, red-polished nails across the stack of designs on Alexandra's dining-room table. "Darling, you were inspired!"

"I guess I was." Alexandra had asked the head of the firm's New York design team to visit her condominium penthouse to take a look at her sketches. Although Alexandra had been back in the city almost two weeks, she hadn't had the energy to make the trip downtown. Barb had been more than willing to drive out to Westchester County, and her response to Alexandra's work was gratifying.

"This line is going to go so fast it'll make your head spin," Barb gushed. "I'll bet we see it in Bloomingdale's, Macy's, Neiman Marcus. And you know the discount chains will be scrambling to follow up. I predict your fabrics will be *the* look for the coming season."

Alexandra ran her fingertip over the detailed rendition of Grant Thornton's green canvas tent with the spiky thorn branches silhouetted in black. "This idea came from an acacia tree in the camp—"

"I'd love to show these to some of the top home interior designers," Barb cut in. "What would you say to that, Alexandra?"

"I guess I could see sheets in these patterns."

"Sheets? I'm talking upholstery! Curtains!" She pointed to the geometric design that incorporated blocks of coral from Fort Jesus juxtaposed against the ocean. "I mean these colors are simply fabulous. The turquoise! The terra cotta! This could go beyond the whole Africa thing. This could be Southwest. Or Aztec. You know how huge the Aztec look is becoming."

"But it's not South America. It's Africa. This is coral from an old Portuguese fort—"

"And the beadwork! Alexandra, this pattern doesn't belong on a fabric. These necklaces and earrings should be created—actually beaded and sold as jewelry."

"I've been thinking about that. There's a tribe in Kenya—the Maasai. The women design and execute wonderful beaded jewelry. And the money they would earn from their handicrafts could go to things like medicine. Their children are suffering. And the water situation is—"

"*Ralph Lauren.*" Barb's eyes had glazed over. "That's who I'm thinking with these beads. Can you see this necklace against one of his dresses? Alexandra, he'd adore it."

Rafloren. Alexandra smiled wistfully. Yes, the Maasai women would agree. All her drawings were very *Rafloren.*

"I almost hate to say this because I know you've been through such trauma, darling," Barb said, "but these designs could propel you to the top. Straight to the top of this industry. You could achieve that goal of yours, you know. You could start your own firm. There are . . . some of us . . . who'd join you."

"Barb? Are you saying you'd step aboard a fledgling business if I'd start it?"

"You've got talent, lady. I've been in this business long

enough to know how important it is to go with the visionary designers. And right now you're it—the one with the dream." She smiled broadly. "Besides . . . you've got the wherewithal to make the whole thing happen."

Alexandra felt her spirits sink. *Money*. That's what it was all about, wasn't it? Although James Cooper had frittered a great deal of her money away, a substantial amount remained. During Cooper's trial, his worth would be assessed. She was bound to be awarded a chunk of his assets.

"No, Barb," she said suddenly. "I don't have the money."

"But I thought . . ." The woman's face paled. "All the papers said . . ."

"I've set up endowments with my father's money. It's going to hospitals like Mayo to fund research into tropical diseases. It'll be used for anthropological research. And I've been thinking about starting a project with the Maasai women. Maybe I'll even try to make that Ralph Lauren connection."

Barb stared unblinking. "You're *not* going to start your own design firm?"

Alexandra shrugged and gave the woman a smile. It still amazed her how good surrender felt. She didn't regret the loss of her dream at all. In fact, she had new dreams.

"Money is a gift," she said. "It was given to me. And now I want to give it to others."

Barb gave an incredulous laugh. "Well, I'll take some of it. Alexandra, I can't believe this. It doesn't sound like you at all. Honey, what happened to you over there in Africa? You're . . . different."

"A lot happened. It was more than just the shooting. It's hard to explain."

"Don't even try. You're scaring me half to death. I hope it's nothing contagious." Barb gathered up the designs. "Look, these are going to be great. The CEO is going to go wild over them. But, Alexandra . . . please. Try to get yourself together before you come into work."

"Together?"

Barb's red nails touched Alexandra's hair. "You've gone . . . soft. Shaggy. You need a trip to the salon, darling. Get yourself a manicure. Have a makeover. You'll feel better, I promise."

"Oh, Barb—"

"And those shoes." She frowned at the rubber-tire sandals on Alexandra's feet. "Really, honey. You look like some kind of a derelict."

Tucking the designs under her arm, Barb headed for the door. Alexandra followed, trying hard not to laugh out loud. *Derelict.* That was exactly what she had first thought of Grant Thornton. How wrong she had been!

"Promise me you'll do something about the hair?" Barb said in the doorway.

"Miss Prescott?" The doorman's voice came over the intercom. "Miss Prescott, you have a package down here. Shall I bring it up?"

Alexandra gave Barb a look that betrayed her annoyance. "Would you please ask the firm to stop sending work to my home? I'll take care of it when I go into the office."

"But *when* are you coming in? You've been out for weeks."

Alexandra rolled her eyes and pressed the intercom. "I'll come down for the package, Robert."

She and Barb stepped into the elevator across the hall.

How could she possibly explain all she'd been through in Africa? The physical trauma alone should warrant a long vacation. But it was much more than that. Her heart felt so sad. Almost barren of feeling. It was as though a part of her had been ripped away, and she doubted she would ever find it again.

"The ethnic look keeps growing," Barb said as the elevator doors slid open on the ground floor. "You seem to have a strong feeling for it."

Alexandra walked across the foyer to the front desk. "I had a strong feeling for Africa," she said. "I'll talk to you soon, Barb."

"OK, honey. Catch you later."

Turning away, Alexandra took the small packet from the security guard. "She thinks I need a trip to the salon, Robert."

The man grinned. "You always look fine to me, Miss Prescott."

Alexandra gave him a wink. As she entered the elevator, she glanced down at the packet—a small box wrapped in brown paper. It bore no return address. Nothing but her name.

The doors slipped shut with a whisper. Alexandra opened the little box. Tipping it over, she slid its contents into her palm.

A silver chain. A chain created of metal links, hammered together one by one. A Maasai chain.

"Grant?" Alexandra hammered on the buttons, begging them to work. The moment the doors opened on the fifth floor, she raced out into the corridor. Running down the carpeted hall, she clutched the chain in her fists. *Oh, Father, please. Please, let him be there.*

She threw open the door to the stairwell and took the fire escape steps two at a time. Her injured chest began to ache. Her heart pounded. By the time she had scrambled down all five flights, she could hardly suck in air. She pushed open the door and raced back into the foyer.

"Robert! Robert!"

"Miss Prescott?" The doorman reached to dial 9-1-1 on his phone. "What's wrong?"

"That package. Who gave it to you?"

"A fellow brought it."

"Where is he?"

"I don't know. I wouldn't let him in. He looked kind of . . . shaggy, you know. Like a . . ."

"Derelict! Oh, Robert!"

"Miss Prescott, should I call the police?"

Alexandra ran to the front door and rammed her shoulder into the brass frame. As the heavy door swung open, she slipped outside.

"Grant?" she called. "Grant!"

The parking lot was empty. Barb had already gone. A light snow was beginning to fall. She watched the first streetlight come on as an early dusk set in. "Grant?" she said, more softly this time. "Grant, where are you?"

"Got a problem?"

She swung around. He was sitting on a concrete planter, his jeans dusted with snowflakes. A bulky winter jacket looked out of place against his tanned skin. The collar of his khaki shirt flapped in the chill breeze, and a curl of sun-gold hair danced on his forehead. He stood slowly, stiffly, as if the cold had half paralyzed him.

"You came," she whispered. She clutched the silver chain, struggling to swallow the lump in her throat as he approached. "Grant, you came to me."

"All the way."

"You didn't write."

"I hate to write anything but research. Figured I could tell you about the rites of elderhood when I saw you."

"The telephone at Oloitokitok—"

"I don't talk much on telephones if I can help it. I prefer face-to-face. Especially when I have something important to say." He untangled the chain from her fingers. "I want you to know what happened to me. It's kind of a journey that started with you. A journey of surrender. On the way up Mount Kilimanjaro I gave up my disbelief and surrendered my life to Christ. Face-to-face with the man who tried to kill you, I surrendered my pride and my rage. And finally— alone in my camp—I gave up my rejection of a world I hadn't tried to understand. Last week I phoned some people I know at NYU. When the spring semester gets under way, I'll be teaching a couple of classes in the anthropology department. Alexandra, I'm here . . . all the way."

"But, Grant—"

"Without you, my old life didn't make much sense. I tried to keep going, but the fire had gone out."

Alexandra brushed back a tear, her soul rocking with disbelief at how closely his words reflected her own life. "Grant, I missed you so much."

"No matter how hard I tried—and I *did* try—I couldn't get that fire burning again. So I packed up my tents. Moved to the house in Nairobi. Tried finding something to do there. I tried everything I knew to make things feel OK again. Make everything right." He shook his head. "Tillie's baby did me in. A little girl. Dimples. Mama Hannah is spoiling her to death."

He touched her cheek. "The baby has a dimple right here," he went on. "And another one on the other side. Just like yours. So I came."

Alexandra nodded, crying openly now. In his halting speech, she understood the depth of desperation that had driven him this far. He stood like a stranger in a strange land, snowflakes gathering on his bronzed cheeks and broad shoulders. A lion in a frozen wilderness—out of time and out of place, yet ready to face whatever challenges came.

"When a warrior gives a woman a silver chain," Grant said, meeting her gaze, "it means he wants her to be his wife. Alexandra, I love you. Will you wear my chain?"

Smiling amid her tears, she took the chain and slipped it over her head. Then his arms wrapped around her, enfolding her in the warmth of his love. She clung to him, hardly able to believe he had sacrificed so much.

"Yes, my love," she whispered. "I will be your wife."

"Thank you, Lord."

She shook her head, wonder filling her at the passion that suffused his expression of gratitude. "Grant, I'm so glad you're a believer."

"Even the demons believe. I am surrendered."

The rough brush of his coat against her cheek filled Alexandra with a rush of memories. The smiling people. The burning plains. The crisp mountain winds. The sweet, musky grasses. The animals.

"Grant, I want you to take me home," she whispered.

Still holding her close, he started for the glass-fronted building. But she stopped him. Lifting her head, she gazed into the gray blue of his beloved eyes.

"No," she said. "Take me home, Grant. Home to Africa."

Epilogue

The first droplets of a warm rain greeted Grant and Alexandra the morning they arrived in Kenya. Then it began to pour. Soaked to the skin, Alexandra helped load her fiancé's Land Rover with tents and supplies. They had decided to use the Nairobi house as their city base—a place where they could come to write, design, and rest—but the plains of Maasailand would be home.

Crammed to the windows, the Land Rover rattled down the streets of Nairobi. Tillie and Graeme McLeod, baby Khatty, and Mama Hannah followed close behind in their car. After them rolled a third car carrying Grant's sister Jessica McTaggart, her husband, Rick, and their son, Splinter, all of whom had flown up from Zanzibar Island for the celebration.

When the three vehicles finally arrived at Grant's old base camp, the Maasai warriors gathered to greet them. A massive raising of four tents was followed by feasting around a campfire. Everyone passed Khatty around until the baby finally fell asleep in Mama Hannah's arms. Splinter joined in the group singing, and then he, too, fell asleep at the old African woman's side.

Alexandra had never known such joy. She and Mama Hannah occupied one of the tents. Around midnight, Tillie and Jessica crept over to join them. The women stayed up late into the night, talking and giggling—trading stories about their childhoods, exchanging family news, and welcoming Alexandra fully into the family.

For the next four days, Alexandra had little chance to talk with the man who was to become her husband. He spent every waking hour in the *kraal,* observing and recording the details of the *Eunoto*. Grant also participated in the feasting and dancing along with the other warriors, who now considered him a full-fledged member of their group. Several times Alexandra joined in the celebration, and she found that the people greeted her as a beloved friend.

Kakombe was chosen *Alaunoni*—the leader—of his age-group. He, Loomali, and the other warriors submitted to the trauma of having their heads shaved of their coveted long locks. Several men wept or fell into frenzies, shaking and foaming at the mouth over this culmination of the highest period of their manhood. Mama Hannah was escorted to the *kraal,* and she shaved Grant's head as he submitted to the rite along with his brothers.

Early on the morning after the final day of the *Eunoto,* Sambeke Ole Kereya and the other elders walked out to Grant's camp and instructed Alexandra to accompany them to the *kraal*. Followed by the whole Thornton clan, she walked slowly toward the future that beckoned.

Grant stood at the gate of the village enclosure. Taking Alexandra's hand, he led her inside. There, the Maasai women surrounded her, slipping beaded collars around her neck and tying green grass onto her sandals and clothing. Then Sambeke Ole Kereya stepped forward.

Speaking first in Maasai and then in English, he addressed

the gathering. "This Grant Thornton is the son of our people, the brother of the brave warriors who have now passed into elderhood. As an elder, Grant has the right to marry. He has chosen wisely. Alinkanda of the long legs wears his silver chain."

The Maasai murmured in affirmation of this excellent choice. Alexandra glanced at Grant. Tall, as nervous as any bridegroom, he gave her a grin.

"We bless you both with the peace and joy of God the Father, Jesus Christ the Son, and the Holy Spirit," Sambeke said. He dipped his hand into a gourd of fresh milk and brushed the traditional Maasai blessing on the skin of the couple. "We pray upon you great prosperity. Strong cattle. Healthy goats. And many children."

Alexandra laughed with delight as the Maasai crowded around her, offering her gifts of beads, baby goats, and even a calf. Though a church ceremony would follow late that evening in Nairobi, to her this was the true moment of marriage.

"Alexandra." Grant stepped over a little brown goat and took her in his arms. His sisters and their families cheered as he placed a kiss on his bride's lips.

"I love you," he murmured against her ear.

She slipped her arms around him and held him close. In the distance the clouds rolled back and the snows of Kilimanjaro gleamed in the early-morning sun. God's gift filled her heart—a treasure more precious than pearls—the union of two souls.

A Note from the Author

Dear friends,

My deepest thanks to those of you who faithfully read each of my books and to those who write to share such wonderful words of encouragement. I praise God that my stories touch your lives and help you grow in your faith walk.

Watch for my first mainstream novel, A DANGEROUS SILENCE, due out in the spring of 2001. Meanwhile, be sure to read the rest of the books in the Treasures of the Heart series, as well as my other HeartQuest novels and novellas. (A complete list appears on page 308.)

May God bless you with peace of mind and heart,

Catherine Palmer

About the Author

Catherine Palmer lives in Missouri with her husband, Tim, and sons, Geoffrey and Andrei. She is a graduate of Southwest Baptist University and has a master's degree in English from Baylor University. Her first book was published in 1988. Since then she has published more than twenty novels. Catherine has won numerous awards for her writing, including Most Exotic Historical Romance Novel from *Romantic Times* magazine. Most recently she has been nominated for the *Romantic Times* Career Achievement Award. Total sales of her novels number more than one million copies.

Her HeartQuest books include both series of full-length novels and novellas in several anthologies. Her first mainstream novel, *A Dangerous Silence,* was released in the spring of 2001.

Catherine welcomes letters written to her in care of Tyndale House Author Relations, P.O. Box 80, Wheaton, IL 60189-0080.

Visit www.HeartQuest.com for lots of info on
HeartQuest books and authors and more!

www.HeartQuest.com

BOOKS BY CATHERINE PALMER

A Town Called Hope series
Prairie Rose
Prairie Fire
Prairie Storm
Prairie Christmas (anthology)

Treasures of the Heart series
A Kiss of Adventure (original title: *The Treasure of Timbuktu*)
A Whisper of Danger (original title: *The Treasure of Zanzibar*)
A Touch of Betrayal

Finders Keepers series
Finders Keepers
Hide and Seek

Anthologies
Prairie Christmas
A Victorian Christmas Cottage
A Victorian Christmas Quilt
A Victorian Christmas Tea

Current HeartQuest Releases

- *Magnolia*, Ginny Aiken
- *Lark*, Ginny Aiken
- *Camellia*, Ginny Aiken

- *Sweet Delights*, Terri Blackstock, Elizabeth White, and Ranee McCollum

- *Awakening Mercy*, Angela Benson
- *Abiding Hope*, Angela Benson

- *Faith*, Lori Copeland
- *Hope*, Lori Copeland
- *June*, Lori Copeland
- *Glory*, Lori Copeland

- *Freedom's Hope*, Dianna Crawford
- *Freedom's Promise*, Dianna Crawford
- *Freedom's Belle*, Dianna Crawford

- *Prairie Fire*, Catherine Palmer
- *Prairie Rose*, Catherine Palmer
- *Prairie Storm*, Catherine Palmer
- *Prairie Christmas*, Catherine Palmer, Elizabeth White, and Peggy Stoks

- *Finders Keepers*, Catherine Palmer
- *Hide and Seek*, Catherine Palmer
- *A Kiss of Adventure*, Catherine Palmer (original title: *The Treasure of Timbuktu*)
- *A Whisper of Danger*, Catherine Palmer (original title: *The Treasure of Zanzibar*)
- *A Touch of Betrayal*, Catherine Palmer
- *A Victorian Christmas Cottage*, Catherine Palmer, Debra White Smith, Jeri Odell, and Peggy Stoks
- *A Victorian Christmas Quilt*, Catherine Palmer, Debra White Smith, Ginny Aiken, and Peggy Stoks
- *A Victorian Christmas Tea*, Catherine Palmer, Dianna Crawford, Peggy Stoks, and Katherine Chute

- *Olivia's Touch*, Peggy Stoks
- *Romy's Walk*, Peggy Stoks

HEART
QUEST.

Other Great Tyndale House Fiction

- *Jenny's Story*, Judy Baer
- *Libby's Story*, Judy Baer

- *Out of the Shadows*, Sigmund Brouwer

- *Ashes and Lace*, B. J. Hoff
- *Cloth of Heaven*, B. J. Hoff

- *The Price*, Jim and Terri Kraus
- *The Treasure*, Jim and Terri Kraus
- *The Promise*, Jim and Terri Kraus

- *Winter Passing*, Cindy McCormick Martinusen

- *Rift in Time*, Michael Phillips
- *Hidden in Time*, Michael Phillips

- *Unveiled*, Francine Rivers
- *Unashamed*, Francine Rivers
- *Unshaken*, Francine Rivers
- *A Voice in the Wind*, Francine Rivers
- *An Echo in the Darkness*, Francine Rivers
- *As Sure As the Dawn*, Francine Rivers
- *The Last Sin Eater*, Francine Rivers
- *Leota's Garden*, Francine Rivers
- *The Scarlet Thread*, Francine Rivers
- *The Atonement Child*, Francine Rivers

- *The Promise Remains*, Travis Thrasher

HEART
QUEST.

HeartQuest Books by Catherine Palmer

A Town Called Hope series

Prairie Rose—Kansas holds their future, but only faith can mend their past. Hope and love blossom on the untamed prairie as a young woman, searching for a place to call home, happens upon a Kansas homestead during the 1860s.

Prairie Fire—Will a burning secret extinguish the spark of love between Jack and Caitrin? The town of Hope discovers the importance of forgiveness, overcoming prejudice, and the dangers of keeping unhealthy family secrets.

Prairie Storm—Can one tiny baby calm the brewing storm between Lily's past and Elijah's future? United in their concern for an orphaned infant, Eli and Lily are forced to set aside their differences and learn to trust God's plan to see them through the storms of life.

Prairie Christmas (anthology)—In "The Christmas Bride," by Catherine Palmer, Rolf Rustemeyer can hardly wait for the arrival of his Christmas bride, all the way from Germany. You'll love this heartwarming Christmas visit with friends old and new from A Town Called Hope. Anthology also includes novellas by Elizabeth White and Peggy Stoks.

Treasures of the Heart series

A Kiss of Adventure (original title: *The Treasure of Timbuktu*)—Abducted by a treasure hunter, Tillie becomes a pawn in a dangerous game.

A Whisper of Danger (original title: *The Treasure of Zanzibar*)—Jessica's unexpected inheritance turns out to be an ancient house filled with secrets, an unknown enemy . . . and a lost love.

A Touch of Betrayal—Stranded in a dangerous land, Alexandra must face her fear . . . and escape the man determined to ruin her life.

Finders Keepers series

Finders Keepers—Blue-eyed, fiery-tempered Elizabeth Hayes is working hard to preserve Chalmers House, the Victorian mansion next to her growing antiques business. But Zachary Chalmers, heir to the mansion, has very different plans for the site. And Elizabeth's eight-year-old son, adopted from Romania three years earlier, has plans of

HEART
QUEST

his own: He wants a daddy—and this tall, handsome man is the perfect candidate.

Hide and Seek (coming in early 2001)—Luke Easton wants to be left alone to nurse his broken heart, raise his daughter in peace, and complete the renovation of the Chalmers Mansion. Jo Callaway prizes her privacy too. She doesn't want her new friends to ask too many questions about her mysterious past. But fighting for common goals begins to forge a bond between Luke and Jo that neither expected—or welcomes.

Anthologies

A Victorian Christmas Cottage—Four novellas centering around hearth and home at Christmastime. Stories by Catherine Palmer, Jeri Odell, Debra White Smith, and Peggy Stoks.

A Victorian Christmas Quilt—A patchwork of four novellas about love and joy at Christmastime. Stories by Catherine Palmer, Ginny Aiken, Peggy Stoks, and Debra White Smith.

A Victorian Christmas Tea—Four novellas about life and love at Christmastime. Stories by Catherine Palmer, Dianna Crawford, Peggy Stoks, and Katherine Chute.